The Fifth River

The Fifth River

Quest for Eden
Book Two

By

Jeanne Desautel Foster

Sycamore Books
Pelham, Alabama

Dedication

Quest for Eden: The Fifth River is dedicated to my two sisters, Nancy and Paula. I am grateful for all their help and encouragement.

Acknowledgements

The cover photograph is courtesy of Matthew Bullard.

Contents

Map A

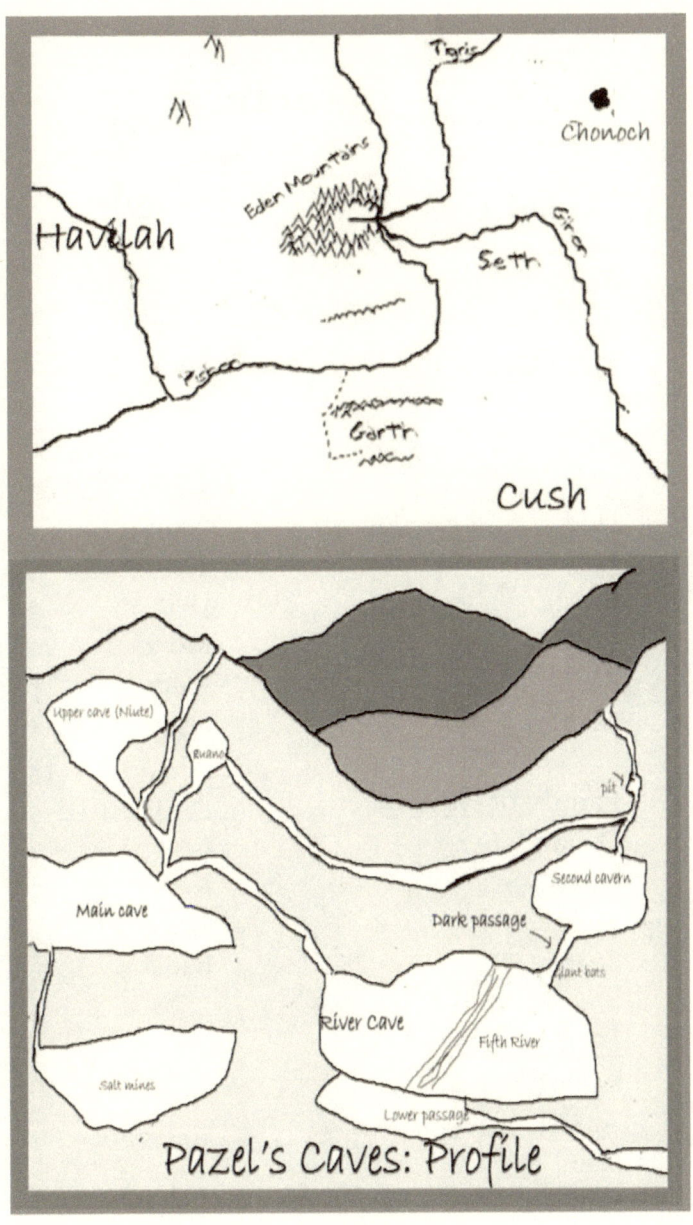

Map B

Characters

Sethians
Seth
Enoch

Family of Elim
Elim
Ahuv
Chay
Hod
Hela
Brosh
Dalit
Abira
Giza

Family of Dolian
Dolian
Neva
Mehri
Shani

Immortals
Remiel
Azazel
Samil
Samyaza

Cainites
Pazel
Juban
Zuph
Tagg
Barush

Lamechites
Niute
Taz
Dolf
Morg
Rahm
Afek

Nephilim
Kron
Kodi
Gradrach
Radek

Introduction

In *The Mission*, the first book in the *Quest for Eden* trilogy, Hod and his friends successfully rescued Mehri—the girl who would someday be the grand-mother of Noah— from the nephilim.

Red-haired Hod, "the fire-hair," left his home in Garth, crossed the Pishon River and then traveled to the Eden Mountains, in the middle of which was hidden the Garden of Eden.

Along the way, Hod found friends to help him and eventually came to the home of his Uncle Enoch—the man who walked with God. Before reaching his uncle's home, Hod was reunited with his brother Chay, who had been captured by the nephilim when they attacked the family home.

Kodi, a young nephil who was raised by his grand-father to worship Elohim until he was taken away by the nephilim, joined with the young full humans to rescue the beautiful Mehri from the Dark Watcher Azazel.

At the end of *The Mission*, Hod left Mehri with his ancestor Seth and returned to his old home, only to discover that the family had moved while he and Chay were gone. Six months after returning home, two nephews come to Garth looking for Hod and Chay. That is where *The Fifth River* begins

As in the first book, I have written *The Fifth River* in modern language. The reader is to assume it is a translation from an unknown, ancient tongue. I have stayed with the truth revealed in the book of Genesis whenever possible, but I have taken liberties of imagination with the possibilities. Of course, none of this story is true beyond what the Bible reveals.

The final book of the Quest for Eden trilogy, *The Tree of Life*, will complete the battle against Kron, king of the nephilim, and will leave the heroes knowing their descendants will be represented in Noah's family.

◁Prologue▷

The Sethians have killed my Hartagga! But you will make them pay!"

Kron's eyes turned to Varqr, the huge silver wolf sleeping at the foot of his bed. He reached down and stroked the lean lupine.

"You will wear the collar now, and the whole world will know you belong to me. You will find the fire-hair—and his brother—and bring them to me!"

The golden collar of Hartagga, the monstrous bear, was too large for Varqr, so Kron, king of the nephilim bent the gold in his mighty hands, shaping the soft metal before fastening it on the wolf's thin neck.

This nephil king—this son of a fallen Watcher—liked his minions to be hungry. He wanted the taste for their prey to tantalize their appetites. Saliva never ceased to drip from Varqr's long tongue.

"Now come, my pet. They have brought the cowards to us. When I have done with them, I will send you out to find those who want to destroy me."

With Varqr at his heels, Kron stalked into his throne room, stepped up onto his gold-covered throne, and surveyed the disgraced warriors standing before him.

"You lost them!" Kron leaned forward and pointed an angry forefinger at the nephilim and Lamechites.

"I'll have your heads!"

The assassin descendants of Cain's murderous grandson Lamech trembled in terror, but one of the nephilim dared to glance up at Kron before speaking.

"Most glorious king of the world, I ask your pardon. The fire-hair had magical powers we could not defeat. He and the other humans ran about quickly cutting our legs until we could not walk from the wounds."

"Cowards! Would I fear one small human just because his hair is red? Do you think I would have allowed those puny creatures to outwit me?"

By now Kron had left his throne and was treading around his defeated warriors, his red eyes glaring out his contempt for them all and his nostrils almost blowing steam. He pushed pointed teeth into the face of the tallest nephil. "Radek, what do you have to say for yourself before I condemn you to death?"

"I am prepared to die, but I have two things to say." The nephil stood tall and straight although his legs were covered with fresh scars from the cuts given him by the humans who had dared to fight back.

"Well, what is it?"

"First, we must find a better way to combat these humans. We must learn to fight their way."

Kron glared and growled but listened. "And what else do you have to say."

"I will tell you this before I die. The fire-hair and his companion the salt merchant had a waterskin containing magic water. While I was on my knees unable to move, I saw them pour it on a Cainite whose arm had been almost severed. I saw the skin and muscles grow back together."

Now Kron was interested. He began to pace back and forth in front of the accused. He said nothing, yet each of his steps shook the bodies of those standing on the stone floor. Finally, he turned and pointed once more at Radek.

"Did the fire-hair speak to you?"

"Yes, he told me to tell you that his mission was completed, and you could stop chasing him."

"Maybe the prophecy of the fire-hair is fulfilled. Maybe they say we are doomed, but I will still kill him!"

Kron suddenly turned his attention on the six Lamechites who stood to the left of the nephilim. Those watching—whether chained or free—dreaded to have that anger turned on them.

"And you!" Kron roared at his captives. "You had the last chance to kill them before they reached the home of Seth! What happened?"

One of the Lamechites, after looking around and seeing that none of the others had the courage to speak, stepped forward. "Sir, we had them surrounded, we were defeating them, their end was near—and then—."

"And then?"

"The four-faced monsters from the gate of the Garden came after us, killing some of us. We fled without thinking."

Everyone on earth feared the cherubim, the creatures who guarded the gate to the Garden of Eden. These ferocious warriors had four faces, three of them the countenances of terrifying beasts and one the face of a man. They carried swords that cut with a fiery blade.

Years ago Kron had sent twenty of his best warriors to try to get past the cherubim and into the Garden where they would pick the fruit from the tree of life. The men he sent to discover what had happened found only twenty headless bodies. The strange part of the discovery was that the severed surfaces were cauterized so that no blood had poured out.

Kron stood for a moment, looming over them all. Finally, he barked out orders to a nearby guard. "Only Radek and Dolf have shown courage. Execute the rest!"

The guilty warriors were led away as Kron climbed back on his throne, planted his right elbow on his knee and leaned his gray bearded chin on his fist. His white-streaked black hair grew down the sides of his face and into a full beard cut into sharp spikes.

Standing to the right of the throne with a group of younger nephilim, Kodi watched Kron's anger rain down on the nephilim and Lamechites. He was glad no one knew he had been part of their defeat.

Much shorter than the rest of his kind, Kodi was still head and shoulders above the tallest Sethian. His golden hair, handsome face, and sparkling blue eyes also marked him as an unusual nephil. All the other sons of Dark Watchers stood twice the size of the ordinary offspring of human women. All the others had coarse, dark hair and fang-like teeth. All the others had eyes that flamed with their hatred for mankind. Only Kodi had a heart capable of compassion.

If Kron had any idea that I no longer share his desire to kill Sethians, he would execute me too.

Because Kodi had been hidden from his father Azazel from birth, the Dark Watcher had not made the many changes in the secret patterns of Kodi's body that would have made him a giant the size of the rest of the nephilim.

His difference was both noticed and resented by the other nephilim, but his close relationship to Kron saved him from persecution. Both Kron and Kodi were sons of Azazel.

Azazel and the other Dark Watchers used human bodies to impregnate the women and then used their powers to change the babies to make them all male and all tall. Kodi was the recipient of this change.

After the babies were born, however, the Dark Watchers would continue to change them until they were aggressive monsters twice the size of the tallest Sethian.

Kodi had been saved from this fate when, at his mother's death, his grandfather Juban had hidden the newborn and later taken him to Havilah where he had told everyone that the over-sized toddler was several years older than his real age.

During his years with Juban, Kodi had learned to worship Elohim and had thought himself the same as the other children with whom he played. This had worked until, when Kodi was eight, some passing nephilim had recognized him as one of them and taken him to Kron.

Separated from Juban, the young nephil had almost forgotten about Elohim. He had begun to think as the nephilim taught him to think. But his experience with Hod and Chay during this last few weeks had changed him again.

He had traveled to Garth with a group of nephilim and Lamechites who were searching for the one called the fire-hair. At the birth of this red-headed Sethian, an old woman had prophesied that he would bring an end to the time of the nephilim.

Kron's spy stole a cradle cloth of the infant, whose family had disappeared from the Sethian lands, and for seventeen years the king of the nephilim had sought this boy.

Most of the Sethians had disappeared by the time the nephilim band arrived, but the giants killed some and their

Lamechite troops had captured Chay, brother of the fire-hair, and taken him back to Kron.

During the trip back to Atlantia, Chay had ridden behind Kodi on his behemoth steed and the two young men had gotten to know one another. Later Chay had convinced Kron to send him and his cellmate Mathu to find his brother Hod, who was now hiding in the Eden Mountains.

Kodi was sent as a guard because he was the only nephil small enough to ride haraanis, the giant eagle-like birds that roosted in the mountains. This was how Kodi met Enoch, who told Kodi of his kinship to Hod's friend Pazel and his childhood friendship with Mathu.

By the time Hod, Chay, Pazel, and Mathu started on their mission to save Mathu's sister Mehri, Kodi was part of the band called the Iron Fist. When his friends had escaped from the castle near the end of their mission, Kodi had been sorry that he was forced to stay behind.

He was relieved to learn now that Hod, Chay, Mehri, and Pazel had made it to the home of their ancestor Seth. The young nephil had struggled with his conscience since meeting Enoch and knew he wanted to follow the true Creator as his new friends did.

After his friends escaped, Kodi had played the role of an obedient subject of Kron, but all the time he could not forget what he had learned from Enoch. Now Radek's talk of magic water brought to Kodi's mind that during the time he spent with the humans, he had noticed Hod and Pazel did not drink from one of their waterskins but had given the water to the human who was close to death.

Kron suddenly turned to look at Kodi. "Radek reports that he saw one of the humans with his arm almost cut off healed by the pouring of magic water. What do you know of this?"

Kodi shrugged as if unwilling to tell all he knew. "I have never heard of healing water."

"I know you were with them for many days." Kron's eyebrows rose straight and black when he glared down from his throne at this smaller nephil. "Do not keep anything from me! Did you see healing?"

"Perhaps." Kodi, after some thought, did not see why he should lie to the king. After all, he knew nothing of this water other than how it had worked. He saw no harm in telling Kron what he knew.

"I saw two of them give water to the brother of the girl —the one who was later killed by the Lamechites. It seemed to make him stronger."

"You saw no miraculous change?"

"Maybe. I thought the man was weak and within minutes he was ready to climb the mountain."

Kron took a moment to stare at the younger nephil. His red-rimmed eyes penetrated as deeply as he could into the mind of his brother, who met his eyes with innocence. He had nothing to hide right now.

"Who had the water?"

"The one called Hod carried the water, and the one called Pazel seemed to know about it."

"You do not know where it came from?"

Kodi shook his head. "No. Even though I pretended to be their friend, they never spoke of the water around me.

They never trusted me. After all, I was their guard when we left the fortress."

Kron moved quickly to Kodi's side and leaned down toward the shorter man's ear. Suddenly his voice dropped from a roar to a whisper

"Even the water flowing through the Garden was never said to heal. Where could this water come from?"

"I have no idea."

Kodi was glad he could not tell the king anything. He cringed to think what Kron would do if he had control of this water. All Kodi's life he had known the king was obsessed with getting some fruit from the tree of life in the forbidden Garden so that he could live forever. With healing water Kron would be able to keep himself healthy for centuries—the nearest thing to immortality.

"I must find that river!" Kron once more bellowed out his words. "I will send scouts all over the world to test the water from every stream, rivulet, spring, well, or river. I will not rest until I find it.

"Do you want me to search too?"

"No! You are more valuable to me here. If I hear word of any of these humans, I will want you to go and bring them to me, since you know them."

Kodi left the throne room after Kron was done with him and wandered aimlessly about the fortress. He had no set duties or responsibilities, so he was bored. His mission with his friends had given him purpose, but now he found himself searching for something to do.

First, he went back to his own chamber, put his torch in a holder on the wall, and straightened the bedclothes he had left tumbled the day he had left with Chay to search for Hod. After an hour he found the small stone room unbearably close after a week in the open country, so he left with his torch and followed the narrow hallway until he was outside.

His wanderings took him out to the landing area where he and Chay had mounted the largest harannis and flown off. As usual several birds were roosting on the rocky area. He saw that a nephil named Gradrach was trying to put a halter on Keoaw, the largest of the birds.

Keoaw shrieked and started to take off, to get away from the giant, but Gradrach grabbed the shoulder of his wing and threw the bird to the rocks. When Keoaw reared up and used his sharp beak to tear a chunk of flesh from the nephil's calf, Gradrach kicked him across the landing.

"That's enough!" Kodi, enraged by the creature's treatment, grabbed Gradrach's arm. "Leave him alone!"

The other nephil jerked away from Kodi, and then, seeing who had accosted him, snarled and stomped off as if he were unwilling to risk the king' s wrath by fighting with his brother.

As soon as Gradrach was gone, Kodi turned to Keoaw, and, with his right hand outstretched, talked softly as he walked slowly toward the bird. He knew that Keoaw, more than any haranni, had a mind of his own. Even though Kron used him for sending messages, Keoaw had never allowed a rider to throw a leg across his back.

Kodi had always thought he would like to see if he could tame the bird and now seemed a good time. Keoaw did not move as Kodi approached. Instead, he let the nephil stroke his neck. "We are going to be good friends, aren't we, fellow? I'll come back and bring you some food. You'll like that, won't you?"

After spending fifteen minutes talking to the haranni, Kodi left him and went looking for a haunch of uncooked meat. As it was nearing mealtime, he headed toward the huge nephilim eating chamber. A rumbling stomach helped him decide to join the others for a meal before feeding Keoaw.

Kodi was sitting alone eating roasted mammoth when Kron strode into the room.

"Kodi!"

For the first time since he had first come to the fortress, Kodi hesitated before obeying. He paused with the meat bone halfway to his mouth before turning his head toward the king of the nephilim.

"Yes. What is it?"

"Sir!" Kron roared. "Has your time with the humans made you forget how to address me?"

"No—sir. Of course not." Kodi quickly stood and dropped his gaze. "I'm sorry, sir."

"Come to me when you are through eating. I want to know all you have learned about the humans."

Kron looked at the meat in Kodi's hand, and then stomped away.

For over a week Kodi answered questions posed by the king, but no matter what he was asked, the young nephil never told of how he had helped Hod fulfill his mission. He told what he had to, yet did not give away his friends.

11

Kodi was once again a part of life in Kron's fortress. He took part in the new training to teach the nephilim to fight humans. He practiced using the new, lighter swords fashioned for the race of giants by the iron-workers of Nod and intended to cut through the air more quickly so as to slash to pieces the smaller but speedy humans.

Kodi was not as handy with this new weapon as his nephilim brothers, but then he had no intention of killing any Sethians.

I am living a double life. How can I continue to pretend to be a loyal nephil when my heart is with my Sethian friends?

◁ 1 ▷

Six Months Later

The two youngest sons of Elim, great great-grandson of Seth, were walking with their nephews near the Pishon River beside the thick trees of Garth when they saw the giant bird flying low and directly toward them.

Chay, the older brother, threw up his right arm and pointed at the distant sky. "Look! A haraani with a rider, and they are flying this way."

"Let's get under cover of the forest and move toward home as quickly as we can," Hod said. "I'm tired of fighting. If he doesn't see us, we'll be safe."

"Don't you want to know what he wants?" Chay asked.

Hod shook his red hair vigorously. "Not at all! I'm a farmer again. Now let's get walking!"

No sooner had he said he was ready to go back to farming than Hod realized he really was curious to know who the rider was and what he wanted. After being chased by Lamechites and nephilim, he could not completely ignore the dangers the world held; moreover, being the leader of the mission had been a responsibility he could not easily discard.

Even though he was now only eighteen, Hod had gotten used to giving orders, so he turned to the elder of the nephews who were leading them to the new home to which the family had moved.

"Brosh, you and Dalit go on and get far enough away to be safe. We'll catch up with you soon."

"All right." Brosh did not hesitate to obey, a fact that gave Hod a prick of pride. "We'll be following that little stream that branches off to the west."

From their hiding place behind a large tree, the sons of Elim watched as the haraani landed on the southern bank of the river, just beyond the trees, and a familiar looking Lamechite got off.

"I wonder what he is up to." Chay pushed his long brown hair out of his eyes as he peered around the tree.

"He seems interested in that rivulet running from the river into the woods."

"Watch out! He's backtracking it and coming this way. Let's get a little farther up in the woods where we can see him without him smelling us."

While they watched, the Lamechite, who had one straight and one severely crooked leg, moved from the riverbank into the forest, all the while concentrating on the little rivulet. The two brothers darted from tree to tree following the man, who eventually came to a small spring.

The man reached for a gourd drinking cup hanging from his belt and knelt to scoop some spring water, which he then poured on his leg. He squatted and watched his crooked limb intently for a while, even stretching and trying to straighten it, before spitting on the ground.

"Healing water!" The Lamechite threw the rest of the water on the ground and turned to the river. "I should have known there is no such thing!"

Hod looked at his brother, whose eyebrows had lifted questioningly at the Lamechite's words. Both of them knew what it was to fear and fight these unkempt sons of an assassin, but it was a shock to hear these villains had learned about the healing water.

"If he knows about the healing water," Hod lowered his voice to ensure the Lamechite did not hear him. "One of the nephilim must have told Kron what they saw."

Chay rolled his eyes and shrugged, leaving Hod to recall the times his brother had told him he should have killed any Lamechites or nephilim who fell into his hands.

Maybe I made the wrong decision when I did not kill that wounded nephil near the Euphrates. If I am a warrior, shouldn't I be willing to destroy the enemy? I did kill the two Lamechites who were trying to kill Pazel and me, but I had no choice. And the nephil—the first life I took? It was almost an accident, and I was protecting my family.

I know my mission was the will of Elohim, but I hope I am through killing.

Thinking of the battles he had fought half a year ago against both nephilim and Lamechites, Hod unconsciously reached for the sword hanging at his side. The weapon was actually a dagger he had taken from the nephil he had killed that day the giant had attacked the old home compound, but since he was half a nephil's height, the dagger made him a good sword.

Hod poked his brother and whispered, "I recognize that man. He is the Lamechite who broke his leg when he was fighting Pazel and me. He doesn't know you. Go find out what he's doing. I'll cover you in case he tries something."

Without a word Chay handed Hod his own curved sword, taken from a dead Lamechite, and stepped from behind his tree.

"What are you searching for, friend? Maybe I can help you."

The Lamechite stopped and turned a suspicious eye on Chay.

"Who says I am looking for anything?"

The man reached for his own curved sword but did not draw it from his belt. Chay pointed at the gourd and then at the spring. "Is this water not good enough to clean your body? Is it not pure enough?"

"I'm looking for special water!" The Lamechite pushed back his dirty black hair. "Do you know of any water that heals wounds—straightens legs?"

"Hmm, I'm not sure what you mean. Why are you looking for healing water?"

"King Kron wants it! If you know about it, he will pay you well for information."

"I have no information to sell," Chay said. "Where have you looked?"

"All over—everywhere except the desert land where there is no water. Are you from around here?"

Chay cleared his throat and chose his words carefully as he answered. "No, I'm from much farther west. I'm on my way from the eastern lands to the home of my father."

"Well, if you come across any water with healing value, send word to Kron, and he'll make you richer than you ever dreamed."

The Lamechite started to limp away, then stopped and turned back.

"Oh, I'm also searching for a Cainite named Pazel, a salt merchant who lives in the mountains. You'd recognize him because he is very short."

Hod looked out from behind the tree where he was hiding. When he caught Chay's eyes, Hod shook his head vigorously. "No, never heard of him," Chay said. "Why is Kron searching for him?"

"Not Kron! *I*, Niute, want to question him—it has nothing to do with Kron."

Once more the Lamechite turned to walk away, but this time Chay grabbed his elbow and stopped him.

"Why do you want him?"

The Lamechite frowned and tilted his head thoughtfully. "It's his fire-hair friend I really want."

"Fire-hair?"

"Yes, he's a Sethian like you but with hair like flames, orange and gold mixed. I have a score to settle with him. Are you related to him?"

Chay met Hod's eyes over the Lamechite's shoulder. "No. I'm Sethian, but I've never seen one of us with red hair. There are many branches of our family. Why do you want him?"

"He did this to my leg." The Lamechite pointed down to the shortened bare leg extending beneath his filthy tunic.

"He knocked me down a hill and broke my leg. It took me weeks to get back to Kron's fortress. By then it was too late to set my leg right."

Chay nodded and then turned his head to sneak a wink at his brother. "Sounds like a mean one to me."

"And when I found out he had healing water and did not use it to help me, I vowed to get him and his friend. I intend to get my hands on him before Kron does—and kill him slowly."

Chay tried to sound greedy and interested. "Maybe I can be on the lookout for them—for gold. Where does the Sethian live?"

"His family used to live near here, but after we discovered them, they moved. We don't know where they went. I'm sure he's with them."

Chay nodded, smiled, and shook the Lamechite's filthy hand. "So, if I hear of this man or the salt merchant, how can I find you?"

"The salt merchant has a dwelling on the southern side of the Eden Mountains, but he hasn't been there for a long time. I have already looked there once and am going back to wait for him. If there is such a thing as healing water, I'll use it myself and then take it to the king.

"I'll be at the salt merchant's if you are looking for me. It has an orange door, and it's a few cubits up from the most southern point of the south side. It's easy to find."

Hod remembered the last threatening words the Lamechite had yelled at him that day when the man had fallen down the incline and broken his leg. Evidently he wanted revenge for his injury.

"And what will you give me if I have some information about him?"

"I have saved some gold. If you bring him to me, I'll give it to you." With these words Niute limped back to his haraani and led it to a nearby hill from which he took off.

Once the man was gone, Hod stepped out from his hiding place and walked toward Chay.

"I knew that was the same man. He blames me for his leg."

"What happened?"

"He and two others followed me from the waterfall and chased me across the desert after you and I were separated. I killed one when I first met Pazel and killed the other a day later up on the mountain. This one had a broken leg, so I left him alive. And now he blames me for not healing him with the water! I could have killed him!"

"You're too soft-hearted. I thought it was a mistake not to kill that giant who saw the healing water working. Now you're paying for not killing this one."

"Maybe that's true." Hod shrugged. "But I couldn't bring myself to kill someone who was defenseless. Anyway, I wanted the nephil to tell Kron we had completed our mission."

Now it was Chay who shrugged, but he did not argue any more with his younger brother. He knew that in the same circumstance he would finish off all enemies he came upon—even crippled ones.

"We need to hurry to catch up with Brosh and Dalit," was all he said.

Hod nodded and quickly followed his brother in the westerly direction their nephews had taken. They found them waiting farther west in the trees that edged the riverbank.

Brosh stepped out as soon as he saw the two younger men approaching. "Could you tell what that rider wanted?"

"He was seeking a spring with healing water," Hod answered, watching to see how the two older relatives reacted to this news.

They had no idea that under his arm was the waterskin Pazel had given him before they separated near the gate to the Garden of Eden. This waterskin was still half full of the healing water as it had not been used since Pazel had poured it on Tagg's terrible wound, the healing the nephil had witnessed.

"Healing water?" Dalit laughed and elbowed his brother. "We could use some of that, right, Brosh?"

"Yeah! Too bad there's no such thing."

Chay looked at Hod as if to ask whether they should reveal to their nephews that they had the water. Hod quickly frowned and shook his head, hoping this would remind his brother that he had sworn him to secrecy about the fifth river to come from the Garden of Eden.

Only Pazel, Hod, and Chay knew of the river that ran through one of Pazel's caves under the Eden Mountains. The four men turned their faces west and continued the journey toward the new home of the family of Elim.

When the nephilim had attacked the family compound almost seven months ago, the family had scattered in many directions. Hod and Chay, the two youngest sons, went out into the northern woods with two other brothers with orders to keep Hod safe from Kron, who feared the prophecy that the fire-hair would destroy the nephilim.

The rest of the younger men of the family had tried to lead the nephilim in another direction while the women and older men were hidden in a secret cave. By the time the two brothers returned home several weeks and many dangerous adventures later, the family of Elim had moved without leaving any hint of their destination. Although Hod and Chay had searched for the family, they had been unsuccessful, so they stayed close to the old home in hopes that someone would come to find them.

Yesterday Brosh and Dalit—sons of Ahuv, the eldest of Elim's living sons—had arrived at the old family compound in search of Hod and Chay. Now they had been found and were on their way to meet the rest of their family.

As they walked along, Hod found himself continually thinking about the Lamechite who was searching for healing water. He was not surprised word of the water had reached Kron, but he was glad the king had not yet figured out that Pazel was the one who knew where the water came from.

Hod could still picture the clear river running through the beautiful cave. Lighted from above by sunlight coming through several holes in a roof supported by three pillars, the cavern ran underground just south of where the Eden Mountains began. Gold, orange, and brown streaks made the room blaze in the shafts of sunlight. And the water? Deliciously cold and amazingly invigorating, it rejuvenated the body and the spirit.

According to Remiel, the Watcher who had appeared to both Hod and Pazel, the river must be kept hidden. The enemies of Elohim must never discover it. But if Niute found Pazel, how long would it take for the king to find out about the salt merchant?

When the four men came to where the Pishon turned north, they noticed a shallow stream dividing off it and meandering westward. They all stopped as Chay pointed out to Hod the hills far to the northwest, which signified the land of Havilah. He had only seen these hills at a distance when he was taken as a prisoner to Atlantia, the home of the nephilim, but he knew this was where Mehri, the girl they had saved, had grown up.

Chay was wondering if Hod still thought about the girl he had seemed to care for when his brother's words showed his mind was following the same train of thought. "Someday I would like to meet the family of Mehri and see her mother Neva again."

"I thought you were tired of missions and wanted to settle down to farming." Chay raised his eyebrows. "After all we've been through, I never want to leave home again."

Hod shrugged and gave a short laugh. "I know, I know. And I meant what I said! I don't want to ever have to fight and kill again, but that doesn't mean I would not like to travel and see more of the wide world—in peace, though."

"As long as Kron rules from his fortress, peace will be no more than a dream," Chay replied.

"Come on." Brosh waved the others forward. "The rest of the way we go down the middle of this small creek to hide our scent."

 H

One day months after Kodi began to train Keoaw, the nephil came out to the landing area on the back side of Kron's fortress and walked over to the haraani. When he reached out to stroke the huge bird's head, it leaned into the path of his hand, its eyes closing as it enjoyed the contact.

23

"How are you doing?" Kodi continued to stroke the bird as he checked out the condition of his feathers, beak, and legs.

"You're holding up very well for all the flying we've been doing."

For months, Kodi had taken Keoaw out exploring the farthest reaches of the world. They had flown as far as the beaches on the edge of the earth, which were surrounded by the great ocean.

Thinking it would comfort this bird of prey that had decided to let a human into its world, Kodi reached down to stroke the soft feathers above Keoaw's legs and smiled as the bird's eyes closed sleepily.

Human, Kodi thought to himself. *That is how I like to think of myself. I suppose we nephilim are human, even if Kron says we are not. But I must be careful in this world in which I live. If Kron knew I considered myself human instead of a nephil, he would turn me over to Marik for retraining.*

Once he had shown the bird he loved it, Kodi strapped on the leather band that worked as a saddle and attached the reins to the beak. At his touch, Keoaw flattened his body into a crouch, making it easy for Kodi to mount him. As he threw his leg over the bird in preparation for taking off from the landing area, Kodi thought back to the time—was it only eight months ago—he had last seen his human friends.

When Kodi had been left behind in the tower-like fortress, he had hoped and believed Chay and Hod would be able to complete the mission without his help. He had watched as Hod ran down the tunnel hand and hand with

Mehri, had listened to their footsteps echoing on the stone floor of the tunnel.

And then he had run back to the cell where Mehri had been imprisoned. He had feigned unconsciousness as he lay alongside the guard he had knocked out. When the king showed up, he had told him that a gang of Sethians had overpowered him and freed the girl and Hod.

Azazel himself had chased the Sethians down the tunnel. Kodi had not witnessed it, but he later heard that Azazel had taken the form of black smoke that sucked the air from the tunnel.

As he was flying, Kodi thought back to the day a couple of months after the mission when he had finally turned Keoaw's face toward Havilah where his grandfather Juban lived. Concerned that Kron might suspect him of sympathizing with the Sethians, Kodi had been careful not to go into their territory when he first had concluded his part in Hod's mission.

But eventually his hunger to see his grandfather could no longer be denied. Knowing nephilim were often checking on the miners of Havilah, he flew in at dusk when he was less noticeable in the sky.

He had hoped he could recognize Juban's hut after all the years since he had lived there and was surprised how the memories of childhood returned as he studied the ramshackle dwellings below.

It was the sight of a small white-haired figure chopping at the dirt in a small garden that drew him downward. He brought Keoaw in to a landing close to the old man, dismounted, and began walking toward the him.

"Grandfather?" Kodi had called out tentatively.

Juban had turned slowly, his creased face breaking into a smile. He had dropped his hoe and then held out his arms. "Kodi? You have returned at last!"

Although short for a nephil, Kodi was nearly twice his grandfather's height and easily lifted Juban off the ground with his hug. Feeling the fragility of the body he held, Kodi tenderly put him down.

"Grandfather, may we go into your hut to talk?"

"Can you fit inside?" Juban's eyes crinkled with humor. "You've grown a few cubits since I last saw you, but you have become a fine-looking young man."

They had gone into the little hut and, after Juban had lighted a fire, sat cross-legged on the floor.

"You have not changed—well, maybe you have a little less hair." Kodi smiled at his grandfather.

"Caused by my sorrow at your loss," Juban's face became serious. "I prayed that Elohim would protect you and help you remember what I taught you."

Kodi leaned toward his grandfather.

"I almost forgot it, but then Elohim found me and used me in His plans."

"I know this. My grandson Pazel came to us to tell what happened to Mathu and Mehri. I learned of the death of Pazel's father many years ago when he was bringing his little boy to Havilah to be with us."

"Yes, Pazel told me his story when we met at Enoch's home."

The old man beamed with pride as he patted Kodi's arm. "Pazel told me how you saved them from Kron's monstrous bear Hartagga and later saved Mehri from the clutches of the Dark Watcher Azazel."

"I was only protecting my friends, for that is what Pazel and the rest had become."

"Imagine my joy to learn that my two grandsons had found each other and were doing the work of Elohim."

"Yes, we were." Kodi looked thoughtfully into the fire.

Juban put a hand out, causing Kodi to meet his eyes. "And now? Do you still do His work?"

"I live back in the fortress of Kron, but I no longer serve the king, although he does not know it. I hope my being close to Kron will help my friends. I will be with them if the need arises."

"That was my hope—that you continue to serve Elohim." Juban rose to get some food for his grandson. "Can you stay with me now? Perhaps you can come live with me again."

"No. Kron would be angry if he found out, but I will keep in touch with you—and my friends. Right now I dare not contact any of them."

Kodi left the hut in the dark and whistled for Keoaw, who had been waiting in the nearby trees. Before leaving he warned Juban that it would be dangerous if he was seen here, so not to expect to see him soon.

Now—months later—Kodi urged Keoaw forward. The bird stepped off the precipitous edge of the landing area, plunged down into the valley below, and then used his massive wings to lift himself and his rider to the skies.

Most haraanis resisted the control of their riders, but Keoaw now willingly did the bidding of the young nephil who rode him. Bird and rider left the area of Kron's fortress and followed their usual circuit.

First, Kodi guided Keoaw east, passing over the home of Enoch before moving farther southeast to fly over the home of Seth.

Far below him, Kodi thought he saw Mehri working with others in a large field. He circled lower and lower until he was sure it was she, and then he landed Keoaw a dozen paces from the girl.

"Kodi!" she called as she dropped her rake and turned toward him. "You're unharmed!"

"Yes, I'm fine."

"I am so thankful you are well!"

He had almost forgotten how stunning this young woman was. Her black hair flowed long and shiny down her back and her blue eyes looked at him in wide-eyed joy.

No wonder Azazel had wanted her for his wife. If I were not a nephil, I would ask for her hand myself.

Mehri ran toward him and threw her arms impulsively around his waist. The top of her head came only to the middle of his ribcage. Tilting her head back, she looked up at him.

"I wanted to thank you for saving me from Azazel, but I didn't think I would ever see you again."

"Were you worried about me?" Kodi patted her head and smiled down at her.

As if she felt suddenly shy, Mehri let go of his waist and moved back several steps.

"Well, I did worry that Kron would punish you for helping me."

"He never knew. I told him I had been attacked by a gang of Sethians."

"How are the rest—Pazel and Chay . . . and Hod?"

"I know they got away, but I haven't seen them since you and Hod escaped. And you? Are you married yet?"

"No. Our aged patriarch Seth has told me that whom I marry is of utmost importance since my husband and I will be the grandparents of the one who will save humanity from the great judgment. He says he is waiting for a sign from Elohim."

Kodi looked far off toward the great cliffs marking the entrance to the Garden of Eden. He took a deep breath and let it out in a long sigh.

"He will be someone very special."

"That's what he said. But he also said my choice could be a sign."

The beautiful young woman took the nephil's hand and began pulling him toward the home of Seth. "Come. I would like you to meet him."

"I don't know how happy he will be to meet me, but I need to ask him if I may climb to the top of that hill behind his hut so that I can take off on Keoaw."

If Kodi had not noticed the hill, he would not have landed here as the haraanis always needed to take off from a high place when they carried a rider. This hill would be barely sufficient, but he trusted Keoaw's strong wings to do the job.

Having heard the story of the mission from Hod, Seth was very glad to meet a good nephil. He spent several hours with Kodi before sending him on his way.

"Promise to find Hod and let me know how he is," Mehri said before he left. "Promise to come back to see me."

"I will if I can."

With these last words, Kodi left on Keoaw and flew directly west across the great desert and the south side of the Eden Mountains, where he knew his cousin Pazel lived.

He wondered if Pazel had returned to his home on the desert side of the mountains or if the little salt seller still lived with his family in Havilah.

Kodi headed for a nearby peak and guided the bird to a perch. After dismounting, he squatted on a boulder that seemed to hang out over the mountainside. As he sat there surveying the land south of the desert, Kodi spotted another haraani flying overhead and coming from the south. It was ridden by a Lamechite he recognized, one who had been injured in a fight with Hod and Pazel.

I wonder what Niute wanted in the land of Garth. If he is searching for Hod and Chay, I may have to get involved again.

◁2▷

A New Home

For several days they walked down the middle of the stream going west from the River Pishon. Chay and Hod followed their nephews without question, but when the water began to deepen, Hod called out to the leader. "Brosh, aren't we going to leave the stream somewhere?"

His nephew stopped and waited for them to catch up with him before he answered. "No, this is to throw off any enemy who might be following. We know the Lamechites have good tracking noses, so we hope to lose them at the water."

"Won't they go up and down the other bank until they pick up the scent?"

Brosh arched a brow at Hod. "We have that figured out. Follow me just a little farther."

After Hod made a gesture for Brosh to lead on, they continued a quarter league more. Finally Brosh turned toward the far bank. By now the water was nearly up to their armpits. They moved toward a place where a large willow grew out over the water. Its branches were so long and thick that they made a tent under which the group could duck. When they were all beneath the willow, Brosh turned to Hod and Chay.

"Down in the roots of this tree, we have dug out a tunnel. You will have to swim underwater a few cubits, but it will not be too difficult. By the time we come out, we will be far enough from the bank to throw off the best tracker."

Hod nodded and looked back at Chay, who had a doubtful scowl on his face, then looked back at his nephew. "How will we be able to find our way in the dark water?"

"Just go down between these two roots and pull yourself down the passage we have made. You can't go anywhere but straight ahead. You have to do it fast to have enough air! Dalit will go first so that he can be watching for you. Hod, I want you to go next. I'll come after to check on you and then come back to help Chay make it."

"Uh, sure." Hod realized he was not too excited about this and wondered if his face seemed as troubled as his brother's.

Dalit immediately dived down between the roots and disappeared. Brosh waited a while, smiling at the concern on the others' faces, and then turned to Hod.

"Your turn. Grab hold of the roots on both sides of the tunnel and pull yourself quickly through. But take several deep breaths first."

Before plunging under the water, Hod peeked through the willow branches at the woods on the other side of the stream. He froze when he saw yellow eyes, followed by an immense body, emerge from the trees.

"Look, Chay!"

Chay peeked through the branches and then sucked in his breath.

"That is the biggest wolf I've ever seen."

"He looks hungry," Brosh snapped. "Hurry!"

Hod pulled in and blew out a deep breath before finally taking in as much air as his lungs would hold and diving down between the two roots. Once under the tree, he realized what Brosh had meant. There was an easy passage between the roots, and even though the water was too murky and dark to tell what was around him, he was able to pull himself through the passage by grabbing the roots on either side.

When he popped out in a watery pool, Hod blew out his breath in an explosive gasp and shook the water out of his face and hair. Dalit, standing by the edge of the pool, reached out a hand to help Hod out of the water.

"We told you it wouldn't be hard!"

"You were right. I don't think Chay will have any trouble."

Within a few minutes all four members of the family of Elim had climbed out of the water and were standing by the pool. Hod looked back through the woods in the direction he guessed they had traversed underground. The woods were so thick that no one tracking them could possibly catch their scent or any other hint of the way they had gone.

"Don't worry," Brosh said. "That wolf won't be able to follow. He'll have no idea what happened to us."

After they had explained to Dalit about the wolf, Hod asked the question that had just occurred to him. "Who ever thought of making a way like this to elude trackers? It was a very inventive idea."

Brosh winked at his brother before answering Hod's question. "You will never guess it in a million years! In fact, it is the last person you would ever think!"

As he looked from one of his nephews over to the other, Hod's mind ran over all the family members who could have devised this ingenious manner of throwing off an enemy. No one he thought of would have been such a cause for merriment.

"Who? I wouldn't be surprised for any of my brothers or nephews to think of this. Chay, what do you think?"

Chay shrugged and then shook his head before an idea occurred to him that made him grin.

"I suppose I would be amazed if they said our mother thought of the idea."

Now Dalit began to laugh. "That's close! It was Hela! Your baby sister Hela! Since we moved, she has had many ideas to make our lives safer and easier."

"I believe it," Hod said. "Hela always was the smartest of us all. Because she is a woman, the family does not expect it of her, but I do. What else has she thought of?"

Dalit nodded and quickly filled in the information. "She made a way to bring water to our homes through hollow bamboo and an idea for disguising our fields from the haraanis. You'll see pretty soon."

"Let's hurry," Brosh interrupted, and they all began to follow him through a thick forest with no discernible path.

"Where are we going?" Chay asked. "It doesn't look as if anyone has ever walked through here."

Brosh chuckled and gave them a mysterious smile. "That is true."

"But I thought you were taking us to the new compound." Chay frowned and looked over at Hod, who looked just as perplexed.

"Grandfather wants no paths to our home," Dalit explained. "If we have to leave home, we come and go from this pool by different routes, and we are bringing you a way never taken before."

Hod nodded as he followed his nephews around a large terebinth tree.

"A wise decision. Although the nephilim have not bothered Chay and me in Garth, we don't know whether or not they are still looking for the family."

"When you see how different our new home is, you will understand how much safer we are," Brosh said.

Within an hour the four men came to a place where the woods ran into a steep hill. The thick trees grew on up the hill with no change in density.

"We're going up." Brosh immediately began climbing the hill, using tree trunks as balance. The other three followed him.

When they reached the crest of the ridge, the woods about them were so thick and the mist coming up from the ground so dense that they could not see much beyond the summit. It seemed to be a complete ring of hills, or rather a ridge that made a full circle. In the center was a low area with treetops sticking through the fog. He saw no sign of habitation.

Brosh and Dalit went down the other side without taking time to rest. Hod and Chay said nothing, saving their energy to keep from sliding down the steep back side of the hill. At the bottom they found only more trees, but after a short, winding trek through extremely thick underbrush, they stepped out into a clearing where barley, beans, and other crops grew right up to the wood line.

"Are these our fields?" Hod cried. "What is that overhead?"

They all looked up at a covering made of woven vines that stretched across the entire clearing. Some tree branches and other green materials were woven into this covering.

"This is what Hela suggested as a way to hide from any haraanis who might be searching for us," Dalit explained. "The covering is very thick over the houses and less over the fields to let in the sun when the mist lessens."

"Good idea!" Chay chuckled as he examined the canopy with interest.

Hod, however, was looking at the many little houses built of logs barely visible at the far end of the field. "So this is our new home?"

"Yes," Brosh answered. "We found a flat area completely circled by this almost impassible ridge, cut the trees to make houses, burned out the stumps, and made farm land."

"What do you do for water?" Chay asked as he and his brother began walking through the green fields toward the houses.

Dalit pointed off to a steep hillside to the right. "There is a large spring that flows down to a good-sized pond in the middle of our compound. We get all the water we need from it. Hela came up with the idea of using bamboo tubes to send some water from the spring to a cistern near our huts."

By this time the four men were in full view of the rest of the family. Hod, thrilled to see his sister running with her arms outstretched, rushed forward, snatched her up in his arms, and spun her in a circle.

Hela's blonde hair flew out, and her dark brown eyes shone with happiness. The strong muscles he could feel in her arms reminded him of what a hard-working girl she was.

"Hela, you've grown up since I've been gone!"

"*I've* grown up?" She held Hod back from her and looked him up and down. "You've turned into a man. I can't wait to hear about all your exploits."

"And I'm ready to tell them. I'll wait till everyone is gathered at the fire this evening to tell about my mission. Right now I want to see Father, and then you must tell me of your ideas for improving life here."

Hod and Chay went from one family member to the other hugging and shaking their hands until they finally reached Elim, their own father. Unable to talk at first, the old man embraced Hod and began crying on his shoulder.

"Father, didn't you know Elohim would take care of us?" Hod asked.

"I tried to believe, but it was very hard. Sometimes I thought I would never see either of you again. We were all sure Chay was dead after the nephilim took him."

Hod reached out toward his brother, beckoning him to move closer. He saw that Chay seemed reluctant to embrace Elim.

"No, Elohim protected my brother. I could not have completed my mission without him."

Elim let go of Hod and hugged Chay tightly to his chest. "My son, my son!"

As Hod watched his brother and father, he was glad to see Chay getting the love he had always wanted. In the old days, most of Elim's attention had gone to Hod. Chay had simply been given the responsibility of watching out for his younger brother.

No wonder Chay resented me. How it must have hurt him to see my father's love fall on me while he was burdened with the job of protecting me. I hope our adventure has changed things. I think Father finally realizes how much he loves Chay. Maybe

*Chay will be able to get over the hurt that had bothered him for
years.*

♓

Using a gnarled stick for balance, Enoch worked his
way to the mountaintop once again. He lifted his long
robe, stepped up on a large boulder, and then raised his
eyes to the pinnacle. Blue sky surrounded the flat rock
marking the highest point.

"Hello, old friend." The Watcher Remiel suddenly appeared on the rock and waved down to Enoch. "We have
much to talk about today."

Enoch finished the climb and then, with his long white
beard blowing in the cool wind, sat on the stone Remiel
indicated. The Watcher sat beside him and put a friendly
hand on his shoulder.

"We are concerned with what we see on earth. The
nephilim have gotten much worse. Kron and his men have
devoured many of the animals on earth. They eat them faster than they breed. The behemoth herds are disappear-
ing."

"What will the nephilim do when they run out of animals?" Enoch stroked his beard.

"Turn to man. Kron has already begun to eat his pri-
soners. It is another abomination that sends a foul odor to
heaven."

Enoch thought a moment before answering. He supposed his young nephews and their friends would be asked to continue their mission against the nephilim when they had so recently gone back to their families.

"I wish you Watchers would destroy them all."

Remiel's smile showed no anger or judgment of the man seated beside him, the only human privileged to really know the Watchers. They were old friends.

"That is not our purpose. We watch. We step in when Elohim tells us to, but we were not intended to always make the way smooth for you."

"I understand that. What will my friends have to do? How can they stop Kron?"

Remiel pointed down the mountain toward the south. "Kron has learned about the healing water from those who fought our young friends. He must not find the river. He will only get stronger with it. The Iron Fist must destroy the cave where the river surfaces."

"How?"

"There are three things available on earth that when combined have great destructive power. The young people will bring these to you, and then I will tell you how to mix them. None of the youths must know all of the ingredients. It is not the will of Elohim for mankind or the nephilim to have this power—not for many ages."

Enoch, agreeing that men should not have this thing, nodded. "How do we destroy the cave?"

"You will put this powder in iron pots, seal them up, and set them on fire. If these pots are placed where I tell you, the roof of the cave will come down on the river and hide the water forever."

"How do I find the young people? They have all scattered to their homes."

"Elohim will bring them to you."

For the next hour Remiel told Enoch about the three ingredients needed to make the powder—how to mix them, how to pack the powder into iron pots, and then how to set them on fire. When he was done explaining this, Remiel again laid his hand on Enoch's shoulder.

"Kron will not be successful finding the river at first. The young people will come to you soon to begin this mission. In the meantime, you will be given the hardest task Elohim has ever set for you."

"Go ahead and tell me. Whatever it is, I will do it."

"I know. He sees your obedient heart. You will go to the place I will take you where you will meet with the Dark Watchers and tell them they have been weighed in the balance and found guilty. For their behavior with human women, they will be punished, and their children will be destroyed."

"All? Even young Kodi, grandson of Juban?"

"He is different. If he continues to keep himself unpolluted from the nephilim corruption, he will survive. If not, he will die."

ℵ

Enoch looked down at the fissure—a jagged, yellow wound cutting across the gray land called Atlantia.

From where he stood on air a league above the earth, the fissure was a bright slash giving the ugly country its only color.

"So that is where the Dark Watchers live," he said to the heavenly being whose hold on Enoch's elbow kept him from plummeting to the ground. "It has a kind of beauty."

"Yes, from a distance, but it has the smell of brimstone. The yellow crystals lining the walls of the chasm are soft and burn in the fire that comes from the depths of the earth."

"I know the smell of brimstone. It burns the eyes and nose. Since you Watchers do not have earthy bodies, it should not bother you."

Remiel smiled at his old friend as he took him down toward the earth.

"But we can smell, and we love the delicious aromas such as roses, jasmine, and cedar. We dislike the stenches of earth. Only the Dark Watchers enjoy the odor of brimstone enough to live in it."

When Enoch's feet touched the ground close to the edge of the yellow fissure, he bent over the rim and looked down. The yellow crystals could be seen embedded in the slightly slanted walls.

"They are beautiful — those crystals. Is there a purpose for these yellow rocks?"

"Yes, they can be crushed into a powder which has many uses. Now I will take you down to the floor below to look for Azazel and Samyaza. I do not talk to them, but you can. You know the message you must give them."

"Yes."

At the bottom of the chasm, as Enoch waited alone for one of the Dark Watchers to appear, his mind suddenly went back to the day many, many years ago when he was standing at the home of his ancestor Seth looking up at the entrance to the Garden from which Adam and Eve had been expelled.

The bluffs rose tall and straight divided by a vee-shaped split through which a mighty gush of water surged before falling on a mass of stones half a league below. From there the water diverted in four directions and became the great rivers of earth, the Euphrates, the Tigris, the Gihon, and the Pishon.

He had been overcome with a desire to see the Garden. All his life he had heard the story of the beautiful place where the first man and woman had lived, and he thought it might be visible from high above.

As far as he knew, no one had been near the Garden since the expulsion. After telling his family he would be traveling a while, he climbed the south side of the Eden Mountains west of the Garden to the highest peaks. He found the back side of the cliffs overlooking the Garden, and looked down for the first time on the glorious sight below.

A many-hued green blanket dotted by circles of pink, yellow, lavender, blue and varied shades of white, the Garden seemed to belong in heaven rather than earth. The river dividing it was as blue as the sky above. After satisfying his eyes with this feast, Enoch had decided to climb to the mountaintop so he could see the whole world. At the pinnacle he had looked at the green lands to the north, south, east, and west and thought that even without the Garden, this was a most beautiful world.

Of course, that was many decades before the first nephil, Kron, was conceived. Since then many more children of Dark Watchers and Cainite women had been born. These giants had eventually corrupted Atlantia, the land they had chosen for their home. Once as green as any place else on earth, Atlantia was now black, brown, gray and ruined.

That first day Enoch had stood and reveled in the cool air and warm sun before lifting his eyes to heaven to thank Elohim for the glory before his eyes. Then Remiel, the Watcher, had appeared to him and had told him his faithfulness and love for Elohim had been noted. Remiel had explained how to better walk with Elohim.

After this experience Enoch found the place on the cliffs above the Garden where he now made his home. For many years Enoch had lived on the mountain, often going home to visit his family, but spending most of his time with the pure Watchers. Now he was an old man—more than three hundred and sixty years old—and he had seen and done more than any human on earth, but until today he had not gone into the abode of the Dark Watchers to meet them face to face.

His friendship with the pure Watchers was a delight, but to speak to Dark Watchers would be horrifying. Remiel's last words before leaving him had been some consolation: "Do not fear the Dark Watchers. They know you have been sent by Elohim to bring them a message from Him. They will not be able to hurt you."

Enoch was not really worried. He knew Remiel would not have left him here if he were in danger. Then the shrieking voice startled him out of his reverie.

"Human! Why are you here in my home? Why have you left your protected garden where no one is allowed to touch you?"

Enoch turned to see a Dark Watcher much like the pure ones he knew so well. He was surprised that the voice held none of the melodious sound he associated with all heavenly creatures.

Tall as he wanted to be—Enoch knew that they could change their size at will—the being had the icy blue eyes and white hair common to his type. His face was beautiful but still terrible to look at while his eyes held a viciousness deep within them.

"You have a message from Him! Go ahead, human! Do not fear to tell me. You are protected."

"I have been sent to tell you that your time for interfering in the human race is at an end. A great catastrophe is coming that will cleanse the earth from the corruption you and your kind have wrought. At that time you and those of you who have slept with the human women will be bound in the bottom of the yellow fissure. You will stay there until the great judgment at the end of the age."

"When will this happen?" Azazel flew at Enoch but was stopped by an unseen force inches from his face.

A second Dark Watcher erupted from the depths of the fissure in a froth of hot, yellow bubbles and darted at the old man. Claw-like hands snatched at Enoch's face.

Again, an invisible power kept the sharp talons away and then began to lift the human into the air.

"Samyaza, do you hear?" Azazel screamed. "We are doomed! He dares to judge us in our world. This is what we were given for our own. Now He will take it away! Kill the man—kill him!"

"We cannot. You know we cannot touch him. We must leave it to your son Kron to thwart His plans."

Enoch looked down at the angry Dark Watcher and then over to the kind being who held his arm.

"I am very glad to be on your side," he said and looked down no more.

♓

Three months after arriving at the Elimites new home, Hod and Chay were once more working together in the fields, but now no one worried about an enemy coming up on them. The new home was many leagues from Kron's fortress and protected by the overhead canopy so probably would not be found by any searching harannis.

As they were chopping weeds, Hod stopped and looked over at Chay, who was working several rows behind him. "Hey, are you bored?"

"A little—why?"

"What would you think about going to visit Mehri's family?" Hod leaned on the mattock handle as he talked.

Chay looked startled. "Are you crazy? We made it back home without dying! Isn't that enough for you?"

"I don't want to go anywhere near Kron, but I would like to hear how Pazel is doing. Mehri's family might know since he was going there. I would like to see more of the world."

Hod turned back to the barley and began chopping again. He understood what Chay meant, but he also knew that his life had changed and he could never be just a farmer again. This new hidden home was a safe place to raise a family, but Hod could not forget about the larger world outside. The safe life no longer appealed to him.

Beyond this ridged ring were rocky mountains, swift rivers, and deep caves that sparkled like jewels. Thousands of people who were not closely related to him populated this world, and Hod wanted to know them. And—in the land just south of Adam's Garden—Mehri, daughter of Dolian, dwelt. Hod had fallen in love with her while saving her during the mission and wanted to see her again before Seth found her a husband.

Chay left his mattock in his bean row and came over to where Hod was working.

"Don't you think we should be here to defend the family in case the nephilim find them?"

"I have studied this place the family has found," Hod said. "The nephilim would have difficulty passing through the forest, and there are no trails. Even our scent was disguised as we entered the forest. They are safe here."

"Father will be upset if we leave, but I think between the two of us we can convince him that we are only visiting and not be in danger."

"We? I don't expect you to go with me, Chay. After all, Kron threatened to eat you alive if you didn't bring me back. Maybe you should stay here."

Chay shook his head with vigor. "Oh, no! If you go, I am going with you."

"I'm not a child anymore, and the prophecy has been fulfilled. You don't have to watch over me now. If that's why you want to go."

"I wouldn't go to look after you." Chay gave Hod a hard look. "I'm just afraid you'll have some adventures that I'll miss out on."

Hod chuckled a little, and then began to laugh. "Fine. Let's go tell our father."

Elim was not happy to hear Hod's plan to visit his old friends, but he did not deny his permission. Instead, the old man looked long at his youngest son, his eyes seeming to bore to the very bottom of Hod's soul.

"You are a man. When I look at you, I no longer see a boy." He shifted his eyes to Chay. "Will you go too?"

"I want to, but Hod doesn't want me to go if it's to take care of him."

Elim smiled at Chay and then at Hod. He put a hand on each son's shoulder.

"Hod is now a warrior. Maybe he should take care of you when you go with him this time."

"What?" Chay cried before realizing that his father was teasing him. "All right! I see your point. If Hod will let me go with him, we'll be equals. And we'll take our swords in case we do confront an enemy."

While they were talking, Hela had come close enough to hear their conversation. Neither brother had noticed, so they were startled when she suddenly interrupted.

"May I go too?"

Her father and both brothers immediately turned to her, their faces reflecting their surprise. Elim spoke first. "Definitely not! You are too young and only a girl. If your brothers encountered an enemy, they would have to worry about you."

"But I would like to see the world too!" Hela protested. "Father, wouldn't I be safe with my two warrior brothers?"

"Not as safe as you will be at home with us," Elim said. The sternness in his eye made Hod wonder if Hela's old strong-willed determination to have her own way was causing their father trouble lately.

"Father is right," Hod said. "After what we have told you about the Dark Watchers desiring human women, you should fear to leave this peaceful cove."

"But Mehri is the most beautiful woman on Earth. I'm just ordinary. They wouldn't want me!"

Hela continued to argue, even though she could tell she would not win. All three males of the family immediately assured her that she was a pretty girl, but only Hod knew the final reason she should not go.

"You are a fine-looking girl. The problem is Azazel knows my face. He saw me escape with Mehri, and I saw the hate on his face. He would gladly ruin my sister just to wreak vengeance on me. You must stay here."

Ж

Hela said no more; however, as she turned to walk away, she was plotting ways to be included in this trip her brothers planned.

Since the boys had left on their mission, she had made a determined effort to be more than just another woman in the family. She had worked hard at coming up with new ways to make the family compound more comfortable. She had worked to devise a new weapon so that she could do her share in defending the family if necessary. And she had paid no attention when her mother had suggested she consider marrying one of the nephews who flirted with her.

"Mother! I know them so well! I would rather marry someone not part of the family."

Her mother had shaken her head and seemed worried. "You are related to everyone in the world. All are your cousins. Even the Cainites are part of the Adamite family."

"I know, but I wish I could meet someone new."

So now she kept her thoughts to herself as she made her plans. Somehow, someway, she knew she would go with her brothers.

◁ 3 ▷

A New Family

The marriage ceremony was short and simple, but the feast would last all day and well into the night.

Pazel stood before Dolian, the patriarch of the family of his friends Mehri and Mathu. Beside him stood Shani, his bride and the granddaughter of Dolian.

As Pazel looked into his wife's blue eyes, he could not help but think how the past seven months had changed his life in ways he would never have imagined.

Months ago he had been going about his usual routine in the Eden Mountains involving scraping salt from the walls of one of his caves and packing it in jugs to sell to the travelers who found their way to him. He also found time to explore the whole of the mountains near his home on the southern side of the range.

His life had been a lonely one. The only contact with humanity he had was with those who either purposely or accidentally found their way to his cave home. He had made his place easy to find by painting the large rock he used for a door with a deep orange-brown dye made from clay from a lower cave floor. Since Pazel traded the salt he gathered for the food that sustained him and the clothing he wore, it was necessary for his home to be easy for customers to find.

And then one day when he was climbing high above his cave, he had seen a small figure running straight and fast across the desert, coming from the ridge to the south and making its way across the southern desert directly toward Pazel's cave.

When he had realized that the human he saw was running for his life from three Lamechites and Hartagga, Kron's evil bear-monster, Pazel had quickly decided what to do. Taking an underground route through caves and tunnels, he had been able to meet the figure at one of his emergency exits—a dry well out in the desert.

The figure he rescued became his great friend, but the red-headed Hod had also saved Pazel's life when one of the Lamechite pursuers had come after him with a sharp curved knife. From that time on, Pazel had stayed with his friend and eventually joined the confederacy that had saved Mehri from the Dark Watchers and brought her to the safety of the home of Seth.

When the mission was over, Pazel had agreed to return to Havilah, Mehri's home, to tell her family that she was safe. That had been six months ago, and still he had not returned to his home in the mountains.

In Havilah he had lived with Juban, the grandfather he had never known as a child but had discovered because of his adventure. He had also spent time with Mehri's family. He still remembered with pain the day of his arrival when he had had to tell both good and bad news to the parents, Neva and Dolian.

"Your daughter is safe in the home of Seth, in the shadow of the gate to the Garden of Eden," Pazel had said to begin his news.

"And Mathu? How is he?"

Neva leaned forward to put her hand on Pazel's hand, Pazel dropped his head but looked up into her eyes.

"My heart breaks to tell you this. He was killed by the Lamechites as we traveled back from the glade."

Neva fell against her husband's shoulder and began a keening moan. Pazel hurried to give her the rest of the news. "He died trying to save Mehri from their grasp. He was brave and faithful."

"Of course, we knew he would be," Dolian said. "But we have lost five sons in the last two months because of Azazel. It brings great grief on our gray heads."

"I'm sorry to bring you this news, but Mehri wanted you to know she was safe, so I volunteered to come here. I hope to stay with my grandfather for a while."

Dolian's family had gathered to hear what Pazel had to say. When he had finished speaking, he looked about at old and young people, men and women, boys and girls, the children and grandchildren of this couple. As he was looking, his eyes met the bright blue eyes of a young girl close to his age. Without thinking, he smiled at the girl, who was shorter than he—and she smiled back.

That was the beginning of a friendship that led to love. Pazel began dropping by to visit with her family who lived in a small house near the home of Dolian and Neva. One day after he had been sitting and talking with Shani, he suggested they go for a walk.

"Oh, I'm not sure my mother will allow it."

"Why don't you ask her and find out?"

Shani's mother had come when they called and listened politely to Pazel's request for her daughter to walk out with him about the countryside.

"If we had not known what a good man your grandfather Juban is, we might have had second thoughts about letting our granddaughter spend time with a Cainite."

"I am thankful then that you know my grandfather well."

Now, months after beginning the courtship, Pazel was wed to the girl of his choice, with Dolian's blessing. After the ceremony, Dolian took him aside for a serious talk.

"You told me you were trying to decide where you would live with Shani. Will you return to the mountains or stay here?"

"I want to take her back to my home in the mountains and show her my place and my business. I mine salt, not gold, so there is no reason for me to stay here. Many people depend on my salt. I've been gone so long that I am concerned my regular traders will be looking for me."

"Then you have made a good decision, it would seem, but I will miss my little granddaughter."

So the young couple left a few days later for the Eden Mountains. They planned to cross from the foothills up and around to the southern face of the mountains. They were only an hour from Pazel's door when they spread out their lunch on a flat space covered by an overhanging rock.

"You rest here," Pazel told his bride. "I am going to climb far up where I can see if there are any dangers near. You are safe to nap in the cover of this rock."

Pazel looked in all directions before finding a comfortable seat on a high and prominent rock that seemed to overhang the entire mountain. He loved the view from the southern side of the range.

The strip of tan desert separated the mountains from the first ridge to the south. The facing side of that ridge was bare of trees, and Pazel knew from experience that it was sandy and hard to climb.

The other side gave way to a land of widely spaced trees, grassy meadows, small ponds, and many types of predatory animals. Next, Pazel turned his eyes eastward where he noticed a small speck in the sky, a speck which grew larger and larger until he could tell it was a haraani.

Pazel's attention remained riveted on the giant eagle coming his way. Eventually he could tell it carried a rider, and by the time it was a league away, he could tell the rider was Kodi, the nephil who had been part of the Iron Fist.

Kodi guided Keoaw to a smooth landing on the hill-top, grinned a greeting toward Pazel, and dismounted his haraani.

"Good morning, cousin!" Kodi called out as he walked toward the little Cainite.

"Kodi! I'm sorry I missed you when you visited our grandfather. We were all concerned about you when Hod told us you stayed in the castle after freeing Mehri."

The young nephil came over and sat on the hillside next to Pazel. "I was all right. Kron never suspected I had helped Hod with his mission. He's cruel but not as smart as he thinks he is."

"So has the king given up on finding Hod?"

"No. Right now, though, his main focus is on discovering the source of that water you and Hod gave to Mathu. One of the nephilim you fought on your way to Seth reported that he had seen a Cainite healed."

Pazel was silent as he looked over the distant landscape. The Watchers had given him the water as a child and for many years only he had known about the fifth river that flowed from the source in the Garden. The water had healed him when, as a very ill child, he had been put in a dry well by his father, who had then been killed by a giant beast. He still clearly recalled when the Watcher Remiel had appeared to him in that well and shown him the way to the river. The crystal water of this river that flowed underground emerged for a short distance in his largest cavern.

When Pazel had saved Hod, Pazel had shared the healing water with him while asking him to keep it secret.

Days later, before Pazel had parted with Hod and Chay at the home of Seth, he had given Hod permission to tell his brother about the river. Even though Kodi had shown himself to be a friend during the mission, Pazel did not feel he should tell him the secret.

"What does the king know about the water?"

"He knows that you and Hod had it. I told him what I knew when he asked, but I told him I didn't know much about it."

"I wish you hadn't even told him that." Pazel looked over at Kodi and saw only an open, friendly face. For a moment he was tempted to tell the nephil the secret, yet did not.

Kodi cleared his throat. "I am not asking you to tell me about it, but I do want to warn you that he's looking for you. If you are going back to your home, you need to be careful."

"Have they been to my cave?"

"Not that I have heard, but they could be there soon."

Pazel frowned and looked from Kodi to the distant mountains and then back over his right shoulder toward his grandfather's home.

"I was planning to take my bride to my cave tonight."

"Bride? You're married?"

"Yes, for a week now." Pazel looked toward the place where Shani waited. "She's at the bottom of the mountain. Shani is the niece of Mathu and Mehri. I wanted to get her out of Havilah where the nephilim feel free to harass the people. She will be freer in my home."

"Are you going there now?"

"I want to take her to my cave where she can help me with my salt business. I want to show her my underground world and all its wonders."

Kodi turned his eyes on the young Cainite, staring at him searchingly. "That is where the healing water is, right? In one of your caves?"

"I didn't say that!" Pazel continued to look away from Kodi.

"You didn't have to. But don't worry about me. I'll never give up you or the secret of the water to Kron!"

Pazel cleared his throat, looked up at the clouds a moment, and then turned his eyes on Kodi. "I would like to tell you, but the water was given to me as a trust to protect. I have had to tell some people, but I must not tell anyone else but my wife."

"Fair enough. I understand how you feel. If I can do anything to keep it out of Kron's hands, just ask me. If my evil brother ever gets his hands on that water, he will use it to live forever."

"Thank you. I believe you mean that." Pazel reached out to grip Kodi's arm.

"Be watchful. They may come for you, but I'm more worried about Hod. Do you know where he is?"

"No, when I left him at the home of Seth, he was going to stay a while before going back to his family home in Garth. I've heard nothing since then, but I was in Havilah for eight months."

Kodi stood and dusted himself off before looking over at Keoaw, still perched on the hilltop. "I have thought about visiting Hod during these last months. Because I was afraid I would endanger him, I have stayed far away, but now I am wondering whether I should warn him that he needs to be watchful."

"If you're careful you are not being followed, maybe you should try to find him." Pazel, confident of his own ability to get himself and his wife safely to his cave, worried more about the well-being of his old friend Hod than himself.

"I'll think about it a while and sound out the king before I do anything. You be careful now. Maybe we'll see each other again soon."

Kodi went back to Keoaw, led him to the edge of the prominent rock, mounted the bird, and urged him off the ledge and into the air. Pazel, who had never watched a haraani take off, marveled at the way the huge bird was able to bear Kodi's weight and lift him to the sky. He waved a final good-bye before returning to Shani.

"Are you ready to continue?" he asked.

"Yes. I've repacked everything. I'm getting very excited about seeing our home."

Pazel smiled at his wife and thought how much he enjoyed looking at her bright, happy eyes. He hoped the news he had to tell would not darken them. She matched his own optimistic spirit. He was sure she would see life as an adventure just as he did.

"I must tell you something before we go any farther."

"Go on," she urged.

"While I was up the mountain, the nephil I told you about—Kodi, my cousin—flew down on a haraani when he saw me."

"Yes. I saw him passing overhead."

"He said Kron is looking for me. We have to be careful, be on the watch for any of his warriors."

Shani grabbed Pazel's arm and turned him to look directly at her. "That's terrible! Why would he want you?"

Pazel debated a moment as he looked at his wife. There was no reason not to tell her about the fifth river; however, he did not want to put her in a position that could cause her trouble. But they were husband and wife now and must share all.

"Come," he said, taking her arm. "Let's talk as we walk."

"Yes." Shani let him lead her across the lower rocks.

"When I was on my great adventure, I carried a water-skin filled with healing water from an underground river. Kron has found out that I had the water, and he wants it—no doubt so that he can never get sick and live to be very old."

"Healing water! I fear if Kron wants it, he will get it. How did you ever find it?"

"I was given the water as a trust by the Watchers when I was a child. I must never allow it to fall into the hands of the nephilim or the Dark Watchers."

Pazel slowed his steps as his voice grew in urgency. "I want to tell you about the water, but you must never tell."

"I promise."

"You know of the four rivers that proceed from the Garden of Eden?"

Shani nodded and pointed off to the south. "I know the Pishon because it passes near Havilah. Tell me about the other three."

"The next river to the east of the Pishon is the Gihon. Our ancient ancestor Seth, who Mehri now lives with, has his home at the mouth of the Gihon. When we took Mehri there—coming from the north—we had to cross the Euphrates, the farthest north, and then the Tigris and finally the Gihon."

Shani took her husband's hand and intertwined her fingers with his as he continued.

"I have seen the water's source, a great spring that gushes from the cliffs above the Garden and then becomes the river that flows through the great stone gap. From there the water falls onto huge stones and is diverted into the four great rivers."

Shani said nothing for a while, merely smiled at him. And then she squeezed his hand.

"What are you thinking?" he said.

"That I wish I could have been with you on your adventure crossing the four rivers. And yet I think that if I can see this fifth river of magic water, it will be better than seeing all of the others."

"Well, you will see it!" Pazel squeezed her hand in return. "There is a passageway from my home cave that leads to the river. I will take you there and let you drink from this water."

"I can't wait!"

By now the painted stone door of Pazel's cave was in sight only a few dozen cubits above them. He stopped suddenly and pulled Shani down behind a large boulder.

"Ssh! Stay down!"

"What's wrong?" Shani stared at him from wide eyes.

"Something's out of place," he whispered. "My door has been moved."

She started to peek over the boulder, but he pulled her back.

"You have been gone a long time. Maybe someone looking for salt moved it," she said.

"Maybe—we must be careful, though. Here! Get down in the hollow behind this rock. Don't come out unless I come after you, even if you have to stay here a long time."

Pazel could tell he was frightening Shani badly, but he did what he had to do to protect her.

"What if you do not come back? What should I do then?"

"I'll be back. I know I will. But it could take a while. I may have to go down into the caves before I return. This is a big space and you have food and water."

"But if you don't come . . . ?"

Pazel sighed and, knowing she would not be content without an answer, finally spoke. "Wait at least until sunrise. It will be full dark in two hours. If I do not come back by morning, go quickly and carefully to your father. I will find you there, if I can."

The southern face of the mountain was composed of sand-colored boulders and huge rock formations with only a few tufts of greenery finding root between the stones.

Above his doorway the mountain sloped gradually up to a low peak. Behind that were layers and layers of peaks and slight valleys—with some grassy or tree-filled glades—all leading to distant and higher pinnacles.

Pazel's orange door stood far to the left side of the entrance. Since he had left it months ago, someone had worked hard to push the heavy stone. Pazel himself never bothered to make more than enough space to pass through.

Shani was right in saying anyone could have done it, but he had a fear that the one who had pushed the stone aside was close by, maybe even inside. Little by little, moving slowly from rock to rock, Pazel approached the door. Every time he stopped, he listened for any sound that did not fit. Eventually he reached the left side of the door, flattened himself against it, and then worked around it.

He slipped noiselessly into the cave, melding into the darkness of the inner wall. Without moving a muscle, he listened with all his might. He knew the sounds of this cave —distant trickling of water, nearer dripping down a back wall, a hollow echo of distant bats.

These sounds he knew, but what was that regular tapping coming toward him? It sounded as if one sandal-shod foot was stepping firmly on the stone floor, but instead of a second sandal, there was only a sliding sound as of something being dragged.

Pazel strained to identify the sound as it came nearer and nearer to where he stood hidden by the dark. Whatever made the sound turned a corner.

The being approaching held a lighted torch in his left hand, but the small light it threw down was on the other side from Pazel. He held his breath when the man passed no more than two bodies' lengths from him.

Now he realized that the unusual sounds he had heard were the result of a crippled leg, which the man dragged as he walked.

While Pazel watched, the intruder stuck his torch in one of the holders installed in the rock wall. He then moved toward the dim arrow of late afternoon light coming in from the open doorway.

When the man stood a moment in the sunlight, Pazel saw that it was a Lamechite, almost as short as he was with shaggy black hair more dirty and matted than usual for the vile sons of Lamech. Just as the strong odor common to these assassins filled Pazel's nostrils, he realized that his own smell might soon be detected.

The Lamechites were used as trackers by their masters the nephilim. How long would it be until this man discovered that Pazel was in the cave and came after him? He watched the man's profile intently. The Lamechite had stepped through the doorway, and his eyes were roaming over the area beyond. Pazel could tell he was sniffing the southern wind, which blew directly into the cave and no doubt kept his own scent from reaching the Lamechite.

Suddenly the man's head stopped turning, and he seemed to hone in on something. Pazel jumped when the dirty man spoke. "Ah! Sethian—and female!"

The Lamechite was looking down the mountainside, directly toward the place where Shani was hidden. Without another thought, Pazel stepped out from the wall.

"Lamechite! Are you looking for me?"

At these words the assassin spun about, drawing his curved sword as he turned. Pazel stepped out into the shaft of light coming from behind his foe and drew the sword he had carried since leaving Hod and Chay.

"You are the salt merchant?" The Lamechite almost growled out these words.

"I am. I repeat—are you looking for me?"

"Yes, Kron knows you are hiding the secret of the healing water."

Before responding, Pazel began to work his way slowly backward into the cave. The Lamechite moved toward him. Both men held their swords in their right hands ready for use while their left hands were held out for balance.

"Healing water? What is that?"

"Stop where you are! Don't take another step! I am Niute, and I am going to kill you. When I am done, I'll find your friend the fire-hair and kill him too."

"Why us? What have we done to you?"

The man pointed at his leg, which Pazel now saw was crooked. "You left me in the mountains with a broken leg, and I swore I would make you pay! But if you lead me to the water so that I can heal my leg, I might forget my vengeance."

Now Pazel was able to put it all together. When he and Hod had been crossing the mountains on the way to Enoch's garden, two Lamechites had followed them on orders from Kron. Hod had killed one and fought this other one until he fell down a steep embankment.

He recalled that his friend had said the man had injured his leg, but who would have thought the man would want to avenge his wound?

Pazel put this aside for the moment as his main concern was for the safety of Shani. He knew the Lamechite had smelled her and had been on the verge of going after her before Pazel had revealed himself. He knew he could run through the labyrinthine tunnels of his home and leave the Lamechite behind; however, if he did this, the man would go after Shani.

The plan that had begun to grow in Pazel's brain was to slowly draw the Lamechite farther and farther into the tunnels until the man was lost. At that point his plan was to go back and get his wife safely out of the man's reach.

Ignoring the words of his opponent, he turned, snatched the torch from the wall, and ran down the closest passageway fast enough to get away but not so fast as to lose the man. Pazel wondered if Niute would take the time to light another torch and quickly discovered that he did not. This would make it easier to lose him.

He probably thinks he can catch me and take my light. He has no idea how well I know this cave.

To encourage his pursuer to keep following, Pazel purposely waited until he was close enough to follow his torch. This passage led away from the river and eventually ended up in a high cavern, but getting there involved many turns—sometimes right and sometimes left. Every time he took one of these turns, Pazel would stop just far enough to be out of the Lamechite's reach but near enough to make sure the torch was seen.

By the time he reached the upper cavern, Pazel was sure once he left the man behind him, he would not easily find his way back, even with his sense of smell. While he waited just inside the door, Pazel put the torch in a wide crack in the wall and held his sword ready for the enemy.

Niute stepped into the room, sword ready and swinging in the usual fighting style of these assassins. Prepared though he was, Pazel was caught by surprise. The wild motion of his enemy's sword drove him back until he came up against a wall.

Pazel took his eye off the sword long enough to glance at the torch he had left in the far wall. If he could dodge the man's blade and dash across the chamber, he could snatch up the torch and leave the Lamechite in darkness.

Of course, the man would follow him by his scent, but Pazel knew that, due to the Lamechite's bad leg, he could gain time on him in the twisting passages. He used his own sword to deflect the next swing but not in time to prevent the blade from nicking his arm. When Niute's sword flew off to the left, Pazel darted to the right and headed straight for the torch. He heard the Lamechite's steps coming after him as quickly as his crippled limb allowed.

Pazel never slowed his pace as he grabbed the torch with his wounded arm and dashed out the doorway. He was barely aware of the pain in his left arm but could feel blood running down it.

He knew the Lamechite would expect to follow him as easily as he had on the way in, but Pazel no longer waited at turns to help the man. Instead, he darted around corners, sped up on straight passages, and then made the next turn.

Eventually Pazel stopped to listen for sounds behind him. A distant scream echoed through the cave, and he smiled to picture the Lamechite lost in the dark. But not really lost. He had his nose to lead him out.

Should I go straight to Shani just in case the Lamechite finds his way out sooner than I think, or should I go down to the river and heal my wound?

Pazel moved to the next place where he had to choose a left or right turn. He glanced to the left where, with a half hour's travel down hidden and hard-to-find tunnels, he could reach the river.

To the right, in almost double the time, he could reach Shani and make sure she was safe. Surely he could go to the river, heal his injury, and reach his wife before the Lamechite found his way out of the dark passages. Pazel thought a moment—and then headed to the right.

◁4▷

A New Journey

ela had concocted her plan for going to Havilah long before her two brothers left. But she had told no one and given no hint of her secret. She was smart enough to know her father would never change his mind about her going. He still saw her as a child.

As the youngest child of Elim, she had been allowed her own way more than any of her older brothers and sisters. However, she knew that in this situation, she would never prevail.

Although he was two years older than she, Hod had been protected by the family because of the prophecy at his birth that he would bring about the downfall of the nephilim.

Once the family had learned that Kron was seeking to kill the infant, they had moved to Garth and tried to shield him from discovery. Hela was the only child born after they moved and, although she was greatly loved by all the family, she never felt as if she were the center of their world as her brother was.

When she was very young, she had thought that red hair meant one was marked for greatness. Her own blonde head was much too ordinary. Because of the family's focus on Hod, Hela had always been able to escape close scrutiny. She had never resented him the way she knew Chay did. To Hela, Hod was the adored older brother who was sweet, loving, brave, and loyal, but Chay sometimes seemed to hate Hod.

As she grew up with these two brothers, Hela often felt as if she were a buffer between them. A few years ago Chay had told her that when he was only seven years old, Elim told him he must always watch over Hod, always keep an eye out for strangers.

Hela remembered how her eyes had filled with tears when Chay had said, "I have always wondered who was watching over me."

No matter how much she loved Hod, she always felt that Chay had been overlooked. As for herself, she had only been liberated by Hod's special place in the family. From early childhood she had climbed trees and played in the woods with Hod, Chay, and the nephews near their age. She had no young sisters and her many nieces cared only for housework.

Her mother insisted she learn to cook and sew, but everyone agreed that the youngest daughter lacked talent in the housekeeping arts. With so many other women to take care of the household chores, no one had stopped Hela from exploring the woods with the boys in the family.

But now that Hod had returned as a man who had fulfilled at least part of the prophecy, Hela's parents were focusing their concern on her, the last unmarried daughter.

Because she felt more akin to her brothers than her sisters and nieces, Hela grieved when they left home last year. A few days after Hod and Chay had fought two nephilim at the gates of their compound and then had disappeared into the woods, Ahuv, their oldest brother, reported that Hod was alive and on a special mission given to him by a Watcher. Chay, they discovered, had been captured and taken away by the enemy.

Hela had imagined herself beside her brothers fighting the nephilim who had attacked the compound, and she had suffered when she was forced to hide in a cave with the women, children, and old men.

While Hod and Chay were gone, Hela had begun to think about their battle with the two nephilim who had attacked the compound. Hod had been able to kill the first one with a well-aimed mattock, which he had thrown and embedded in the giant's chest, yet the second giant had run off only because they had stabbed his legs. With her inventive turn of mind, Hela had decided she would devise a better way to defeat and destroy this enemy that was twice their size. She had spent the intervening months working on this problem.

One day when she was sharpening stakes to use for propping up plants in the garden, she had accidentally poked her leg with the point of one stick. She had quickly staunched the blood with some moss and then had snatched up the stick and thrown it away in anger. Feeling foolish for her temper tantrum, Hela had gone to retrieve the stick and found that it had stuck straight up in the soft garden soil.

It's too bad we don't have a way to throw sharpened sticks at the nephilim with enough force to hurt them, she had mused.

After that, Hela bent her keen mind to finding a better way to propel the sharpened sticks than throwing them. It was while she was helping one of her older sisters make thread from flax that the idea had come to her.

Abira and she had stripped the long threads from newly harvested flax plants. Next, they had twisted the fibers together into threads they could use to weave the linen for the family's clothing. Abira soaked the thread before stretching it tightly from one end to the other of an ash ox yoke to dry. The next day Hela came back to gather the flax, which was now dry and shrunken until tight. She unwrapped the thin string little by little, rolling it into a ball as she did.

When she reached the last few threads, Hela became curious about how much it would stretch. She pulled it out a hand's length and then released it to see if it would spring back to its original state. It did, and with a sharp whoosh. She suddenly stood up straight as a new idea began to form. She dropped the ball of flax fibers and ran to the field to get one of her sharpened stakes. Attaching the stick to the thread she had just pulled back and then letting it go propelled the stick a few feet. Hela repeated this until she was content that this new idea had possibilities.

Hela experimented with different threads until she found that a four cubit line of twisted flax rubbed with beeswax and tied at each end to a five cubit peeled ash staff worked best at propelling the arrows with force.

The staff had to be bent enough to keep the line taut. The sharpened sticks needed to be as straight and slim as possible, but with the right combination she might have a weapon to strike the nephilim right to their hearts.

When she could find the time away from her work, Hela practiced with this bowed wood, waxed string, and slim, swift arrow until she was able to embed it in the bark of a tree. Aim and straightness of direction was a problem, but she felt that if she were close enough, she could hit the neck of a nephil. Hela worked with different types of arrows. The best were made from the slim but stiff reeds that grew in the pond where the water from the spring collected in the compound. By fraying the ends slightly, these arrows would fly true for at least a hundred paces.

The day her brothers left, Hela hugged them both and said her farewells, trying her best to look sad and disappointed, yet all the time planning to join them on their journey. "Please take care. Watch out for haraanis overhead."

"We will," Hod hugged his sister. "We're only going to Havilah. I don't expect to come across any enemy."

"Yes, but you said the nephilim rule over the miners. If any are near, they'll spot your red hair right away."

Hod reached into his pack and pulled out a brown linen scarf. "I intend to keep my hair covered."

"Do you mind if I walk with you until you are out of our valley and over the ridge? I already told Father I would, and he said it was all right."

Hela began to walk beside them before they could answer. She knew both her brothers had their minds on the trip ahead and were not concerned about her. Watching the path and direction they took, she saw they were going to exit through the pool rather than cut north through the woods.

"It is a good thing you are using the underwater tunnel. I thought you might go out of the compound over the western hills and straight to Havilah."

Hod studied the woods and shook his head. "No, I don't want to leave a trail that might bring the nephilim to our home."

When they came to the pool with the secret tunnel, they all stopped.

"Chay, let's make sure there is no sign of that wolf. We need to make sure it did not follow us," Hod said.

Once they had looked around the area and were sure the wolf had not discovered the way to the compound, Hod turned to his sister and took her hand. "This is where you go back. I need to know that you have headed home safely before we go on."

Hela glanced to the east and then back where they had come from. She had paid much attention to the land near them when the family first moved here, so she had a good idea of where they were.

"Which direction will you take from the stream?"

Hod and Chay glanced at each other, seeming to ask whether they should tell her their plans.

When neither of them answered her quickly, Hela restated her question. "Are you going to continue straight to the east and stay with the valley until you reach the Pishon?"

Chay looked the direction she was pointing and shook his head. "No, Havilah is northeast of here. Hod and I thought we would cut through the thickest part of this forest rather than following the clearer path east to the river."

"Why? The woods there appear nearly impassable."

Hod nodded. "Chay's right. We'll be out of the sight of haraanis and no nephil would pass easily through such a tangle. Also, we'll have a shorter route."

"You'll have slow going. You'll have to make a path."

"We've done that before." Hod smiled at Chay. "Reminds me of when we left home last year."

"You're right! I had almost forgotten about that. Anyway, we need to get moving. Hela, you go straight home."

Hela did as Chay ordered, but after she got home and made sure everyone saw her, she began to gather her own supplies. She had her bowed staff and twenty arrows she had made, a full waterskin, and a sack with bread and dried fruit.

When the family finished the noon meal and scattered to their varied chores, Hela slipped into the hut where she lived with her parents, tied her long, blonde hair back with hemp twine, put on new sandals she had made, reached for her supplies, and slipped out the back door.

No one would miss her until the evening meal, she knew. But when they did notice she was gone, would they be terrified for her and send men to find her? Deciding it would be better if someone knew where she had gone, she found her niece Giza.

"Tell them I am going with Hod and Chay. They are not to worry about me or come after me, for I will be safe with my brothers."

Giza frowned and glanced over her shoulder to see if one of the older family members was near enough to hear.

"You mean that Hod and Chay agreed you could go with them?"

"Um hmm," Hela mumbled as she turned her head away from her niece. It wasn't exactly lying, she told herself.

"Then you know where to find them?"

"Oh, yes, they pointed out their path to me and said they would be moving slowly." Hela avoided Giza's eyes.

"So you could catch up?"

"I suppose that might have been their purpose for going slowly."

Hela bustled around as if she were in too much of a hurry to explain more.

"Anyway, they'll take good care of me. Tell everyone good-bye."

Before Giza asked any more questions, Hela hurried out of the hut and into the woods beside it. She slipped around the compound until she had found the path made by Hod and Chay. Hela easily swam through the tunnel and popped up in the stream. Before getting out of the water, she looked around for any sign of the wolf they had told the family about. Seeing nothing, she got out and followed the stream until she could tell where her brothers had entered the forest.

Based on her many years of exploring the woods of Garth, Hela could tell that her brothers had tried not to leave a trail. But she was still able to discern the path they had taken by the way the thick foliage was bent or pressed aside. She moved quickly, wanting to be close to her brothers before dark, yet not too quickly as she did not want them to hear her until more time had passed.

Before the sun had set, she caught up with them; however, when she saw that they were bedding down for the night, she found a place to sleep well out of their sight or hearing.

When they started off the next morning, Hela stayed even closer. The forest was growing much denser, to the point that she saw her brothers were having difficulty finding a way through it.

It almost seemed as if vines and briars were growing back as quickly as they cut them. The trees became strange. The leafy vines covered every cubit of the thick trunks until they seemed as if they were wearing furry garments. Some of them—with their arm-like limbs stabbing at the sky—ceased to resemble trees at all. Instead, they reminded her of odd behemoths rooted to the ground and grabbing at their prey with claws hidden in leaves.

From her spot forty paces behind them, she saw Hod draw his sword. For the nephilim these daggers were the lengths of their forearms and were slim and swift to use. For Hod, the dagger made a very useful sword, although a little clumsy for cutting brush.

Hod was just beginning to use the sword to hack at the tangled underbrush when Chay stepped forward. "Let me use my sword. These curved blades of the Lamechites are perfect for cutting brush."

Hela was not far behind Hod, who closely followed Chay as he chopped a passage. She noticed that this thorny, twisted underbrush almost totally surrounded her, leaving barely enough room for her body. Since the only direction she could move was forward through the path Chay was cutting, she did her best to stay close without giving herself away.

As she persisted in her pursuit, Hela suddenly realized the tangled vines were brushing her head, even dropping down to touch her face and choke her neck. It was hard to see in the gloom, but it was almost as if the forest was clutching at her, trying to make her part of it.

"It's getting too dark," she heard Hod say, so she hurried to close the distance between them.

"I think we're going to have to spend the night in here," Chay grumbled. "I can't see well enough to make a path anymore."

Hod almost snapped at his older brother. "I say we should go on."

"You're not the boss now! We're not on a mission!"

Hela cringed at the sharp words between her brothers. The last weeks she had thought the boys were finally becoming friends. She held her breath as she waited to see what would happen.

Neither one made a sound. In the near dark she could see them facing each other with their arms cocked tensely and their fists clenched.

"All right!" Hod finally spoke but his voice held an edge of authority. "We'll camp here."

Peering through the underbrush, Hela watched Chay clear roots and sapling trunks until he had a smooth spot for them to sleep. She noticed that Chay lay down as far from his brother as the clear space allowed. Once they were quiet, she went back a little from where they were and sat with her back against a tree so she could watch without being seen.

Her brothers were so tired from the effort of working through the thick forest that after eating they quickly fell asleep. Hela watched a while, determined to stay awake, but eventually she lost the fight and slept with her head leaning back against the trunk.

During the night the mist they knew so well rose from the ground in snaky tendrils, wafted upwards, and combined with other plumes until it made a diaphanous, wet canopy over the sleepers.

A tickle on her cheek just as the darkness of night was slipping away made Hela reach out to brush at her face. When she touched something cool, she sat up, and immediately ran into wet vines over her forehead.

Hela tried to get to her feet but could not until she tore away the creepers that were beginning to tie her to the tree where she had slept. She stood and peered into the area Chay had cleared, but no sign remained of her brothers.

She stumbled out into the area but fell on her hands and knees as she tripped over the thick layer of intertwined vines covering the ground.

"Hod! Chay!" she called out. In the dim morning light she couldn't see anything but mounded vines. "Where are you?"

"Help us! We can't move." Hod's muffled voice came from under the greenery.

Realizing the vines had grown over both her brothers as they slept, tying them to the forest floor, Hela pulled at the foliage and found that it was green and fresh and not hard to rip loose. She tore at the foliage until she found Chay's sword lying near him and then used it to start cutting her brothers free.

When Chay was loose, he snatched his sword from her hand and took over the work of freeing Hod. "Get up off the ground as soon as you can. Pull the vines away from you until you can use your sword."

Hela realized these vines were so fast-growing that they were twining about her feet as she stood there. The only way to avoid them was to keep moving and to knock them away before they could attach.

"Hela!" Hod cried as soon as he was free. "What are you doing here?"

"I wanted to come with you so much. And it's a good thing I did. How would you have gotten loose? You might have died here."

By now Chay had also come toward her. "Does anyone know you followed us?"

"Yes, I told Giza. I confess I let her think you did not mind, but it was important that I show you what I've devised something to help you fight the nephilim."

Hod stepped toward her and sternly took charge, ignoring the scowl from his brother.

"All right, you can show us after we get away from these vines. Look, they're growing around our feet right now."

"I'm hungry," Chay protested. "I think we should we eat first."

Hod shook his head. "Not yet! There will be time to eat once we have gotten to a better spot. We have to get away from these vines."

Chay rolled his eyes and halfway turned his back on his brother; nevertheless, he immediately set to work chopping a path northward through the woods as quickly as he could. It seemed as if the vines were growing only slightly more slowly than they were cutting them.

Hod would not allow them to rest until he sensed the viney woods seemed to be lessening.

Finally, he ceased work and looked around. "I think we are far enough away from that strange plant. Let's stop here to eat."

Chay let his curved sword fall to his side. "That's what I was about to say. I don't see any more of it. We need to rest a while for Hela's sake."

"And we all need some food," Hod added. "It seems as if we can get through the woods now without cutting our way.

While they ate, Hod turned to Hela with the sternness of a father and grilled her about her reasons for following them. "Why? Why did you lie?"

Hod's frown began to make Hela doubt for the first time her decision to follow them. She dropped her pack to the ground and reached behind her for her bowed staff and sharpened sticks.

"I did not really lie. I just avoided telling Giza the whole story. Father will know I'm with you."

"He will still worry," Hod growled.

"But I've been working on a new weapon ever since you first left Garth. I think it will make it easier for you to kill nephilim."

She held out the bowed staff and showed them how to fit an arrow into the string and shoot it at a tree. Hod and Chay studied it with interest, each shooting one arrow, but since they needed to keep moving, they decided to wait until later to see if it really worked.

"I already like this," Chay said after flashing a contemptuous glance at Hod. "You deserve to go with us."

"As you've come this far, we will have to take you with us. We cannot go back through those vines, but if we meet any more danger, you must obey us instantly." Hod held Hela's arm while he gave her his most serious frown.

"I promise I will do whatever you say. I really do want to see more of the world, and I believe my new weapon will help you. Thank you for letting me go with you."

Hod shrugged his shoulders. "You did not give us much of a choice."

$)($

The next morning, before they continued on their trip, Hod and Chay practiced shooting arrows from the bent staff and found that they were able to send the sharp sticks at least fifty cubits with enough force to make them stick into a tree.

"They're not extremely accurate, but you should be able to hit a nephil's heart if you're close enough." Hela peered anxiously at her brothers to see how they would accept her creation.

"We need to make more arrows," Hod said as he gazed with approval at the device. "If we run out, we would be in trouble."

Chay felt the point of one arrow with his fingertip. "How did you make these so sharp?"

"I tried different methods. Finally, I hit on the idea of burning the end of the reed until the wood was stiff and dry. Then I filed it to a point on a rough stone."

"This is a good weapon, Hela. I wish we had more bowed staffs. Maybe we can make some in Havilah." Hod smiled at his sister and then turned to lead the way on to Havilah.

While they walked, Hela was thinking how glad she was her brothers had not only accepted but approved of her bowed staff and sharp sticks.

The forest at this point showed no sign of ever being disturbed by humankind. Centuries-old oaks interspersed with relatively young timber only a few decades old made it impossible to follow a straight path. The high-reaching branches and thick leaves created a canopy so dense that only a little sunlight filtered through. Beneath this leafy ceiling, the forest floor was spongy with layers of old moss and fallen leaves that deadened their footsteps. Ahead in the depths of the woods was a mysterious darkness that did not give any hint of a path or outlet.

"Are you sure we can get to Havilah from here?" Chay asked.

Hod just laughed and kept walking. "All forests end somewhere. And I have a good sense of direction. I am almost sure we're heading toward Havilah."

Hela followed joyfully. For the first time in her life she was adventurously free. She strolled through the woods, feeling almost as liberated as her brothers. Of course, she was still under their protection, but thanks to the staff and arrows she carried, she could fight with them if the need arose.

No matter how dark the woods appeared ahead of them, when they plunged deeper and deeper into the forest, they always found a little light filtering down through the leaves above. They walked all day with only a short stop for their noon meal and eventually came to a hill as steep as a cliff, which seemed to run left and right a long way.

"If we want to be sure we're going the right direction, we should climb this hill," Hod said. "Maybe we can get a good look at the country. I'd like to try to spot the Eden Mountains or at least the hills of Havilah."

Chay studied the steep hill. "I think only one of us should go to the top and spy out the land before we put Hela through the effort of climbing."

"All right, I'll go up while you stay here with her. It's a good thing we brought rope this time. We might need it to help Hela."

When Hod patted her on the shoulder, she felt like hitting him. "Do not talk about me as if I were a child! If you can climb it, so can I!"

"Be patient, little sister," Hod said. "Before our trip is done, you'll have much more time to prove how strong and brave you are."

She said nothing more as Hod took the rope and scurried to the top of the hill, appearing almost as if he were climbing a ladder. He had to search for hand and footholds on the trees that grew almost sideways from the hillside.

Eventually he disappeared from sight, and she was left waiting with Chay.

"Do you mind so much that Hod is the one giving orders?" she asked.

"Sometimes I do." Chay cleared his throat and avoided meeting her eyes. "When I was taken captive last year, I blamed him for my situation. I mean, if it had not been for him and that prophecy, the nephilim would never have attacked our home."

"But that wasn't his fault." Hela laid one hand on her brother's arm.

"I know. And during the time we spent with Enoch and saving Mehri, Hod and I settled most of our disagreements."

"Most—not all?"

Chay shrugged and walked around as if he were looking for a lurking enemy. "Don't say anything to him about what I'm telling you!"

"I won't, Chay. You can trust me."

"I know. It is just that I do not like taking orders from my younger brother. We said we would be equals this time."

Hela ran after him and hugged his arm to her cheek. "I know how you feel. All my life I have been the youngest in the family. Sometimes I feel a bit of jealousy toward Hod myself."

"I didn't say I was jealous of him!" Chay cleared his throat and straightened his shoulders.

Hela decided it would be better to say nothing more about the relationship between her brothers, but she promised herself to do whatever she could to help them get along.

◁5▷

Kron's Command

K odi stood before Kron as the king gave orders to the giants who had been training for eight months with the new Cainite swords. Along with three nephilim, six Lamechites were lined up before him.

Kron sat upon his golden throne, which lifted him five cubits above those before him. In his right hand, he held one of the new swords high above the heads of his warriors. As he spoke to them, the high domed rock ceiling echoed back his words.

"I'm done with this halfway effort to find the water. I'm sending you out in three groups. You have all fought the Sethians before and have been preparing to fight them with new weapons. You will each take two of our greatest Lamechite warriors and go out on special missions.

"Gradrach, you know Garth. I have already sent Varqr after the fire-hair, but it has been weeks and he has not returned. You follow him to the Elimite compound. Use these Lamechites to track his scent to their new home. Find the fire-hair!"

"Yes, my king. I will take the best Lamechite trackers."

"Bring the fire-hair to me—alive!" Kron turned to the nephil whose life he had spared. "And you, Radek, you and two Lamechites go to the salt merchant's home and find him. Bring him to me!"

"Yes, sir!"

"Choose your men and go."

Now the king looked at the last nephil—his brother Kodi, who was wondering what task Kron had set for him and how he could avoid turning in his friends.

"You have been to the garden of Enoch. You and two Lamechites will go there and see if the old man controls the source of the water or whether he knows its source. Also, find out if the fire-hair is there."

"He will not allow the Lamechites to enter," Kodi said.

Kron slammed an open hand down on the side of his golden throne.

"You had no trouble entering. If you can't bring them in, they will wait for you outside."

Kodi dropped his eyes at the anger in Kron's glare. For a moment he wondered if his brother suspected his friendship with the Sethians.

"Go! I want you to be ready to leave after midday. You! The Lamechite I saved from execution. Stay with me! I have a word for you in private."

Kodi left the room, sent his remaining Lamechite to gather food for their journey, and then slipped back to the hall outside the throne room to listen to what the king was telling the Lamechite who had stayed behind.

Evidently he had come in time to hear the end of some long instructions Kron had given—instructions involving Kodi.

"You are to report back to me. And keep this to yourself! Do you understand?" Kron finished his orders to the man. "Kodi will be your leader, but I want you to report any strange behavior from him. Try to find a way into the old man's home if Kodi leaves you outside the garden."

"Yes, my king. I will keep an eye on him."

Kodi hurried back to the eating hall before the Lamechite, whose name was Dolf, saw him. Kodi was sure Kron would have executed him without regret if he knew Kodi had killed Hartagga and saved the Sethians.

Before Dolf could find him, Kodi hurried to the haraani landing and called Keoaw to him. As always, he was gratified to see the bird's willingness to be his partner. Even though Kodi was in a hurry, he took a moment to stroke Keoaw's neck and murmur a few loving words to him. During the months since he had gone on the mission, this creature had become his only friend.

Since no one was near, he quickly mounted the bird and took off from the steep cliff that was the western rim. After Keoaw recovered from the plunge toward earth and lifted his rider to the sky with powerful wings, Kodi immediately flew south to Garth. Without landing he searched the place from the air but found no sign of human habitation.

I have to hurry. If I am not back before Dolf discovers I have left, he could report me to Kron. I will make a quick sweep over Garth and back. If I can't find Hod, I'll look for Pazel. I have to warn someone of what Kron is doing.

Kodi flew many leagues to the south and then swung to the west, covering twenty leagues before working his way back north. Always searching the ground below, Kodi turned toward the thick forest south of Havilah.

Seeing no sign of his friends in this tangled woods, Kodi decided to go back to the fortress. To avoid the eyes of any of Kron's scouts who might be near, Kodi flew just over the treetops. Below were closely growing trees that allowed him no place to land, and then, some leagues ahead, he saw a long ridge running east to west.

And then his keen eyes spotted a human figure—a figure with red hair—standing atop the ridge.

♓

Having left his brother and sister at the bottom of the ridge, Hod pulled himself up and over the final outcropping of rocks. As he was reaching upward, he remembered that he had not put the rag over his head to hide his hair.

Oh, well, I'll put in on when I get to the top.

Glad to see that the crest was clear of trees that would block his view, Hod stepped up to a broad, flat rock where he could see in all directions, even back toward the new home of his family. Before looking around, Hod pulled out his rag and covered his red hair.

As he expected, they had reached a point where directly to the north lay the rolling hills of Havilah, some to the west of the Pishon River and some to the east of it. Far past the river, many miles to the east, were the Eden Mountains. On the closest side of these mountains—the southern side—his good friend Pazel lived.

High up in the mountains and overlooking the Garden of Eden was the home of his uncle Enoch. On the northern side of the mountains, and not visible from this southern side, was Atlantia, the land ruled by the nephilim and their king Kron.

Hod had never seen that land, but his brother had described it to him. After Chay was captured, he had been taken by the nephilim to Kron's fortress, a tall, pointed, stone mountain carved into many rooms and passageways.

According to Chay, this land was bleak and ugly and showed no sign of farming or grazing animals. His brother had seen only a small part, for he had been taken into the fortress and thrown in prison.

Now, as he looked toward the closer hills of Havilah, Hod saw some signs of mining and some huts, which he estimated they could reach in another day's walk.

Hod was relieved when he looked down the other slope of this hill to see that it was long, grassy, and gradual. There was even a fairly level area near the top where they could camp for the night. In the morning they would be able to walk down it easily.

He quickly glanced toward his goal—Havilah—and could make out what seemed like houses and upturned land. Mehri had described the ugliness of this land chewed up by mining of gold and silver. Before he turned to go back down the hill, Hod cast one look back at their old home in Garth.

Just as he turned, Hod saw a haraani with a rider coming at him from the south. Hoping he had not been seen, he began backing down off the hill's rock cap, but before he could conceal himself in the lower boulders, the haraani glided to a gentle landing on the summit.

"Hod, it's me!"

The sound of Kodi's voice halted Hod's rapid descent. He peered upward and saw the nephil who had been a vital part of the mission to save Mehri seated on one of the largest haraanis he had ever seen.

"Kodi! What are you doing here?" Hod quickly climbed back to the top of the hill.

"I've been to Garth looking for you. I was giving up when I saw you standing on this rock pile. "

"Do you have any news?"

"Yes. Kron just gave orders to find you and Pazel. He knows you have healing water. I came to warn you that he is sending a force to Garth to try to track you to your new home, another force to find Pazel, and I am to lead a group to Enoch's garden. But I won't let them get to the old man."

Hod took a step toward Kodi. "They won't find my family this time, but do you know where Pazel is?"

"I saw him two days ago with his new bride and told him Kron was looking for the healing water. I didn't know then that he was sending out warriors to find you."

"Did you say 'bride'?"

"Yes, I did! He met and married a girl in Havilah and when I saw them, he was taking her back to his home."

"Can you warn him now?" Hod cast his gaze over to the Eden Mountains.

"I can't because if I don't get back to Kron before he knows I left the fortress, I'll be in trouble."

Remembering what a good friend Kodi was to Pazel and himself, Hod made a gesture back toward the waiting haraani. "Then hurry back before they miss you!"

"You wait here a while. If I can, I'll bring you back a haraani so you can go to Pazel."

Hod glanced back over his shoulder to where his brother and sister waited for him down the hill. Going on to Havilah was no longer an option. He must either go back to warn his family or go to help Pazel.

"You had better bring three haraanis," he finally said to Kodi. "Chay and my sister Hela are with me."

After working halfway back to Chay and Hela, Hod called down to them, tied his rope to a strong tree, dropped the end so he could tie it to Hela, and waited until his brother climbed up to where he was. Together they kept the rope taut as Hela climbed toward them.

When she finally drew even, Hod smiled at the fire in her dark brown eyes. "I told Chay I could do this myself!"

"I knew you could," Hod said. "We just wanted to be sure. You go on ahead of us the rest of the way up the hill."

As they followed their sister, Hod told Chay about his meeting with Kodi. "If he can, he is going to bring us haraanis to go to warn Pazel. If he does not return, one of us will have to walk there."

♓

When he heard Hod's news about Kodi, Chay looked over at their sister. "We can't take Hela to the Eden Mountains. She'll have to go back home."

"I can't go back through those woods alone!" she protested. "I want to stay with you!"

"Kodi said Pazel got married in Havilah and is taking his wife back to his caves. Hela wouldn't be the only woman." Hod knew from the expression in his sister's eyes that she would not be easily sent back.

Chay looked from his brother to his sister. "It will be too dangerous to cross the desert to the mountains. There is too much of a chance that we will be seen."

"But what if Kodi is able to bring some haraanis for us to ride."

"All right," Chay said. "If we can fly, I'll agree."

By the time the three they reached the flat rock, haraanis were visible in the northern sky. They watched the birds draw closer, easily recognizing Kodi on Keoaw. Soon the four giant eagle-like creatures had settled on the mountaintop.

Kodi quickly dismounted and hurried over to embrace his old friend Chay. "I've been feeding these haraanis.

They are used to being ridden and will stay with you if you feed them."

Just then Hela walked up and smiled at Kodi.

"This must be your sister," he said to Hod.

"Yes, this is Hela. Do you think she will be safe riding a haraani?"

"I'm not sure." The nephil looked Hela over. "Are you strong?"

When Kodi gave her a skeptical glance, Hela's temper flared. "I am! I can do anything my brothers can do!" She wheeled on Hod and Chay as if daring them to contradict her. "Tell him, Hod!"

"She is strong—for a girl. You can see that she's nearly as tall as I am. I'm sure she can ride a haraani as well as Chay or I."

Kodi accepted Hod's word and quickly showed them how to ride.

"You sit on this wide leather band across their back. Take a firm grip on these straps on their beaks. You still need to let them know you are in control. Guide them gently yet firmly."

Chay, who had ridden a haraani on the mission, demonstrated how to prod the bird to step off the hilltop. His mount dropped at first before lifting to the sky with powerful wings.

Just as Chay was safely circling them, Kodi suddenly drew in a sharp breath and bent his eyes on the distant base of the hill.

"What is it?" Hod asked. "What do you see?"

"It's Varqr, Kron's new pet. I heard he sent him off alone to seek you."

Hod followed the direction of Kodi's eyes "It's the wolf I saw two months ago when we were going to our new home. We better get going!"

"So have I. The two Lamechites who will go with me were not around when I went back, but they will miss me soon. You can get away before Varqr can get up here."

"What did you call him? *Vock*?"

"No, Varqr. Look! He's trying to climb the hill. You three better go!"

The nephil put Hela on the smallest haraani, which seemed to understand that this human was more fragile than its usual riders. Kodi watched her take off and smiled at the ease with which she took to this new activity. By now Varqr was closing the distance and only thirty paces from the top of the mountain.

"Watch out!" Hela called from her position in the sky. Kodi and Hod were surprised to see her pull her bowed staff from her back and fit an arrow to the string.

"What is she doing?" Kodi cried.

"That is her new creation—a device to propel sharp sticks."

They watched as Hela let one stick fly at the wolf but were not surprised when she missed her target. Varqr was moving and she was moving. It seemed an impossible task. But when the arrow landed near it, the wolf stopped to look up just as Hela's haraani swooped down. She let her second arrow fly. This one embedded in Varqr's flank, causing him to yelp and try to bite at the intruder.

"Quick! You need to go. He's not badly hurt—only angry." Kodi helped Hod get on his haraani. "I can't help you anymore. I've been gone long enough. But I have a feeling we'll meet again soon." With these words, the nephil got on Keoaw, waved good-bye to his friends, and headed for Atlantia.

Chay and Hela had already flown in the direction of the mountains, so Hod took a last look down before turning his haraani to follow. As his bird headed northeast, he saw that Varqr was trying to follow the shadows cast by his haraani. Kodi was right. The arrow had only enraged this beast. It had barely slowed it down. Hod shuddered to think of how difficult it would be to battle this monstrous animal.

Q

◁6▷

Escape from the Cave

Shani! Shani!" Pazel called for his wife as he ran from his cave and hurried down the hill. The sound of his voice brought her out of the spot where she had hidden for the past hour.

"Come here! Quick!"

Without a question, she scrambled up the mountainside and met him as he came down toward her. The sight of the blood dripping from his arm brought her to a sharp stop.

"You're bleeding!" she cried as her hands flew to her mouth. "What happened?"

"I ran into a Lamechite who wants to kill me, but I led him into the passages until I lost him. We have to hurry back into the cave before he finds his way out."

"Let me look at it." Shani's expression changed from horrified to disbelief, and she snatched at his uninjured arm. "I need to stop the blood."

"Don't worry about this. It's not as bad as it seems. I will be fine if I can get to the healing water."

She shook her head and planted her feet when he began to move toward the cave. "We're not going back in there?"

"Yes, we are. The fastest way to get to the fifth river is through my cave, and we need to make haste! Don't worry. He will not have found his way out yet."

The young bride's face appeared to consider this a moment, but then she nodded and squeezed the arm she had been clutching. With no more questions and making no more objections, Shani ran alongside her husband up the mountain and through the open door.

The sun was nearly gone behind the western hills, so they ran from murky dusk into the total darkness inside.

"I threw my torch down when I left the cave," Pazel said. "But we'll be safer in the dark. I know the way by memory."

"Are you sure? It's so dark I feel as if my eyes were shut—or gone."

"I know the feeling. Hold on to my hand tightly and don't say another word."

Pazel stood quietly listening for any sound warning that the Lamechite was near. Hearing nothing, he led Shani down the series of passages leading to the river. He held the hand of his injured arm high so that the blood did not drip while he let his fingers trail along the wall to keep himself oriented. He gave his other arm to his wife.

When a cool draft of air on his left cheek told him they had reached the intersection where he had lost Niute, Pazel stopped once more to listen. His sharp ears detected a regular sniffing sound distant but drawing closer with each sniff. He knew that Niute was using his nose to find his way to them. If he and Shani kept going toward the river, they could lead his enemy there.

In an instant of decision, Pazel rushed forward past the intersection and pulled Shani with him until he came to a place where the wall to his right disappeared. This was the exit to the river. He turned a corner and came to a stop.

"Shani, I have some torches just ahead. I'm going to take you to the turn I want you to take. Once we turn, I'll light your torch. You need to be far enough away so he can't smell the smoke. After that, I need you to go on by yourself while I throw off that Lamechite."

After Pazel took Shani to the turn, he lit the torch and gave it to her. "Now I want you to go straight ahead until you come to the second right turn. Take that one—it's just a wide crack, but you'll fit through. Follow it through all its twists and turns, and it will take you to the river. When you think you are at a dead end, look to your right."

With these whispered words, Pazel handed the lighted torch to Shani. As his hand touched hers, he realized she was trembling and wrapped his good arm around her shoulder. "Don't be afraid."

"What if I get lost?" Her wide eyes stared into his, making his heart tighten.

Pazel knew without a doubt that he loved her with all his heart and would die for her—and maybe would die without her in his life. "You won't get lost if you don't turn off the main passage. If you're confused about what to do at any time, just sit down and wait for me."

"What are you going to do?"

"I have an idea for disguising our scent so he can't find the river. I need something strong to cover our smell. There's no time to tell you now. Start on your way. I'll probably catch up with you before you get there."

Shani kissed Pazel's cheek and turned to leave but stopped and came back to kiss him again. When Pazel saw that she was safely on her way, he backtracked, turned right, and hurried as quickly as he dared to a cavern large enough to hold a massive colony of bats—which it did.

When he ran into the cave, the male bats began shrieking an alarm, followed by a concerted flapping of wings, and then the entire colony swept over his head and out of the cavern.

If I had not startled them, they would have stayed on their roost. I had better hurry before they lead Niute here.

Pazel followed his nose to what he was searching for, the thickly layered bat droppings coating the cavern floor. Closing his eyes to avoid the burning smell of the acrid stuff he then scooped up and held against his chest, he moved up and down the passage, depositing some of the bat waste at every exit off the main way.

When he drew close to the exit he wanted, Pazel heard the Lamechite sniffing some way up the passage. After taking a wide step into this smaller tunnel, he turned and spread the bat manure carefully across the entire entrance. Then he backed away several cubits and waited to see what would happen.

The sniffing came closer and closer, stopped for an intensified moment, and then continued down the passage. Pazel waited—not moving or even breathing deeply—until he heard Niute coming back toward him.

The man did not even pause at this passage. Instead, he headed back toward the cave's entrance. When he realized the Lamechite was muttering under his breath, Pazel crept toward the entrance and leaned his head out enough to make out his words.

"Can't take this darkness. Can't bear it. Blind—going blind. Must get out."

This was enough for Pazel. Now he knew the man was more concerned about getting out of the dark than finding him—at least for the moment. He turned and followed his wife down the passages he had directed her to take. He went slowly since he had no torch, but before long reached a place where he had stored some pine knots he used for light. Using his flint, he immediately lit one of the torches and continued down the passageway.

He was near the last turn when he spotted a torch ahead. "Shani? Are you all right?"

He found her sitting on the stone floor with her head between her knees and her back against the wall. But when she heard his voice, she looked up, and he saw she was smiling.

"Oh, yes. I just wasn't sure I should take this turn, so I decided to wait for you. I was thinking about what to do if you never found me."

Pazel reached out one hand and pulled her to her feet. "I promise I won't let anything happen to you. You will always be safe with me."

Then he led her through the last gateway into a short passage that seemed to come to a dead end.

"This doesn't go anywhere!" Shani exclaimed.

"Yes, it does. Walk right up to the end."

She did as he said, and just as she reached what appeared to be a dead end, she looked to the right and saw a tiny opening. It was shorter than she and Pazel and only wide enough for someone small to enter. One after the other, they slipped through, and then, on the other side, Pazel gathered enough stones to fill the space from bottom to top.

"There! Even if that Lamechite does backtrack and follow us, he shouldn't notice this."

It was night by now. No light came through the three overhead holes, so Shani had no way to know that during the daytime this very large cavern was alight with orange, gold, and red hues. To her the three pillars that held up the roof were streaked with only brown and gray. By the light of their two torches, Pazel led her to a narrow river that ran through the middle of the cavern.

He pulled off his tunic, knelt, and immediately immersed his injured arm in the water. His wife watched as his cut pulled together and made itself whole again. She impulsively reached out and touched the place that had only moments before been bleeding and ugly.

"It's amazing! This feels like baby skin! It's better than it was before."

"You must bathe in the water. It will take away all your travel fatigue. But hang on tightly to the edge because there is a strong current that could carry you off. If you get caught by it, it will take you underground and you would end up who knows where."

Shani slipped out of her linen garment and into the water. "It's so cold! But it feels wonderful."

Pazel watched her moving her legs in the water while she held on tightly to the rock bank. He loved to look at her and realize that she belonged to him just as he belonged to her. He thought about the many solitary years he had spent in his caves, often here at the river.

It's wonderful to have a companion. I'll never have to be alone again.

"Don't stay in there much longer. You'll get too cold."

"Why don't you come in too?"

"All right. I will."

After Pazel and Shani were through washing themselves, they picked up their torches, and he led her farther down the bank to a place where the river disappeared into the south wall of the cave.

"This is the end of the river, at least in the cave," he said. "It comes out of the rocks at the north end of this cavern and goes back in the wall there at the south end. As far as I know, this is the only place this river comes out from underground."

He led his wife up to the rock wall where she noticed there was a level area that seemed almost like a carved bridge.

"This is where we cross the river," he said. "It is the only place where you can."

Shani studied the other bank, barely visible in the light of their torches. "It is only twenty cubits to the other side. Isn't it possible to swim across?"

"No." He shook his head. "I told you the water is swift. I tried swimming it once and the current caught my feet and swept me all the way down to this end. If I had not grabbed hold of the rocks here and pulled myself out, I would have drowned down in the depths of the earth."

Pazel's vivid picture of near drowning seemed to have a strong effect on Shani. She took his hand and looked into his eyes. "Thank Elohim you survived. It terrifies me to think that you could have died."

"So promise me you will never swim in the river or go in it unless I'm with you."

"I promise."

The next morning Shani woke up and stared at the beautiful cavern. The early sunlight slanted through the holes in the roof of the cavern, illuminated the gold and orange streaks down the walls, and highlighted the three stone pillars.

"I have never seen anything so gorgeous in my life!" Shani said in a breathless voice. She was looking in amazement at the glorious hues painting the cavern.

"Yes, I suppose it is beautiful. I've lived here so long that I take it for granted."

"You wouldn't if you had grown up in Havilah. With all the mining, the country is ugly."

Pazel reached over and took her hand. "I never did think it was ugly because I met you the first day I came there."

The young couple shared a meal and talked over what the next step would be. Since they had crossed to the other side of the river, Pazel felt that they were safe from the Lamechite—if he were to follow them—but he was afraid to take her back to his main cave above.

"We could go back to my home," Shani said. "We would be safe with my parents."

"I think that would be too dangerous. Niute may be outside my door or somewhere on the southern side of the mountains."

"Where else can we go?"

Pazel was silent a moment as he thought about his options. There were many places on the mountain to hide, as he knew very well; however, none of them would be comfortable for a young woman.

"I know! I'll take you to Enoch! I told you all about him. He invited me to come back any time, so I know we will be welcome."

The quickest way out of the cavern would be through the Dark passage Pazel had taken with Hod, but he was not willing to subject his bride to the dangers it held, so he decided on a tight, winding route that would take him up to one of his western exits. It would take longer, but it was safer, even though it emerged farther west than the other would.

Pazel carried a waterskin filled with the healing water and a bag of dried fruits, and he knew that when they reached Enoch's home, they would be offered bread and vegetables to fill their stomachs. After a day spent leaving the caves and another two days crossing the higher reaches of the mountains, Pazel and Shani looked down on the rock corral where he and Hod had met Kodi, Chay, and Mathu months before.

"Look, Shani. We will come down in that little wooded area with a rivulet on the other side. Enoch lives just beyond it."

They hurried on and within an hour reached the narrow stream that ran just outside Enoch's home.

"How do we cross the water?" Shani asked.

Pazel did not let go of her hand as he walked into the stream. "It's shallow. Come on!"

Shani noticed that on the other side of the stream was only a narrow strip of land up against a monolithic rock wall. She wondered where they would go once they had crossed the water.

When her husband walked straight to the wall, she realized that what had looked like a solid sheet of rock was two overlapping walls with a slim gap between them.

Without hesitating, Pazel led her through the gap. On the other side of the wall, Pazel looked for Enoch but seeing no sign of him, led Shani on toward the little garden where Enoch made his home. Soon they came to the group of mushroom-shaped rocks where Pazel and his friends had sat and talked to Enoch when they first met him. Still there was no sign of the old man.

"He must be up in the area where he has his house."

Pazel eventually saw the little hut where Enoch slept. "He should be here." But he was not—and night was not far off.

"Maybe he has left," Shani suggested.

"That's possible. He does sometimes travel around the world with the Watchers."

"Well, I guess we'll just have to wait. Will you show me the Garden? I mean *the* Garden—Adam's Garden?"

"I don't know if I should. I mean, it is almost as if that is Enoch's privilege. I don't feel worthy even to show it to you."

Shani dropped her eyes. "I will trust your feelings. You know more about it than I do. But I hope he returns soon."

Pazel found a spot some distance from the hut and laid out their bedrolls. While Shani pulled out their remaining food, he gathered wood and made a campfire. Later they sat side by side next to the fire, their arms around each other.

"This is the first time in days that I have felt safe," Pazel said.

His wife laid her head on his shoulder and rubbed her cheek on the rough linen of his tunic. "I have felt safe ever since we've been together."

Pazel kissed the top of her head and then laid his cheek on her hair. It was wonderful to have love like this, but it was also a great responsibility. He must never let her down.

Reunion

As Hod, riding his haraani, led his brother and sister straight to the doorway of Pazel's cave, he had time to wonder what his father would think about him taking her into danger.

What kind of brother leads an inexperienced young girl into what could be battle with Lamechites? I should have sent her back with Chay to our family. I do not need them just to warn Pazel.

Hod made up his mind to insist that Hela return home as soon as they landed. He was prepared for a fight—with both of them—but it had to be done. First, however, he must make sure no enemy was waiting to attack before Chay and Hela could leave.

He had little trouble spotting the orange door from above so brought his haraani to a soft landing on a rock some distance above it. After Chay and Hela had dismounted from their birds, he led them to scramble down the rocks to the level area outside the open door.

"Let me go in and investigate first." Without waiting for them to answer, Hod crept into the cave, using the shaft of sunlight coming through the door to scout out what seemed like a dwelling place.

A pile of fur and old cloth marked someone's bed, and a ring of blackened rocks looked like a fire spot. Against one wall were a few jugs, probably for salt Pazel sold to travelers, but nothing in the cave looked recently used.

"Doesn't look as if anyone is here," he called out to the others. "I suppose it is safe for you to come in."

Chay peered into the darkness. "You said Pazel uses pine knots for torches. Do you see any?"

"Not in here. There are probably some farther in. He told me he had quite a few of them stored around."

"At least we have the light coming through the doorway." Hela did not seem too concerned. "Do you think your friend and his wife have come back here? I am anxious to meet them."

"It does look as if someone has been eating in this area near the door, but the scraps appear at least a couple of days old." Hod pointed at some fruit seeds and the bones of some small animal, perhaps a rabbit.

"It's a meat-eater?" Hela looked from Hod to Chay and then back at the bones.

Chay grunted cynically. "I'm sure it was no Sethian staying here. It could have been Pazel, but his wife is Sethian. She would not eat meat. It could have been a Lamechite. You'd better pray it wasn't."

Despite her efforts to be as tough as her brothers, Hod saw that Chay's words made Hela shiver. During these days of traveling, she had shot arrows at only the wolf Varqr. Facing a human enemy was something different. No matter how brave Hela thought she would be, her courage had not been tested.

He should send her home, Hod knew, but first he wanted to find out if Pazel was here. It might be perfectly safe for Hela to stay and more dangerous for her to fly so far in skies where they might meet Lamechites on haraanis.

"I see an opening to another passage at the back of the cave. Let me go down there and call for Pazel. Maybe he will hear me."

While his brother and sister waited, Hod walked about calling out to his friend. His words echoed off distant cavern walls, bouncing back to him with reverberations of his friend's name; however, Pazel did not answer or return.

Hod rejoined his siblings near the cave door. "I don't think he's here. You take Hela home while we have the haraanis. I can wait here for Pazel."

"I'm not going home now!" Hela stamped her foot as she yelled at Hod.

"You will if I say you have to."

Even though his sister was younger, she was not used to taking orders from him. Just then Chay stepped between them. "Hela's right. If you were going to send her back, you should have done it when we first took off on the haraanis. We were much closer to home then."

"Maybe you're probably right." Hod knew Chay had found a flaw in his thinking. "Why didn't you say something before?"

Chay's lip curled slightly as he shrugged. "You're the leader. I will say I think it is too dangerous for Hela to fly home now, even with me escorting her."

Hod's head swam as he tried to make a decision. He closed his eyes and made a silent plea to Elohim. When he spoke, he had found some peace with his decision.

"I think we should fly on to Enoch's garden while the haraanis are still roosting here," Hod said. "They might take off at any time. Hela would be safe with our uncle. We can come back and look for Pazel later."

"More flying?" Chay groaned.

"It's not that far by air, and there is a good chance Pazel is there. Knowing that he has a wife, I can see that he would want to introduce her to Enoch."

"I want to meet him too." Hela's eyes shone with excitement at the suggestion. She did not even protest that she did not need to be protected.

Chay merely threw his pack down and sat on the floor by the open door. "I don't feel like going to Enoch's place or anywhere else right now. I have not had a good night's sleep in days! I think we should stay here and wait for Pazel."

"Well, I think we should go to Enoch." Hod insisted.

"You and Hela go and I'll wait here in case Pazel returns."

"What will you do if that Lamechite you talked to comes here?" Hod cocked his head questioningly at his brother.

"Niute? If he was here, he would probably have made himself known since you're the one he wants. It has been two months since he said he was coming here. I'm sure he did not hang around."

Hod shook his head at his brother's stubbornness. "But he said he would wait a year if he had to."

"I'm not afraid of a cripple even if he is here. I can handle him by myself. And if Pazel does return before you do, I can tell him what's going on and where you are."

Hod thought about this a while before nodding briskly and taking his sister's hand. "There is no use talking to him when he's like this. All right, we'll leave you here, but I don't know how long it will be. If you see Pazel, tell him to come to the garden."

Soon Hod and his sister were once more on the haraanis. As his bird made a wide circle, he squinted far across the desert south of the mountains and saw that the silver wolf was still following them, undeterred by Hela's arrow. Wanting to distract the animal from Chay, Hod called to his sister.

"That wolf is still after us. I don't want him to find Chay. You circle here while I draw him away."

Hod made a wide turn, passed over Varqr, and—acting on a sudden thought—swung back to the south. He crossed over the ridge that made the southern border of the desert in hopes that the wolf would follow him.

In the savannah land between this ridge and the next one, which as he remembered was half a day's travel south on foot, he saw some of the animals he had seen months before, including the razor-toothed behemoth.

As he flew directly over the monster, it jerked up its immense head, stretched wide its lethal jaws, and roared upward. Hod's breathing quickened when the behemoth lumbered after him straight toward the wolf.

When the two beasts spotted each other, Hod turned and headed directly for his sister and on toward Enoch's garden. He hoped the wolf would be eaten by the behemoth but knew not to count on it. True safety from the beast could only be found with his uncle.

As he flew minutes later with Hela beside him, Hod recalled the days of travel he and Pazel had gone through to find Enoch months ago. Looking down from high above the mountains, he spotted the place where they had emerged from the cave between two large boulders. He also saw the flat spot where they had fought the two Lamechites, one of whom was Niute.

He saw where they had entered into the crevice in the rocks to escape Hartagga and where they had emerged from the rocks in the stone corral. This was the spot where they had met Chay and Kodi. His brother and the nephil had flown in on haraanis, having been sent by Kron to search for Hod.

Then he spied the little stream separating Enoch's home from the rest of the mountaintop. Unsure whether the haraanis would be allowed to enter the air above, Hod motioned his sister to bring her bird down to the ground.

After they landed, he explained to Hela his concerns and pointed out the little stream with a rock wall beyond it.

"I am not sure Enoch will allow the haraanis inside. While we were staying there, we could see the birds flying at a distance, yet they never entered the air above Enoch's place."

"But these haraanis are not doing Kron's bidding. They are just birds, after all. Do you think they are evil—at least some of them?"

"I don't know. That is something we can ask Enoch."

"Did I hear my name?"

Hod and Hela turned when they heard the voice not far behind them. Walking toward them from the little woods where Hartagga had slept while waiting for them to leave Enoch's home was an old man with a white hair and beard, wearing a long linen robe and carrying a gnarled staff.

"Hod! What are you doing riding haraanis? And who is this young lady you have with you?"

"This is my sister Hela."

As he introduced them, Hod studied his uncle's face. It radiated peace and kindness as well as something else he could not quite explain. Although he was definitely flesh and blood, Enoch had an aura of someone who spent part of his time in another world.

The old man hugged his young niece before looking questioningly at Hod.

"How about my first question."

"Oh, Chay, Hela, and I were traveling from our home to visit Mehri's family when Kodi found us. He warned us that Kron was searching for Pazel and me because he has found out about the healing water Pazel has."

"Yes, I know about the water coming from the fifth river. The Watcher Remiel told me of that long ago. Where is Pazel?"

"Kodi brought us haraanis so that we could get to Pazel's cave quickly to warn him. Kodi is still pretending to serve Kron. He had to return. Pazel was not there, so Chay stayed behind to wait for him while my sister and I came to see if he was here."

Enoch took in all this information before gesturing toward the wall. "I have been gone for several days. Let us go in and see if he is here. It looks as if your haraanis are staying with you."

They all followed his eyes and saw that their birds were perched on the rocks above Enoch's home. When they reached the area of Enoch's home where he had a small hut to sleep in, they found Pazel and Shani having a meal together at a small table in the area outside the hut.

"There they are!" Hod hurried toward his friend while his sister and Enoch followed more slowly. "Pazel! It's good to see you! And this must be your new wife."

Pazel jumped up and held out his arms, his usual merry grin stretching his face wide.

"It's good to see you, old friend! How did you know I was married?"

Before he could answer, Hela was at his side, so he first introduced her to Pazel and then let his friend introduce Shani. Enoch walked up in time to join in the introductions.

"I'm glad you young people made yourselves at home. How long have you been here?"

"Two days," Pazel answered. "We hoped you would be back soon. We have plenty of food if anyone is hungry?"

Since they all were, they quickly availed themselves of the meal. Enoch went into his hut and came out with some dried fruit to add to Pazel's provisions.

Finally, Hod turned to his friend. "You asked me how I knew you were married. We were on our way to visit Mehri's family when Kodi found us and told us Kron was looking for us. He said you had a wife."

"Yes, he found me a few days ago when we were almost to my cave and told me about Kron. Did he have any more news?"

"He said Kron was sending three groups out: one to search for me and my family, one to search for you at your cave, and one to come to Enoch's garden. Kodi will be leading the last crew, so we don't have to worry about them."

Pazel listened with a frown of concern on his forehead. He glanced at his wife and sighed. "It is a dangerous time for these girls to be away from their homes. When we got back to my cave, there was a Lamechite waiting for me, but he said he was not doing the work of Kron. It was the one that fell down the hill when we were leaving the caves—you know, the one you said you thought had broken his leg. His name is Niute."

"I know," Hod said. "Chay and I came across him a couple of months ago when we were leaving Garth. But we just left Chay in your cave to wait in case you came back. Do you think Niute could still be around? Maybe I should go back and get Chay."

"It has been three days since we fled. I hope he has left the cave and is looking for us elsewhere."

"Do not worry about your brother." Enoch gave Hod an inscrutable look. "He will soon be on his way here. Now I want to hear Pazel's story."

Since there was no hurry, Pazel filled in the details of his flight from Niute.

"And so I left him sniffing for me in the dark," he concluded. "I knew the strong odor of the fresh bat droppings would foil him, so I felt safe enough taking Shani to the river."

"Are these droppings from the giant bats that attacked us when we went through the Dark passage?" Hod asked.

"No, the bats in the higher caves are the smaller type. But there are thousands of them, and they leave a lot of droppings. It's too bad I cannot find a use for it. I could collect that with a lot less trouble than salt."

When Enoch chuckled at Pazel's words, the young people all turned to look at him.

"Why is that funny?" Pazel asked.

"It reminds me of a recent conversation I had with one of my Watcher friends about you and Hod."

Enoch motioned the four to gather closer, and they quickly obeyed him. Each was listening carefully, but the young men paid particular attention to the old man's words.

"I have been to the highest part of the mountain to meet with Remiel. He told me Kron had turned his attention to the healing water and that he would be coming after my nephew and his friend. He told me the river must be buried where it could never be found."

"How can that be done?" Hod asked.

"You must bring down the top of the cave."

Without thinking, Hod jumped up. "Bring down the roof of the cave! How are we supposed to do that?"

Enoch smiled patiently. "There is a way. Remiel has told me how to make a black powder that will release great power when you set fire to it. You will use this powder to bring down the columns holding up the roof of the cave."

"How do we get this powder," Hod asked.

"Remiel wants you to gather the ingredients and bring them here to my home. When you have brought them, he will show me how to make the powder."

"Where do we find the ingredients?" Pazel asked. "Will Remiel get them for us?"

These words seemed to trouble the old man, who stood and paced back and forth a while before coming back to the young people. "I fear you young men have never understood about the pure Watchers. They watch us but only occasionally interfere in our lives. It is in their power to protect us from all the danger and evil of our world, but this is not their purpose."

"Then why did Remiel save me from Hartagga and from falling into the pit in Pazel's cave last year?" Hod asked.

"Remiel was sent to start you on your mission. Once you had been given your work, it was yours to do."

Hod sat down and dropped his head into his hands, elbows on his drawn-up knees.

"I don't understand. Surely Elohim wants us to be safe and happy. Surely He does not want Kron to get the healing water. Why doesn't He just get the Watchers to destroy the cave?"

Now Enoch came up to Hod and leaned over to peer into his eyes. All of the young people held their breath waiting for his answer.

"Elohim did not want Adam and Eve to eat the fruit in the Garden. He wanted to give us a perfect, safe world. He wanted to fellowship with us every day. But when our ancestors disobeyed, they were sent out into the harsh world where food is hard to grow, where animals may eat them, where their children might kill and lie, where they would get sick and die. Yes, the Watchers could snatch away the danger before it hurts us; however, that it is not His plan. Hod, you and your friends must do this. The burden is yours."

A sudden oppression squeezed Hod's chest, and he glanced at Pazel, then at Hela and Shani. Would he have only these three to help him—and two of them women?

"We need more help. Will Chay arrive in time?"

"Yes. Kodi also will join us, and then you will make your plans."

"When will Chay come here?" Hod asked. "How long will it take?"

"He will take a dark path, and he will be tested along the way, but he will have a part in this dangerous deed. He will be here soon."

Enoch would say no more about the new mission. Instead he told them he would wait until all were gathered. Hod knew there was no sense bothering his uncle. He would have to be patient. He decided to change the subject.

"Uncle Enoch, would you show Hela the Garden of Eden?"

"Certainly! Come with me, niece. And you, Shani, has Pazel shown you the Garden?"

"He wanted to be sure you would not mind," she responded. "We waited."

Pazel quickly explained. "I did not feel I was worthy to show her."

Enoch motioned for them to follow him. "Let's all go now."

When they reached the edge of the immense circular cliffs that surrounded the Garden, both girls drew in their breath before sighing it back slowly. Down below were clearings and treetops and gorgeous flowers of every hue, including some colors they had never seen before. A wide, light blue river bisected the garden and flowed through a gap in the ringed cliffs at the far side of the enclosure.

"I wonder how they crossed from one side of the river to the other," Hela mused. "If I had lived there, I would have devised a walkway of logs."

Enoch gave Hela a closer look, as if he were analyzing her.

"I think this river is shallow and wide enough to be slow-moving."

"Oh, I see. I guess they just walked across." Hela cleared her throat and looked off at the far horizon before looking back down at the Garden. "As you said, they were protected from all danger. They did not know fear."

Above the cliffs the sky was filled with watery clouds. Far beyond she saw leagues of pale green land she supposed must be Nod, a place filled with humans who lived far from this beauty.

"What a shame!" Hela sighed and took her brother's hand. "We must risk our lives to stop Kron because our ancestors made the wrong choice."

Shani held her husband's hand as she leaned over the edge of the cliff and looked down. "I see where the water gushes out of the cliff and falls to the pool below. Is this the same water that becomes the fifth river?"

"Yes," Pazel answered and then glanced at Enoch, who nodded his approval for Pazel to continue.

"The water from the pool flows through the Garden and out the gateway where it becomes the four great rivers. But where the water goes deep down in that pool, some of it exits through an underground tunnel."

"So—where does it go from there?" Shani asked.

Now Enoch answered her question, pointing down and then drawing an imaginary line to the southwest.

"I have been told the river—deep and cold—runs through a rock passage under the mountain, under the desert, far under the Pishon River, and many leagues more until it reaches the end of the earth and mingles with the great ocean that surrounds our world."

Pazel bent his head to the side and seemed to be considering what he had heard. "Hmm, couldn't Kron get the healing water there?"

"No, it enters the ocean at a great depth and quickly loses its healing properties."

"Remiel told me many years ago that the river only emerges from the rocks in my cave," Pazel said.

"There is also a hole where a tiny bit of the water bubbles to the surface. It is in a hidden den in the mountains."

They all waited for him to tell them more. Hod guessed he would say that their mission also included eliminating this place. He noticed Enoch was staring at him intently.

"Anyone, man or beast, who drinks of this water on a regular basis not only stays healthy but will be able to live for centuries."

Hod nodded. "We Sethians already live for centuries if we do not die of an injury. Can any animal live for longer than two hundred years?"

"You know one who has lived for hundreds of years." Enoch's eyes burned into Hod's. "You have had a conversation with him."

"You mean Dracon?" Hod's hair prickled on his scalp.

He suddenly pictured the old serpent that had tempted Eve in the Garden, coiled upon itself, fat and shiny from its diet of haraani eggs. Dracon had thrown his spell over Hod when the young man had stumbled upon him in his flight through the mountains.

It was Pazel, pulling him back from the opening into the serpent's lair, who had saved his life. Hod had filled up the hole with loose stones and had made his friend promise to never come back. How could they defeat this creature?

As if he were reading Hod's mind, Enoch gave his answer. "First, we will destroy the cave. After that, we will worry about Dracon."

◁ 8 ▷

The New Mission

After warning Hod and Chay that Kron was sending nephilim and Lamechites to find them, Kodi remounted Keoaw and flew straight back to the landing area on the south side of the fortress.

When the two Lamechites assigned to him came out of the narrow doorway, Kodi was leaning against a tall boulder scowling as if impatient with waiting.

"Where have you been?"

The two men, short and filthy as all of their kind were, hustled over to the nephil who was their leader for the assignment they had been given. It was ingrained in these men to grovel before the race of giants, and they knew that Kodi was Kron's youngest brother and a favorite of the king—if it was possible for such an evil creature to care for anyone.

For these reasons they were careful not to offend Kodi. Yet even as they hurried to obey him, Dolf, the one who had been given the task of watching this nephil, studied Kodi from under half-closed eyelids.

What does the king have on his mind? Why would he want me to watch his brother? I know this one spent time with the humans last year. And I know he was there when the woman escaped. Could it be Kron suspects he is a traitor?

Noticing that the nephil was scowling at him, Dolf quickly changed his expression and turned blank eyes on the leader.

Kodi's neck stiffened as he returned the man's look, but, knowing his safety depended on damping down any suspicion this Lamechite might have, he refused to give away his thoughts by any word or action. Still it seemed like a good idea to pretend to be impatient while the Lamechites chose haraanis from those roosting nearby.

I can play the game as well as you can, Kodi thought. *You can pretend you are not watching me; however, I can pretend I know nothing about it. I think I will win this game.*

Kodi distrusted Dolf, knowing from earlier dealings that he was a treacherous devil, but to his relief both men apologized for keeping him waiting and gave no sign they knew he had flown off without them and had been gone half an hour.

"We were searching for you in the fortress, sir," Dolf explained. "That's why we're late. We searched it from top to bottom for almost an hour. I guess we were looking in the wrong place."

Without replying or even acknowledging this explanation, Kodi urged Keoaw off the edge of the landing. As always he exulted in the excitement of the plunge earthward and the sudden veering upward as the great bird used its wings to mount to the cloudy sky.

Although he purposefully did not look back to see if the Lamechites were following, he breathed easier when he heard their shouts and the cries of the haraanis and knew they were in his wake. When Kodi finally reached the little rivulet with the rock wall on the other side that indicated Enoch's garden, he motioned the others to fly close enough to hear him.

"I've met this old man before," he shouted as he leaned toward them and swung his arm in a wide circle. "He won't let Lamechites into his garden. You land beside the stream. I'll go inside and find out if the fire-hair or the salt merchant is here. Wait here until I come back."

Kodi glared at Dolf, as if daring him to argue, but—even though he frowned at the orders—the man said nothing.

♓

After the haraani had disappeared from sight in the sky beyond the rock wall, the Lamechites landed by the stream as they had been told. As soon as they were on the ground, Dolf turned to his companion Morg, his face marked with cunning.

"I don't care what you do, but I'm not staying out here! I'm going on into that garden! I don't believe there is anything that can stop me." Dolf snarled out his words and started for the stream.

"We should obey the nephil." Morg said.

Dolf's eyes seemed to be assessing the other man. Kron had told him to obey Kodi but to also keep his eyes on him. Staying out here did not fit those orders; however, he knew better than to tell Morg about his assignment.

If Kodi was doing nothing wrong, Dolf could be in trouble for talking about him. After all, he was a nephil. Morg would take delight in turning him in if it would make him look better in Kron's eyes.

"I just want to make sure he's all right. We're supposed to be with him. The king will be angry if anything happens to his brother."

Morg said nothing else, so Dolf waded into the narrow stream and in two steps was at the other bank. He reached up with his right leg, intending to plant it on the pebbly shore, but his foot ran into something unexpected that threw him off balance. He abruptly fell on his backside in the water.

"What in the name of Azazel was that?" Dolf quickly jumped to his feet and made another attempt to leave the water.

This time he stepped carefully, making sure his foot did not trip over anything. But again he was thrown back into the water.

"What is it?" Morg asked.

Dolf stood right at the edge of the water and felt the air in front of him. His hands slid over the clear space as if it were a wall as solid as the visible one three cubits away.

"I don't know what it is! Some sort of Sethian witch-craft, I suppose. I can't move past the edge of the water. Some power is holding me back."

Morg hurried over to the stream but stopped just short of the bank. His face was contorted with fear as he stared at the place where Dolf was feeling the air.

"It can't be real. You must be imagining it. There's nothing there."

Dolf snorted his disgust. "Well, look at this!"

While his companion watched, Dolf leaned his right shoulder into the invisible barrier. He pushed at it with all his strength.

"Do you believe me now? How could I lean this far without falling over if there was nothing?"

"I suppose you're right. I have heard this old man has great power. It is said he is friends with the Watchers."

"I know—magic, like I said."

Morg shrugged and turned to go back to where he had left his pack. "So the nephil was right when he said the old man won't let us in. I suppose that means we'll have to wait for Kodi."

"Probably, but I'm going to explore farther up in that woods and down the mountain to see if there's another way in."

Morg made himself comfortable on the ground some distance back from the stream while Dolf set off on his explorations.

♓

Meanwhile, Kodi had flown easily into the space over Enoch's garden. No unseen force, no invisible wall, no heavenly being stood between Kodi and the beauty below. Enoch's home was on the rim of the Garden of Eden, and evidently the Watchers who guarded the sky above the garden knew Kodi.

Down below him several people were gathered about Enoch's table. As he came closer, he recognized Hod and Pazel, the two Kron sought. Kodi circled them twice—waving as he grew closer—and brought his haraani down to an easy landing. With a wide grin on his face, he dismounted and walked toward his friends.

"Well, this is a surprise. What are you all doing here?"

"We have been expecting you," Hod said before introducing Kodi to Shani, the only one he had not met. "And I am glad you are finally here. Enoch has been telling us about our newest mission from Elohim, but we need you."

Kodi first fed Keoaw and the other birds some fresh meat he had stowed in his pack and then with wide strides quickly covered the distance between his friends and him.

"I may not be much help for you. I have two Lame-chites out there across from the stream, and one of them has been told by Kron to watch me. I think I may be under suspicion."

Enoch's face betrayed no concern as he studied Kodi closely. "That will not be a great problem. You should be able to do your part even with these men watching you."

"What is the mission? What do we have to do?"

Before answering him, Enoch stood, walked around the small area where they all sat at the table, and ran his fingers through his beard. He was more excited than they had ever seen him.

"I have spent many days with Watchers. They have told me it is up to mankind to stop Kron from obtaining the healing water. Kodi, you do not yet know that the water comes from a river in Pazel's cave. If Kron finds the water, he will be almost impossible to destroy. After you young people cover up the access to the river, your final mission will be to destroy Kron."

Kodi frowned at Enoch and ran a hand over his golden hair. It would not be easy to kill the king. He rarely left his fortress, and even if one were to come face to face with him, he would be hard to destroy. He was the strongest man—or half man—in the kingdom.

"Can you fight him, Kodi?" Enoch seemed to read his mind. "He is your brother."

Kodi's countenance hardened as he squeezed his eyes shut and gritted his teeth.

"Will I have to kill him—myself?"

"I cannot say. It has been prophesied that Hod will destroy the nephilim, but I do not know if that means he will kill Kron. I do not know what your part will be in the final next step in the prophecy when Kron will be judged and condemned."

Kodi stood and began to pace the area around Enoch. "I am a nephil! How can I be asked to help destroy myself?"

"Not every nephil will die," Enoch said. "If there should be any more young ones who have not been contaminated and corrupted by the evil of the Dark Watchers, they—like you—will be given a choice."

Hod cleared his throat and then spoke. "What of the prophecy of the great judgment to come within the next millennium? Will any nephilim survive that? You once said only eight people will live. Will that be the end of the nephilim?"

"So much depends upon the actions of you young people," Enoch replied. "If the river is hidden, Kron will be destroyed. If Kodi perseveres, his seed will be saved. If Pazel and Shani survive the mission, their seed will be saved. If Hela is faithful, her descendants will be saved. If Hod endures, his seed will be saved."

"Each of us has the opportunity to save our grandchildren from destruction," Pazel said as he scratched in the dirt with a stick.

"One descendant of yours, one of Kodi's, one of Hela's, and four of Hod's."

Enoch's enigmatic answer left them all puzzled and yet more than ever aware of the importance of doing the will of Elohim.

"You did not mention Chay," Hod said.

"No, but he also has to prove himself." With these words, Enoch left them to ponder the meaning in silence.

Eventually the rest fell into a discussion of the meaning of Enoch's prophecy while Kodi found himself pondering the wonder of it.

I do not deserve to be saved. What am I but a nephil, a child of a fallen being? If only eight people will be righteous enough to survive, how could one of them be a nephil? I know eight good people right now—Enoch, Juban, Mehri, Hod, Hela, Pazel, Chay, Mehri's mother—and I am sure there are many more. Will the world be so evil in a thousand years that only a few will still honor Elohim?

"I will do whatever you say." Kodi said when Enoch returned. "I will find some way to either use or get rid of my so-called helpers. What do you want me to do?"

"I have already told the others that Remiel has said you must gather the ingredients for a black powder to which you will set fire, causing it to erupt and bring down the roof of the cave where the healing water flows." Enoch glanced from Kodi to Pazel as he spoke.

Kodi gripped Pazel's shoulder. "I understand why you had to keep the river a secret. The temptation to drink from this water and live a long, long life could sway any man. Kron must not ever have it!"

While Pazel merely nodded, Enoch gestured for them all to be silent.

"Three ingredients must be gathered, but you will only know yours. I will tell one group at a time. You, Kodi, will take Chay with you when he comes, but I will explain your job to you. Come aside with me."

After the nephil followed the old man to the rim overlooking the Garden, Enoch gave him his orders.

"You must go to the great yellow fissure that cuts deep far in the north of Atlantia. Down in the canyon you will find yellow crystals. You must bring back many of them, enough to fill two large sacks."

"Bring them here?"

"Yes, but you must go quickly and carefully! Remember, tell no one your ingredient but Chay. Now go to the others and send Hod and Hela to me.

"I will and then I must go outside and hunt some more meat for the haraanis to keep them with us."

⊬

Enoch waited until his nephew and niece met him on the rim.

"Hod, you and your sister will go to the city of Chonoch. You must bring back from there three iron pots as big as a nephil's head, each filled with charcoal."

As Hod considered these words a moment, he glanced at Hela and then back at Enoch. "I don't think the two of us can carry back three full pots."

"Before you go to Chonoch, go to the home of Tagg, the young Cainite whom you freed from prison. Ask him to help you come back here. He will not say no."

Hod said no more, merely nodded as he was sure their old friend would be glad to help. Still he wondered if they would have difficulty getting the pots and charcoal ingredients from the Cainites in the city of Chonoch.

"I have nothing to trade for the ingredients."

"You do not need anything. The man you ask will give you what you want. Now go get Pazel and Shani."

"First, may I talk to you about something that has been bothering me," Hod asked.

"Certainly. Niece, you go on and send the other two while I talk to Hod." Enoch waited until Hela was out of earshot. "Now, what is your question?"

Hod stretched his neck and worked his shoulders before clearing his throat. "Am I the leader of this mission?"

"Is that a problem?"

"In a way. You see, I don't think I'm old enough or smart enough—or maybe I mean wise enough. Oh, I am willing to lead but sometimes the others argue with me."

Enoch nodded and looked at Hod with understanding. "A leader is not always liked. Remember, Elohim chose you. I hear the others coming. Hear this. When the crucial time comes, your leadership will save this mission. Do not hesitate to seize the opportunity. Be daring!"

Hod stepped back from Enoch when Pazel and Shani came to the rim. After nodding at them, he went back to find Kodi and Hela, leaving the newlywed couple with his uncle.

♓

"What about Shani and me?" Pazel turned to Enoch. "What do we do?"

"Your job will be easy. You will return to your cave and bring back two bags of guano. Your wife will help you carry them."

The look Pazel gave the old man showed the maturity marriage had already brought him. He glanced from Enoch to his wife and then reached over and took her hand into his.

"Do I have to take Shani with me? I would rather she were safe with you."

"It is good that you are concerned for your wife. She *will* be going into danger at your side; however, it is the will of Elohim that she shares this assignment with you. Even though she faces great peril, she has a part to play in your mission."

With his eyes turned thoughtfully to the sky, Pazel pondered these words. It had only been since meeting Hod and Enoch that he had come to learn about the Creator. Since then he had begun to trust Him and to feel Elohim was guiding his life.

It is much easier to trust when it is I and not Shani I am worried about. How do I know He wants to keep her safe? Maybe it is part of His plan for her to die. How can I let that happen? But if it is part of His plan, how can I stop it?

Enoch's eyes crinkled with humor as he watched the expressions chase across Pazel's face. "Let me explain this. Trusting Him means that your opinion of His will cannot change it, and what seems bad to you at the time is still part of His plan."

"So trusting is a matter of blind faith that He knows best?"

"Of course, what did you think?"

"Then I have no more questions. Shani will go with me."

Shani squeezed his hand tighter. "I was going to insist on it anyway. You're not leaving me behind."

"It looks like you will get what you want. As your husband I say that I would rather you stay here; however, we are doing the work of Elohim, so we must do it His way."

♓

When, a couple of hours later, the sun began to fall behind the western peaks, Enoch gathered his little flock of young people around him.

"You all need to rest another day before you leave on your assignments. I suggest you all prepare to get some sleep tonight. In another day Chay will join us. Then we will be able to begin the plan. Kodi, can you gather the haraanis you and the others flew? They are roosting above us. After that, I think you must go out and speak to your friends."

Kodi hastened to gather the birds in preparation for Chay's arrival. He saw there were only two beside Keoaw and assumed Chay would fly in on the third one. He was not sure how many Enoch would need, so he hoped that last bird would be enough.

Afterward, he headed for the gateway leading out of Enoch's home. While he walked, he planned how to handle the two men waiting by the stream.

Morg had fallen asleep on the ground while the other one was nowhere near. Kodi strode over to the sleeper and kicked the soles of his sandals.

"Where's Dolf? I need to talk to both of you."

"He's scouting the area. He went up the mountain into those woods." Morg pointed to the north. "Oh, here he comes."

"Good. Dolf, get over here!" Kodi barked his order in hopes of quashing any suspicion.

"I've talked to Enoch—the old man. The fire-hair and the salt merchant are here, but I cannot get them to come out with me. The Watchers protect this garden, so you can't help me. You'll have to wait until they leave on their own, which should be in a day or two when they go back to the caves."

While he was speaking, Kodi noticed that Dolf was eyeing him doubtfully. Even to his own ears, his explanation sounded unbelievable, and he was not surprised when the man protested.

"Why do they let you in? It seems as if the Watchers wouldn't let a nephil in. I can't understand why they trust you!"

Kodi called on all his powers of invention to answer Dolf. If he were to continue to stay in Kron's good graces, he had to keep this wary Lamechite from reporting him as a traitor.

"I made them think I was helping them—last year when I was thrown with them. But all the time I was helping Kron. He knows that."

"But the Watchers?" Dolf shook his head.

"They are not all-knowing. They can be fooled. Now I'm going back in there to work on getting the fire-hair to leave. You two wait here for orders."

For a minute Kodi thought Dolf would continue to argue with him; however, he turned his back on the dirty man and headed back across the stream. When he reached the other bank, he felt a resistance, as if a slight wind were pushing against him.

"There's some magic stopping us," Dolf called to him. "I already tried to cross. I guess they don't trust you after all."

Kodi turned and pushed against the barrier. Immediately it gave and, with a triumphal smile back at Dolf, he stepped onto the bank. With one mighty step, he was through the gap and headed back to his friends.

Q

<1**9**▷

Captive Again

C hay woke with a start as rough hands grabbed his arms. While still half asleep, he tried to fight off the coarse rope binding his arms behind him.

"What—what's going on?"

"You'll find out soon enough! I've got you! I smelled you, Sethian! Did you think you could hide from me in this dark corner?"

Chay tried to sort his tumultuous thoughts into some kind of order. A little way off a torch cast a circle of yellow light on the wall of the cave, but it was not near enough to illuminate the face of his assailant, although there was something familiar about the voice.

"Who are you?"

"You know who I am! And I know who you are! We met in the forest of Garth a few months ago—and you fooled me then! But I recognize your smell, and I know the fire-hair was here with you. Where is he? And don't lie to me again!"

By this time the unseen character was dragging Chay toward the light of a torch fixed to the wall, and he was able to make out the man's face. It was the Lamechite with the injured leg who had been searching for healing water when they were leaving Garth for the last time.

"There's no use lying to me. I would know his smell anywhere. He was here in the cave not long ago and standing close to you."

Chay's mind was racing with ideas for protecting his brother and sister. "He was here, but he left. He won't be coming back."

"Where did he go?"

Knowing that no enemy could attack Enoch's garden, Chay decided that sending this Lamechite there would not hurt. He expected Hod and Hela would return before long, and he wanted Niute to be far away from here by then. "To Enoch's garden?"

"Is that where the healing water is?"

Chay cut his eyes to the left and cleared his throat. "Uh, I don't know."

"Where is Enoch's garden?" Niute grabbed Chay's tunic at the neck and pulled him toward him.

"On the top of the cliffs surrounding Adam's Garden, above where the great spring gushes from the cliff."

"You are going with me. You can guide me. Is that where the healing water is?"

"I told you that I don't know."

"Then take me to the fire-hair. I'll make him tell me."

Chay resigned himself to once more being a captive. His best chance for escaping this enemy could be in pretending to take him to Enoch.

⠀

♓

A couple of hours later Chay and Niute had made their way out a small passage far at the back of Pazel's domain. When the Lamechite lost Pazel several days back, he had followed an old scent and found this way out of the cave complex.

Niute led Chay with the rope that tied his arms to his side. Although they made slow progress due to the man's lame leg, they met no obstacles in the cave and soon emerged into the afternoon sun high in the mountains.

"I won't be able to climb up and down all these rough boulders with my arms tied at my sides," Chay complained. "Why not untie me? You have my sword. If I walk ahead of you, you would have the advantage over me."

Niute stared at Chay as if he were out of his mind and then jerked at the rope so hard that his prisoner was forced to step toward him. Chay almost choked at the man's foul odor.

"I'm keeping you tied up, Sethian! Why should I trust you?"

"You shouldn't, I guess. I wouldn't trust me in your place. What do you plan to do to me after you find my brother and Pazel?"

"I might take you to Kron," Niute shrugged and led the way off toward the east with the bound Chay stumbling along behind him.

"Are you going to take Hod and Pazel to Kron if you find them?"

"No, I am going to kill them with my bare hands! Or at least your brother—unless he gives me the water. I might take the salt merchant to Kron, though. Now shut your mouth!"

For three hours captor and captive worked their way through the rough terrain of the almost treeless mountain range. Once in a while, Chay lost his balance. He even stumbled to his knees a few times. Niute only paused long enough for his prisoner to get to his feet again before leading him off.

Finally, Chay could not keep his thoughts to himself. "My knees are bloody from falling on this rough stone, and I'm hungry. Can't we stop a while?"

"It's almost time to stop to eat anyway." Niute looked around as if searching for a good place to camp. "I think I see a cave ahead. That could be a good place to rest a while."

When they reached the spot, both saw that it was not a true cave but merely a deep horizontal cleft in the monolithic face of the mountain. The Lamechite pushed Chay ahead of him until they reached the back of the cleft where there was a stone wall only a little higher than their heads.

"I'm going to untie you so you can take care of your needs and eat some food."

Remembering how he had worked to make a friend of Kodi months ago when he had been captured by the nephilim, Chay thought it would not hurt to be cooperative and even friendly to this crippled man.

"Thank you. I appreciate that—I really mean it."

Niute snarled back at him. "Don't expect me to act like a weak Sethian!"

"I don't. Believe me; I have great respect for you Lamechites. You are better fighters than the nephilim."

"Don't let them hear you say that."

Chay shook his head vigorously and leaned forward so that Niute could untie his bonds.

"I didn't mean they are not terrifying. It's just that they don't really know how to fight well since no one ever fights them."

"That's going to change. Kron is training them to fight against smaller people. They now have lighter iron swords specially made by the Cainites in Chonoch."

"Hmm, that will make life harder for Sethians. Aren't you afraid I will go back and tell the rest of my people about this new way of fighting?"

The Lamechite's humorless smile showed his yellow chipped teeth. "I don't think you'll ever see your people again."

Chay fell silent at these words, discouraged that his efforts at friendliness were falling flat. For a long while they both ate in silence, except for the sound of grunting and chewing from the Lamechite. Eventually Chay became aware of a distant, muted groaning seeming to come from behind them, behind the rock.

"Do you hear that?" Chay jumped to his feet and stared at the wall in the gloom of the cave.

"Ugh! I don't hear anything."

"Your ears are not as keen as your nose." Chay held his ear cocked toward the wall and moved slowly toward it, intent on tracking the distant sound.

He moved his hands over the solid stone until he felt a ledge a half cubit over his head. When he pushed his hand into the space behind the ledge, he found it filled with loose stones.

Chay reached in and pulled some rocks out, and then stopped when he heard a voice beyond the rocks speak distinctly.

"Who is out there? Sethian, is that you? Are you coming to visit me again?"

Immediately Chay knew he had come upon the lair of Dracon, the old serpent from the Garden of Eden. Hod had told him of his own encounter with this talking beast, and his description was vividly alive in Chay's mind. The serpent had grown to an enormous size and was covered with shiny green scales.

"If you should ever come upon him, do not take the stones away. Never talk to him. He is a deceiver!"

Hod's words still lingered, even though months had passed. Chay quickly went back to Niute, who had evidently heard the words from the wall.

"You were right! There is someone farther on in this cave," the Lamechite said. "Did you find the way in?"

"There's no door—only a window."

"How do you know?"

"My brother came here. He told me who lives in the chamber beyond this place. We should leave him alone."

Niute snarled at Chay before getting up and searching for the window. When he found it, he turned back at his captive. "Get up here and move all these stones."

"You shouldn't," Chay said. "My brother told me that the serpent Dracon lives in there."

"Dracon? That's good! I've heard the story about him. He'll be on my side. I want to see him. Now dig!"

While Chay pulled out the stones, he tried to stay back from the opening, remembering that Hod had said Dracon had tried to kill him.

I have no intention of becoming a meal for that creature.

Niute pushed the final stones back into the hole and stuck his head through the opening into the dimly lighted cavern on the other side.

"Who's there? Who are you?" Niute barked fearlessly into the space beyond him.

"I am Dracon. And who might you be?" The smooth voice flowed past Chay's ears, easing some of the fear he had of the creature.

The voice was soft and easy yet filled with a quiet power Chay had never heard before. It seemed to be pulling him toward it. It was as powerful as his uncle's voice, but not as kind and comforting. Even though Chay knew this might be a good time to break from Niute's grip and run from the cave, curiosity and the desire to see this creature overwhelmed him.

He moved up in the window where Niute had scooted forward until only his legs extended into the first cave. There was not room for Chay alongside him, so he could only listen as the other man conversed with Dracon.

"I am Niute, a Lamechite who serves Kron, king of the nephilim."

"You are not alone. I heard another voice."

"I have a Sethian captive with me."

Silence filled both caverns. Chay wondered what the serpent was thinking.

Finally, Dracon spoke again. "Does he have red hair?"

"No. He is the brother of the fire-hair, who is at the home of the old man who lives on the mountain."

"Let me talk to this one."

Niute looked back at Chay and then gestured for him to come up beside him. "There is room for you to come up beside me—at least to stick your head in. Dracon wants to talk to you." Niute pulled back until just his head protruded.

Chay wriggled up onto the ledge and stuck his head into the hole. "You wish to speak to me?"

"Yesss. I have talked to your brother. Now I am very pleased to meet you. What is your name?"

"I am Chay. And I know you are Dracon. I know what you did to Eve in the Garden. Don't try to fool me so easy."

A dry chuckle was the first response, but then the serpent spoke. "You seem different from the other one. More intelligent, I would say."

"Hod is smart enough," Chay said, knowing he need-ed to defend his brother even though what Dracon said was true. He had always been the smarter one.

The serpent's large head bobbed on his thick, sinuous neck, and his amber eyes never left Chay. The young Seth-ian remembered that his brother had described the creature as loathsome and hideous, but he did not agree.

There was something beautiful about the green scales that covered Dracon, something soothing about his soft voice, something fascinating about the golden eyes with their thin black pupils. Of course, Chay knew this animal was dangerous.

"Smart is one thing. Wise is another. Your brother was very foolish. He tried to argue the secrets of life with me. He, heh, heh—as if I have not been alive since creation while he is so very, very new."

"Yes, Hod is the youngest son in our family and has always been protected."

Chay found himself impressed with the serpent's in-sight. He was jealous that his brother had talked so long with him, and he wanted to know the things Hod had learned from him.

"Perhaps you have a question for me?" The serpent seemed to read his mind.

"I would like to know what secrets you told my broth-er. What did you tell him? He would not share them with me."

Dracon's head drew closer to Chay, yet the young man did not pull back. At this moment he was filled with a de-sire for the knowledge this aged animal could impart.

"We talked about the first man and woman, we talked about living forever, and I was about to tell him about the tree of life when he ran away."

At these words Niute pulled Chay back and squirmed even farther into the hole. "Tell me about the tree of life!"

It occurred to Chay that with a little effort he could push the Lamechite down into Dracon's den and escape before the dirty man could crawl out. But he held back because he wanted to hear Dracon's answer.

"Kron will pay well for that information!" Niute added.

Dracon pulled his head back sharply. Chay perceived that the serpent was offended by Niute's words. "Pay me with what? Food perhaps? I've lived here all alone in this cave. I have grown too fat to leave. I must await haraani eggs dropping from the nest above to feed me."

Both humans immediately looked up at the diffuse light coming from small holes in the ceiling of the cavern. Chay could tell the light was coming through sticks and straw he supposed were the nests Dracon mentioned.

"Would you tell Kron about the tree if he freed you from this cavern?" Niute asked.

"Perhapssss. I will think about it. Now I would like to spend some time with my Sethian friend. He is sssuch an exemplary young man."

"He is my prisoner. Will you guard him for me while I search for food?"

"Yesss. Send him in here."

Niute pulled back and pushed Chay toward the ledge. "Go in there and talk to him."

Chay recoiled in horror at what Niute was ordering him to do. "In his den? He could kill me!"

"And then, so could I."

The Lamechite used the point of his sword to push Chay to the edge of the ledge and then over and down into the serpent's den. When he found safe footing, Chay was only a few paces from the serpent. Dracon's head twisted to one side and then the other. He seemed to be studying this human with amused curiosity—and a little speculation.

"Here, my friend. Sit here on this comfortable rock."

Dracon flicked his forked tongue toward a stone pedestal that would raise Chay several cubits from the floor.

After climbing up on the seat, Chay put his hands on his knees and leaned toward the serpent. "Will you tell me what you and Hod talked about?"

"Of course. If I can remember."

"I should tell you that my brother warned me about you. He didn't trust you."

"How foolish he was. I was only trying to enlighten him. But he feared my words. And how can words hurt?"

Chay shook his head. This was one thing they could agree on. "You are right. They cannot!"

"Your brother wanted to know about my old friend Adam." Dracon closed one eye. "Is he still living?"

"No, he died when I was a child. He lived a long time, though."

Dracon's chuckle reminded Chay of a snake's rattle. But Dracon was no rattlesnake. Chay shivered a little and shook off the eerie feeling coming over him.

"So I have outlived him," Dracon said. "I told him I intended to when we left the Garden, when we found out we would all die. I am as healthy as ever, although rather larger than I expected to be"

"You are old for an animal," Chay said. "I have never heard of any living past two hundred."

"Some do, I have heard, but not serpents. Of course, I am not an ordinary serpent. For one, I had a special friend who taught me to talk. He visits me still from time to time."

Chay's curiosity forced the question from his lips. "Taught you to talk? But you talked to Eve! So you learned to talk that long ago. Who else was in the Garden beside her and Adam?"

"Not in the Garden. No, *he* was not allowed in. He was forced to roam the world outside. That is where I met him."

"I didn't know you could go in and out of the Garden."

"We animals could—if we wanted—but none did but me. I found a secret way out. Now—what would you like to ask me?"

Chay thought a moment. So many questions churned in his brain. Which should he ask first?

"Who was your friend and what did he teach you?

"Samil is his name, a Watcher of Watchers, and he taught me that obedience is for the weak. Strength comes from making yourself lord of your own life. He gave me the fruit and suggested I tell my friends of the wonders of knowing good from evil."

"A pure Watcher—like Remiel?"

"Of course. They are all pure. You have not fallen for that old idea that some are evil, have you?"

"I have always heard that."

"A lot of bad information came out of that time in the Garden when Eve ate the fruit."

These words needed some digesting, so Chay wrinkled his forehead and tried to decide if the serpent was telling the truth. He decided Dracon's version very believable.

"I have another question. Did you go back and forth from the Garden after everyone was cast out?"

Dracon now began slithering around his den in fretful loops that folded on each other and seemed to fill the gloomy room with dread. "When we were driven out, I found this den to hide from everyone. Before I could try to sneak back out of here, I outgrew that hole where you entered. I was surprised at how fast I grew."

"I also would like to know how you have lived so long," Chay said.

"Yesss, I have wondered about that myself. It is possible the water from my spring has kept me healthy."

Before Chay could respond, Niute elbowed his way back into the hole, obviously excited by what he was overhearing. "What water?"

Dracon's head whirled at the sound of the Lamechite's voice, and his eyes dilated into straight vertical lines. The only movement in the cave was his tongue moving slowly in and out.

"I thought you had gone, Lamechite. So you were skulking and eavesdropping. Why do you ask about my water?"

"Kron wants to find healing water. He suspects it is underground in the mountains. This one's brother and his Cainite friend know where it is. Kron wants that water."

"I have only a very small hole at the bottom of my den where I lick water. It might be the same."

Niute held out a pleading hand. "I would do anything for water that would heal my leg. If you have healing water and will share it with me, I would do whatever you want."

"Perhapsss. I will think about it while I visit with your prisoner. Now go farther outside and wait."

After Niute left, Dracon turned back to Chay. "Now you and I can talk of serious things. Your brother was interested in the immortality of his soul. How about you? Would you like to live forever?"

"Sure. Who wouldn't?"

"There is a way to live forever—body and soul—the way He intended it when He created us. It is all part of the plan, but someone has to put us back on the right path."

His intelligence completely engaged, Chay leaned closer and looked into the depths of Dracon's eyes. "How do we do this—drink the water?"

"Forget the water for now! There is a tree . . . ."

"A tree?" Chay whispered.

"The tree—of life!"

"The one in the middle of the Garden?"

"Yesss. If you would help me get free of this cave, I could show you the way into the Garden. The salvation of mankind is in that tree if you could just get to the fruit."

The shiver that shook Chay's frame felt like a warning—but he ignored it. "But that fruit is forbidden!"

"No, no. Not that one. The fruit of the *other* tree was forbidden. He always intended you humans—indeed, all of us—to eat from *this* one."

Chay was having trouble thinking clearly. Although these words made sense, he had to reconcile them with his old ideas, those taught by his parents. "My father said—."

"Forget your father's words!" Dracon hissed. "He was not there. I was!"

That is true, Chay told himself.

"Your guard will tell Kron about me. The king will be glad to help me get out of here. I could tell him about my way into the Garden, but I do not really like the nephilim. I do not want to help Kron. The nephilim are evil and untrustworthy. They want to become gods. I would rather work with you."

"But you told the Lamechite you would help Kron."

"I said that to get rid of him. My Watcher friend Samil has told me that your brother is going to destroy the cavern where the healing water emerges. Remiel is teaching him how to blast the rocks with black fire powder."

"They are learning this right now? At Enoch's home?"

"So I have been told." Dracon moved closer and lowered his voice. "If you could get some of the powder, you could open the way for me to leave. I could take you to my secret entrance to the Garden. We could get the fruit and become immortal. Together we could free the world of the nephilim—the source of evil."

Rubbing his forehead to clear his brain, Chay pondered these words. If he helped Dracon, they could free the earth from the scourge of the nephilim—except for Kodi, of course. His family would not have to hide. Peace and safety would rule. They could put everything back the way it was in the Garden. Everyone would live forever.

"We would share the fruit with everyone, wouldn't we?"

Dracon almost smiled. "Certainly."

"We could make the world good again!" Chay sat up straight, his eyes wide with excitement.

"Good? Of course!"

He makes sense. The prophecy said we would destroy the nephilim, but I never thought we could really do it. How could anyone expect five small young people to kill so many giants? We need someone with extraordinary strength on our side. Dracon could be the one to make the difference.

The serpent stopped moving a cubit from Chay. "Will you follow me?"

Finally, he made up his mind. "If I can, I'll help you."

"Good! You go on to Enoch. Join your friends and find out how to make the powder and then bring it to me as soon as you can. I will take care of your captor. But you must keep our plan secret."

"What will you do to stop Niute from following me?"

The old serpent began to move feverishly back and forth in the cave.

"Well, I have not eaten in three days."

"What do you mean?"

"Never mind. Tell the Lamechite he can come into my den and drink my water. You go on to Enoch, and come back as soon as you can."

In moments Chay was up the wall and out of Dracon's lair. Niute was waiting at the edge of the outer cave but came toward Chay as soon as he saw him.

"What did he say?"

"He has a plan for the three of us to become immortal and rule the world. Right now he said for you to come into his den, and he will give you his water."

"First, I must tie you up."

Chay stepped backward. "You can trust me. Ask Dracon."

"He is now with me." From inside the den, the snake's sibilant voice spoke. "Let him go. I am inviting you into my home. Come now if you would drink."

As soon as Niute disappeared through the hole, Chay ran from the cave and in the direction of Enoch's home. Nothing slowed him, not even the blood-curdling scream he knew was the last sound Niute would ever make.

Although his stomach churned and he almost threw up the little he had eaten that day, Chay's legs responded wildly to the horror of what he had done. He ran and ran and ran until exhaustion took its toll and he had to fall to the ground to rest.

A half day later he stopped at the edge of the woods beside the rivulet, startled by what stood in his way.

Lamechites! Camped outside Enoch's garden. I wonder what they want. They could be looking for Hod and Pazel. Maybe they don't know about the gap in the rock wall.

It was close to sunset, so he waited until dark. He watched the campfire made by the two Lamechites until it died down to coals, and then he made a wide circle to skirt around them. Seeing that they had fallen asleep, he went on to ford the stream and enter Enoch's home.

◁10▷

The Deceiver

As Chay stepped up on the far bank of the small stream, he was suddenly exhausted down to the marrow of his bones. It felt as if a huge invisible hand was pressed against his chest, holding him back from entering Enoch's home.

Knowing this place was protected by Watchers, he wondered if they might be keeping him from entering. Did they know about his meeting with Dracon?

No, he said his den was beyond their realm. They could not suspect me. I'm just tired.

For a moment he considered giving up and going back to the woods to rest.

"Come on, you can do this," Chay grumbled at himself and, exerting the last bit of his strength, stumbled onto the bank. From there he lurched the two steps through the gap in the rock wall.

Uncle Enoch has done a good job of making his home into a beautiful garden, Chay thought as he walked in the bright moonlight. *He must have tried to come as close as possible to what he sees below.*

The little grove Chay passed through on the other side of the wall gave way to the circle of rocks where Enoch had first talked with them last year. Chay remembered sitting on those rocks with Hod, Pazel, Mathu, and Kodi while they listened to Enoch tell them how they were related to each other. It seemed that he had been so young and innocent, yet it was not even a year ago.

How he had changed! And now he had found access to more power than he had ever imagined possible. He would help heal the earth.

Off to the right, not far away from the rocks, was the cliff edge with the Garden of Eden below.

They will be sleeping now. I will make my bed here and wait until sunrise to find Enoch. The mornings are glorious with the sun rising over the Garden of Eden. Maybe if I take the time to meditate on its beauty when I wake up, I will feel better about what I am planning to do. No, I don't want to see it. It is foolish to pine for that lost, forbidden grandeur. The world Dracon and I will create will have a more realistic beauty.

The next morning, without even looking toward the Garden, Chay headed toward Enoch's hut and found his uncle, Kodi, and Hod breaking their fast together.

"Brother, you made it!" Hod jumped up before anyone else could move. "Enoch told us you were coming."

These words stopped Chay's steps, and his eyes flickered nervously to his uncle and then back to Hod. He had forgotten how prescient the old man was. What if he knew about Chay's deal with Dracon? What would he do Chay?

"Pazel is here . . . and Kodi. And this is Shani, Pazel's wife." Hod pointed out the two just emerging from Enoch's hut and waited while Chay greeted them before continuing. "I'm glad you didn't wait for us in the cave."

"Well, I—ah—."

Chay wondered whether or not he should tell about Niute. He knew that if they found out about him later, it would seem bad that he had not told them. He looked up to find Enoch's eyes on him. Once more he quickly glanced away.

"I was captured in the cave by Niute, that Lamechite we saw when we were leaving Garth. He was searching for Pazel as he said he would be. He found me sleeping and tied me up. He was taking me to Kron when I escaped and came here."

Knowing he was lying and concerned that his uncle would know it, Chay avoided meeting their eyes.

"Do you think he followed you?" Kodi stood and clapped a hand on Chay's shoulder. "I can go look for him if you think he is a danger."

His friendship with Kodi, developed during the mission, and the eagerness with which his friend had volunteered to defend him pricked Chay's conscience. He hated the thought of lying to him.

"I . . . uh . . . I think he might be . . . dead now."

"How?" Kodi's eyebrows shot up.

"I didn't see him die, uh, but I heard him scream—a death scream—somewhere behind me in a cave."

"Did you cross the pit? Or the giant bats?" Hod asked.

"No, we went out another way."

Pazel shook his head. "Hmmm. I wonder what he ran into."

"I have no idea."

With this lie, Chay could not help looking at Enoch. He halfway expected to see accusation in the old man's eyes, but all he saw was kindness.

He does not know about Dracon, at least not yet. The Watchers must not see everything. Anyway, if I can find a way to free the serpent soon, it will not matter what they know.

"I hoped you would fly here on the haraani I brought you," Kodi said.

"No. I never went out the front door after Hod and Hela left. I never saw that bird again."

Kodi shrugged. "Oh, well. I am sure he returned to his roost. I hope we can get by without him."

"We will work that out." Enoch gestured for Chay to sit with them. "Nephew, we are making plans to destroy the cave where the fifth river emerges. I have been told we must do this to keep the water from falling into the hand of

Kron. Our first step is gathering the ingredients of the black powder we must make."

"Black powder?" Chay knew this was what Dracon had spoken of but could not allow his friends and family to know that he was not surprised to hear of it.

"Yes. A powder that will release great power when set afire. You young people will bring me the three ingredients, but none of you will know what they all are. It is important that none of you have the secret of the black powder. Elohim has told me that mankind is not ready for such knowledge."

Kodi stood now and Chay knew by the look in Kodi's eyes that he was hurt.

"Is it me? Is it because I'm a nephil? Are you afraid I will tell Kron about the powder?"

Chay was also wondering if he was the reason for keeping the ingredients secret, but before he could comment, Enoch explained himself.'

"It is not just one of you I worry about—it's mankind! I know man is not to be trusted with this powder. It has the potential to kill, maim, and destroy—and in our short time on earth, man has shown himself to be destructive. Only I will know what is in the black powder. I will make it by myself, but you all will use it this one time. Then at the end of my days it will fade from human memory."

This powder would add to the control that Dracon and I will have over evil. I must discover the ingredients.

Chay glanced about furtively, afraid someone might read his thoughts. Knowing he had to hide any such ideas from the others, Chay put them out of his head and concentrated on Enoch's plans.

"Kodi, now that Chay is here, I will send you out as soon as he has eaten and rested. You and Chay will go where I have told you already. You explain it to him. I will also leave it to you to deal with the Lamechites waiting for you on the other side of the stream."

Chay had looked at Kodi to try to ascertain how much he knew of the black powder. "I saw them and had to go around them. Why do you have Lamechites with you?"

"When I went back to Kron that day I warned you of him, he sent me with a group to come here to seek Hod and Pazel, but the two Lamechites could not pass the stream. The power of the Watchers held them back."

Chay looked up with a start, remembering the restraint he had felt on crossing the rivulet. Had it been the hand of a Watcher against his chest? And if so, why had it finally let him go? Maybe it was a warning. Maybe the Watchers had seen him with Dracon, even though the serpent had told him they could not see him in his den.

I wonder if Elohim sees us all the time. Probably not since he uses Watchers to observe us. After all, He must be very busy with more to consider than we humans. He must be disappointed in us if He plans to destroy the earth. Perhaps if Dracon and I destroy the nephilim and put things right again, He will change His mind. How proud my father would be if I could do this.

"What will we do about the Lamechites?" Chay asked. "They will tell Kron what you are doing?"

"I've already considered that. I'm thinking of a story that should satisfy them. Don't worry."

While filling his stomach, Chay listened as Kodi went into great detail about their mission. He told Chay they would take Keoaw and another haraani—the one Hela had originally ridden.

"We will take off from the cliffs, fly out over my Lamechite companions, and tell them to follow us."

"Can they take off from that flat ground?"

Kodi grinned and then began to laugh. "No. That's my plan. They will have to walk all the way back to the stone corral and try to get their harannis to follow them there. We should be at the fissure and have gathered the crystals by the time they are in the air. Right now you need to get some sleep. I'll talk more about this later."

When Chay woke up from his nap, Kodi was not around, so he walked through the garden looking for his brother and sister, whom he found about to leave on their mission. "Are you flying out now?"

"Yes, but we will both ride one bird. You are using the one Hela flew on." Hod turned and pointed up at the three haraanis perched on the rocks above them.

"Where are you going?" Chay asked.

"Hela and I are heading to Nod. We're going to try to get Tagg to help us carry everything. Besides our ingredient, we are getting iron pots to put the powder in. They'll be too heavy for the bird, so we'll have to walk back. Where are you going?"

Chay paused. If he was very careful what he said, he might get Hod to tell him his ingredient.

"Somewhere in Atlantia. What else of value could you find in Nod? The iron pots must be your contribution. Enoch couldn't expect you to carry anything else."

"No, we are getting an ingredient," Hela interrupted. "The other stuff should be light, and it will be carried in the pots. After all, it's only cha—."

"Hela!" Hod yelled.

"What? Oh, no! I almost said what we will be getting in Nod! Well, it's only Chay. He's our brother! We can trust him!"

When Hod scowled at their sister, Chay's hope to discover their secret dissolved. "Hela, if you're going to be part of this mission, you have to accept that Enoch knows what he is talking about. And he said not to tell anyone."

Chay shrugged but in his mind was trying to figure out what she was going to say. What could "cha" mean?

While their brother watched, Hod and Hela took off on their one haraani from the cliffs above the Garden of Eden. The bird, although carrying two riders, did not fall far before veering sharply upward. Chay watched until they were distant specks in the southern sky.

Eventually Kodi showed up, laden with some woven bags and a coiled rope. "There's no reason to wait, Chay. Let's take off."

Soon they were mounting Keoaw and the other haraani on the high rocks above Enoch's garden. Enoch stood below and watched as the birds dipped down toward him before curving toward the west. They circled around and passed low over the two Lamechites, who had set up camp beside the stream.

When the men looked up, Kodi called down. "I have captured one of them and am taking him to Kron. You two come with us."

The men below waved their acknowledgment and began bustling about. Kodi led Chay toward the fortress for half an hour before turning Keoaw northward.

"I didn't want those Lamechites to doubt where I was going. Kron told one of them to keep an eye on me. We should be back before they find out I'm not at the fortress."

Feeling considerably more comfortable with Kodi than he had in the company of his brother and Enoch, Chay followed Keoaw through the gloomy skies over Atlantia.

Far off to the west was the forbidding peak of Kron's fortress. Down below was the black and brown wasteland he remembered from when as a captive he had climbed the steep stairway carved up the side of the mountain, which had been made into a mammoth dwelling for the king.

He remembered being surprised that Atlantia had no sign of green fields with grazing herds or the varied colors that signified crops being grown. It was a ruined land, a used up land. He wondered how the nephilim were able to feed themselves.

He noted that the Euphrates, the first river they had crossed when they left Enoch's garden to take Mehri to Seth, circled from the east to the north and then cut through the middle of the dark land. Along the banks of the river were thin strips of green. Chay noticed a few behemoths drinking on the side of the river.

Kodi motioned with his right arm for Chay to bring his haraani closer.

"Look up ahead," the nephil yelled. "See that jagged, yellow scar in the ground. That's the fissure we're looking for. I came here once to collect some of the yellow crystals. The nephilim crush them and use them for medicine."

After both haraanis had landed on the bare soil beside the great break in the earth, Chay dismounted and followed Kodi to the edge where he could look down at the smoking depths.

The fissure was actually a great chasm with a yellow, bubbling pool running the length of the bottom. Golden smoke or steam—he was not sure which—rose from the pool and gave off an acrid smell that stung their noses. The slanted walls were covered with rough and jagged yellow rocks.

"We'll have to climb down to the bottom for the purest crystals," Kodi said. "Here. I brought rags to tie around our noses.""

"I don't think I can stand this air long even with the rag. I can barely breathe now."

Although Chay watched his companion start climbing down, he hesitated to follow. Kodi stopped and looked back up at him.

"You stay up here if you want. I can handle it. When I get to the bottom and find the rocks, you can use this rope to haul the bags to the top.'

"All right. I'll do that." Chay grabbed the end of the rope Kodi extended to him.

"Keep an eye out for nephilim or haraanis coming this way."

As Chay watched his old friend descend rather easily, he saw that the area about him was flat and treeless with no place to hide. He almost wished he had gone down with Kodi. Up here by himself, he would be easy prey to any nephilim who approached, but he had to stay close so that he could pull up the rocks Kodi found. Chay immediately scanned the sky to assure himself that there were no haraanis in sight and then sat cross-legged and thoughtful while he waited.

When he felt a tug on the rope, Chay pulled up the sack as quickly as he could considering how heavy the rocks were. After putting the sack aside and dropping back the other end of the rope, Chay scanned the sky again. He noted a few of the birds far off, but none coming this way. Then he studied the bleak landscape farther off.

Only a few shrubs were visible for many leagues in all directions; however, some rock formations stood like towers, as blackened and blasted as if the land had been burned over by a great fire. As he studied the area around him, Chay saw two nephilim suddenly appear on a rocky ridge half a league away. They were pointing at him.

"Kodi!" Chay hung over the edge of the chasm and called down to his friend, who stopped stuffing rocks in his sack and looked up.

"Nephilim about half an hour away. I think they saw me."

"Pull up these rocks. I'm coming up."

With another glance over his shoulder at the giants, who were now coming his way, Chay began frantically pulling in the rope. Kodi stayed even with the sack and reached the top at the same time.

"Can the haraanis carry us and the rocks?" Chay asked as Kodi whistled for the birds to come to him.

"I think so if you take both bags. They may have trouble gaining altitude, so we'll probably have to fly low. Let's get going before the nephilim know it's me."

Chay glanced around before mounting his bird. "We don't have time to get on top of one of these rock towers to take off. How do we get off the ground?"

"Follow me and do what I do."

Chay watched nervously as Kodi led Keoaw to the rim of the yellow fissure, threw his leg over the bird, and then nudged him off the edge. Immediately bird and nephil plummeted toward the bubbling bottom of the fissure. Chay leaned over and, with a knot in his stomach, saw Kodi pulling up on the reins.

Keoaw's breast feathers seemed to touch the liquid sulfur before he finally leveled off. Chay pulled his head back at once and mounted his own haraani. In the meantime, he lost sight of Kodi until eventually he saw Keoaw rise into view a quarter of a league to the south. They were flying down the middle of the crevice well down into the yellow pool.

The sight of the approaching nephilim made Chay prod his haraani with his knees so it also dropped over the edge. He gripped the reins tightly as—only a cubit from the crystal-studded walls of the chasm—they fell and fell until he thought they would surely plunge into the liquid at the bottom.

Just as he had seen Kodi do, Chay sawed at the reins, pulling and pulling upward at the bird's head as he was enveloped in a cloud of stinking, yellow vapor. When the suffocating air and searing heat sapped his strength, he had to quit pulling and throw his arms around the bird's neck. Even with the rag around his nose, he could not breathe.

The haraani trembled so that Chay wondered how it could stay in the air. He expected for the haraani to pass out and plunge into the pool any moment.

I'm going to die. I'm going to be boiled in that nasty yellow porridge. I should never have come with Kodi. I should have gone back to Dracon and told him what I know. We could have figured out some way to get him out of the cave. If I die now, I'll never be able to save the world from the nephilim.

But before he could plunge into the pool, his bird also leveled off and shot down the canyon after Keoaw. They gained altitude but still were well below the rim. Chay looked back to see the nephilim peering over the edge far behind him. He was sure they had never seen Kodi. In fact, he could barely make out his companion in the distant reaches of the canyon. He saw Keoaw veer upward just in time to miss slamming into the narrowed end of the fissure. Chay did not even have to steer his haraani, which was dutifully following its leader.

Once out of the fissure, Kodi slowed and soon the two birds were flying side by side. The nephil called over to Chay. "We did it, and probably before my two friends figured out I was not at the fortress. Once we drop off these rocks, I will fly back to get them. I'll think of some story to throw them off."

"I think you should stay with Enoch," Chay called to him. "You're taking a chance by going back."

"I'll consider it."

They said no more until they had reached Enoch's garden and landed their haraanis. Kodi turned to Chay before they went in search of Enoch. "You were right. I'm not going to worry about those Lamechites. They will probably come looking for me soon enough."

Of course, they were the first group back. Pazel and Shani were just entering the back passage leading to his cave while Hod and Hela were walking toward the city of Chonoch and would not be back for two days. Kodi and Chay's mission, though hazardous, had taken only two hours. The two old friends carried their bags of crystal sulfur rocks to Enoch and plopped them on top of his table. Enoch immediately poured the crystals out on the top.

"Good!" The old man said as he ran his hands over the yellow rocks. "You have brought enough for our needs. While we wait for the others, you can help me crush these to powder."

Enoch laid the first crystal on his flat grindstone and showed them how to smash it with a heavy stone. He then swept the resulting powder carefully into a bowl.

"Every drop is precious. Don't lose a grain if you can help it."

"How will this powder help make an exploding fire?" When Chay asked his question, he turned an innocent look on Enoch, but his uncle only shook his head.

"Do not ask. It is enough for you to know that this is one ingredient."

Chay shrugged, yet he studied Enoch's face in an effort to read what was behind the kindly expression. Did he have any idea of what was in Chay's mind? Did he know he had talked with Dracon?

How could he? He is only a human even if he does walk with Elohim. And if he suspected what Dracon and I have planned he would not include me in this mission.

Just then Kodi brought Chay's thoughts back to the business at hand.

"Give me that rock. I can easily pound all this crystal into powder. Chay, you gather it in the bowl."

Enoch only nodded and handed the rock he held to Kodi. The old man watched a while to make sure they were doing it right before turning to go to tend to other chores. Before he had gone far, Chay hurried after him.

"Uncle Enoch," Chay said without fully meeting the wise eyes that turned to him. "Are you sure there is not something else I can do while Kodi crushes the rock. I would be happy to help you make the powder."

"I cannot do more until I have the rest of the ingredients. Help Kodi and then get some rest. The hardest test you will face lies ahead of you."

Chay said no more. Instead, worried about the meaning behind Enoch's words, he walked back to Kodi.

Q

◁ 11 ▷

Making the Powder

As Hod and Hela took off on their one haraani from the cliffs above the Garden of Eden, Hod felt as if they had hit a force pushing them upward, repelling them away from this forbidden place.

Although his plan was to fly straight to the little village where Zuph and Tagg lived, Hod knew they were only a short distance from where Mehri lived in the home of Seth. He would like to see her and tell her of the new mission, but that would have to wait until they were finished.

To make sure he found the location, he veered the haraani back to the east so that he could retrace the path they had taken on the last mission. By counting off the rivers they had crossed, he easily found the village and landed in a field just outside it.

Knowing there would be no place high enough for the bird to take off with the weight of riders, Hod left the haraani to do as it wished. He had decided that the return trip to Enoch must be made on foot.

As they neared the small collection of dwellings made of logs and thatch, Hod saw the two brothers he had rescued from Kron's prison hurrying toward them with drawn swords. He noticed that other men of the family following them. But the weapons were lowered when they recognized Hod.

"Hello, old friend," Zuph called as he met Hod with an outstretched hand. "I was worried when I saw the haraani with two riders. I'm glad to see it is you. Who is this young woman with you?"

"My sister Hela. We are on an important errand for Enoch and hoped you could help us."

Zuph nodded. "What can we do to help?"

"I need to go to Chonoch and obtain some iron pots and charcoal and take them back to Enoch. We'll have to climb back up the mountain as the bird we had could not carry us and three pots. I hoped you might help us find an easier way up than that vertical climb we made down the eastern side of the mountain months ago."

Zuph's brow furrowed with concern when he heard the plans. "We know a way up that's not too difficult; however, it is on the northern side. You would have a good chance of running into nephilim. Do you want Tagg and me to come with you and show you the way?"

"No, just Tagg. Enoch told me to ask him to help us carry back the iron pots we need. We'll send him back as soon as we can."

For a moment the two men were silent, only looking at each other with unspoken words in their eyes.

"So you don't need me," Zuph finally said. "I see. Tagg will be able to help you if you have to fight nephilim, but I worry your sister will be in danger."

"Don't be concerned about me. I'm prepared to fight!" Hela grabbed her bowed staff and held it out before her. "I have a weapon I can bring down a giant with. Let me show you."

While she demonstrated her new bow, Zuph appeared skeptical, but Tagg—who had been standing by and taking in Hod's words —was instantly interested. He reached for the bow and, when Hela gave it to him, studied how the arrows worked.

The young man looked at her with admiration. Hod guessed Tagg did not meet many girls he was not related to. "I want to make one of these. Do we have time before we leave for Chonoch for Hela to show me how?"

"If you can do it in the next hour," Hod answered, but he was surprised that he even asked.

Zuph's concerns for Hela's safety had reawakened his own worries. He needed to hurry and get her back to

Enoch's garden. And he would do all he could to make her stay there whether she liked it or not.

"I will start now," Tagg said. "Hela, would you help me?"

She blushed a little, gave Tagg a shyer look than her brother had ever seen on her face, and nodded. "If you would really like to make one, I'll help you. And I can show you how to shoot it."

"Sure! Let's go find the right kind of wood."

Hod watched thoughtfully a moment as his sister and Tagg walked off together. Then he turned to Zuph.

"I want to spend the night outside Chonoch. How far is the city from here?"

Zuph pointed toward the northeast. "A few hours that way. You can spend the night in the forest outside the city, go in early in the morning to get what you need, and be on your way before midday."

"Do you know an ironmonger? Enoch said the right man will give us what we need if we say it is for Elohim."

"I have a cousin who makes iron pots in a furnace outside of town. He should be able to supply charcoal too."

"Good. We'll leave when Hela and Tagg come back."

When they returned, Tagg held a bow made from a thick staff bent by a cord. He had collected several dozen stiff reeds to make into arrows.

"I'm going to work on adding sharp points to these when we stop to rest," he explained.

Hod handled the arrows with interest, picturing how they could come in handy in a fight with the nephilim.

"What will you use for points?"

"Well, I've been looking at the burnt ends on Hela's arrows. That will not work with hollow reeds, so I'm thinking of tying sharp stones on with some of this leather cord. I have a good-sized ball of it."

"You make that from the skin of sheep," Hod fingered the stretchy material. "That is an advantage you Cainites have over us Elimites. We don't eat meat, so we only have the skins when they die naturally or we sacrifice."

"We are all learning from each other. I expect you two will be on the hunt for sharp stones all the way to Enoch's."

"We will!" Hela nodded and looked at Tagg, who had his own ideas to add.

"I want to make a holder for our arrows too. Maybe Hela and I can work on all this at Enoch's home. I think we should have at least fifty arrows ready in case we face a large number of the enemy."

⊬

They approached Chonoch cautiously. Having spent the night in the forest, they had not attracted the attention of any citizens of this busy city Cain had named for his oldest son.

They studied the place from the top of a small hill overlooking it. Neither Hod nor Hela had ever seen such an amazing sight as this collection of houses built close together with narrow dirt streets running between them. Even early in the morning the roads were crowded with more people than belonged to the entire clan of Elim.

"Do all those people live in Chonoch?" Hod asked. "I do not see any crops growing nearby. I wonder how they feed everyone. And what kind of work do they all do?"

Tagg laughed at the wonderment of his friends. "Most are working to make things for others. There are pot makers, ironworkers, bakers, weavers, wine makers, builders, carpenters—the food is brought in from the farming villages like ours. They trade with each other to get what they need."

"How can they stand to be so packed together?" Hela turned questioning eyes toward the young Cainite.

"I've always thought the same thing. I suppose they grow up that way and are used to it. Some of our young people give up farming and learn trades so that they could move to Chonoch. They seem to get used to this type of living easily enough."

Hod glanced up at the sun and then over at Tagg. "It's getting late. We'd better find the ironmonger."

Following Tagg, the group slipped through the crowded city to the forge on the far outskirts of town where his cousin had his business.

The city streets were made of dirt paths between rows of wood and mud houses. The houses had oak doors and windows shuttered with wooden slabs, some closed and some propped open. From open doors and windows came the odor of burning charcoal mixed with the scent of food being cooked.

"What is that smell?" Hela asked.

"It makes me hungry—and I already ate. Maybe we can get some of it."

"Lamb pottage. Tagg winked when his new friend turned pale when she realized it was forbidden food.

"Never mind. I didn't know how meat smelled, but I don't want to taste it."

They found the man they wanted working at a charcoal-fueled fire where he melted down iron ore and shaped it into various tools. A selection of iron goods hung on the walls around the forge.

"Barush, I have some friends I want you to meet." Tagg walked up to the middle-aged man, who wore a leather apron, and pointed to those with him.

"This is Hod and his sister Hela. Hod has something to ask you."

Barush held out a large, black-stained hand to Hod. "I am glad to meet you. How can I help you?"

"We have been sent by Elohim on a special mission. We were told by our uncle Enoch, the old man who lives on the top of the mountains, that the man we asked would gladly help."

"I am one of the few in this city who honors the Creator. It is His hand that led you to me. What do you want?"

"We need three large iron pots with handles and with openings the size of my palm. Also, we need enough charcoal to fill them halfway."

"Is that all?" Barush's booming laugh reassured the brother and sister. "You have them. All I can ask is how large do you want them?"

Hod thought a moment before answering. "Well, we have to carry them filled with charcoal to the top of the Eden Mountains."

"Do you think these will do?"

Barush indicated some round iron pots small enough to be held in a man's encircled arms. They also had handles, which allowed them to be held at the side.

"From what I have heard of the plans, these should be large enough." Hod hefted one pot to assess the weight.

"I'm not sure the two of you can carry three of these up the mountain. Is Tagg going to help you?"

Hod nodded at this question and Barush continued. "He's a strong lad. He should be able to handle two so your sister does not need to carry one of them."

"I can!" Tagg grinned before looking proudly at Hela. It was obvious that he was thrilled to be able to prove his strength to her. "I'll carry two, and you can carry my shooting sticks."

Hela drew herself up and glared at all of the men around her. Her knotted fists trembled at her side. "I am strong enough to do my share, but I will let you carry my pot for a while until you get tired. Then I'll carry it—and yours when you're tired."

"Well, I suppose that will be all right."

Hela watched Tagg's eyes as if she could read his motives there. Hod was surprised his sister gave in. Hela had been trying to prove she was the equal of any man. Now the influence of young Tagg seemed to be softening her.

He had noticed the friendship that had so quickly developed between these two and wondered how he would ever be able to explain to his parents if Hela were to want to marry a Cainite. It was bad enough that he had taken his sister across Eden without his father's permission.

He knew he should discourage their friendship, but he also knew Tagg was a young man who worshipped Elohim and would make his sister a good mate.

Soon they were headed back toward the Eden Mountains. They would have two rivers, the Tigris and Euphrates, to cross on their trip back, and the first one was a rapidly rushing stream.

Using ropes to keep from being swept away by the Tigris, the three young people crossed this first obstacle with little difficulty.

Tagg, however, made two trips to carry first his and then Hela's pot safely across. He held them high above his head with one hand while holding the rope with the other. Hela, who clung to the rope with both hands when she crossed, did not protest.

When they reached the edge of the shallow and slow-moving Euphrates half an hour later, Tagg glanced around a moment and then shuddered. "This is where the nephil cut my arm almost off. If it hadn't been for the healing water, I would have bled to death."

These words made Hod think of the small pottery jug of water he had filled with healing water and put in the bottom of his pack. Since he had had no use for it yet, he had almost forgotten it was there.

"I remember that well. It is hard to believe that now we are on a mission to destroy all access to that water."

"I don't understand why! It seems that Elohim would want mankind to have something like the water to keep us healthy and living long."

Hod pondered this idea. He had had similar thoughts.

Why not let everyone use the water? Why keep it a secret when it could help mankind?

He understood that it came from the perfection of the Garden of Eden and traveled through clean rock without encountering human or animal waste. He knew men corrupted everything they touched, but if he and Pazel had been allowed to use it, why not everyone else?

"I think I have a clue to the reason," he finally said. "Elohim hid the river underground and only allowed Pazel to be saved by the water when he was a helpless little boy lost in the desert. It is not His will that man live forever—at least not since the fall. He gives us Sethians long lives, but at last we are gathered to our fathers."

"But why not let us have a way to heal? It would make our lives better."

"Maybe it's because the nephilim would use it to perpetuate their power." Hod turned thoughtful eyes toward the heavens. "Maybe all men would be tempted to use it for power."

Tagg sighed as he accepted this answer. "Well, then, we should be getting on our way. We should not waste any time. It's past midday."

Until they had crossed the Euphrates, Tagg refused to surrender the second iron pot to Hela. "I'm going to take one across and then come back for the other as I did last time. We need the charcoal, so I'm going to have to lift them high out of the water. You carry the weapons."

"He's right," her brother added. "We need to hurry. No time to argue."

While Tagg made his trips across the river and Hod checked out the security of his pack, Hela inspected the bowed staffs, making sure the strings were tight and the arrows she had brought with her were ready.

Before long all three had crossed and were rapidly covering the two leagues from the river to the place on the north face where Tagg suggested they climb.

He had told them that the northeastern face of the mountain was gradual enough to be climbed without ropes. Even though they would be taking the chance of running into nephilim, it was the easiest way to get back to Enoch. They traveled quickly from Chonoch to the river before stopping to eat a meal on the grassy bank.

Tagg finally allowed Hela to carry one pot. Both she and Tagg had their bowed staffs slung over their shoulder, ready to access quickly if necessary.

They began climbing boulders, stepping from one to the other when they could and then walking between them when they had to. Before they had covered a fourth of the distance to the top, they reached a wide, flat area covered with scruffy grass and sloping gradually upward.

At the far end of the area, Tagg stopped and looked back at Hela, who paused when he did. Hod had fallen fifty paces behind them to keep an eye out for any nephilim.

"It will be steep going from here on," Tagg said. "I'll carry both pots."

Before Hela could answer, Hod called out. "A nephil—coming up the mountain!"

Hela and Tagg both whirled around, dropping the pots, and reached for the strung staffs over their shoulders.

"We need to be much nearer," Hela said, moving back toward Hod as she spoke. "These arrows are not accurate unless we are closer."

Tagg said nothing, only matching his actions to hers. He had practiced some the day before, but he had only a few of her arrows and looked to her for guidance. By the time they were ten paces from her brother, who had pulled out his sword, the giant was almost upon him.

Hela stopped, planted her feet in a wide stance, and fitted an arrow's notched end to the string. By now Hod was trying to hold the nephil at bay by darting in and stabbing at his thighs.

The nephil, however, had one of the new lightweight swords Kron had decreed. Unlike the old heavy weapons, this one could cut swiftly through the air, allowing for deft maneuvers necessary for fighting a small, quick opponent.

Seeing her brother had jumped back from the rapid onslaught, Hela let fly her first arrow and was relieved to see it embedded in the giant's shoulder.

The nephil roared and, noticing her for the first time, stepped past Hod. Although Hela and Tagg both began shooting arrows as fast as they could, none of them went into his body more than a finger's length. Even so, they were definitely slowing him down.

As the giant headed for Hela, Hod followed, continuing to distract him from Hela and Tagg. The nephil turned to Hod once again, lifted his sword, and jabbed it downward. Hod, trying to avoid the blade, fell backward on the ground.

Meanwhile, seeing her brother in danger, Hela pulled her string back farther than she ever had, held it a moment, and sent her last arrow into the giant's back.

This one buried itself between two ribs through a gap in the armor over his torso. The nephil groaned thunderously before falling slowly first to his knees and then to his side. The huge head was only a cubit from where Hod lay on the ground, the sword that had wounded him sticking out of his stomach.

With only a cursory glance at the fallen enemy, Hela ran to her brother. The nephil sword had found its target.

"Hod! Hod! You can't be dead!"

She started to throw herself on her brother, but Tagg grabbed her arm and held her back. "Wait! Don't move that sword until I see if he's breathing."

Tagg leaned an ear close to Hod's mouth and then felt his chest.

"He's alive, but I wish I had some healing water."

Tears running down her cheeks, Hela could not say a word. She took one of Hod's hands and held it tightly and then suddenly looked up at Tagg.

"He squeezed my hand. Hod! Oh, Hod! Don't die!"

"Look! His lips are moving. He is trying to tell us something. Can you make out what he is saying?"

Now Hela put her ear to Hod's mouth in an effort to understand the soft sounds he was making. Moments later, he became still as death.

"He said, 'my pack' and 'jug.' See what you can find in his backpack."

Tagg quickly obeyed and found a small pottery jug that just fit his palm. "What is it? The water? Do you think it is the healing water?"

"It must be. But he fainted before he told me what to do with it."

"I know what to do. He used it to repair my arm when it was almost cut off. Just pull out the plug and pour the water on his wound as soon as I remove the sword."

While Hela fumbled with the leather plug, Tagg gently began to move the blade. When Hod moaned and stirred, he held it as still as possible.

"Hurry, he'll begin bleeding badly when I move this. Pull his tunic aside as soon as the blade is out."

Blood began to spurt from the wound as soon as the sword came out. Hela opened the jug and began to dribble the contents on Hod's wound. They watched in awe as the cut began to close up and the blood ceased to flow.

"It does heal!" Hela breathed in awe. "I don't know if I ever truly believed in it. Hod, wake up!"

"I knew it worked," Tagg said. "See. He's opening his eyes. Let him rest a minute while I check to see if there are any more nephilim about."

Tagg borrowed Hod's sword as he left to scout the mountainside. Hela held her brother's hand until Hod began trying to sit up.

"Good! You found the water. I was fading out. I tried to hang on long enough to tell you about the jug of water in my pack. I wasn't sure you understood what I meant."

"Why didn't you tell me before that you had some of the healing water with you?"

"I almost forgot about it. I came home from the mission with half a waterskin full, and I hid it away where no one would accidentally waste it. You know I promised Pazel to keep it secret. I decided to bring a little bit with me in case we needed it."

By now Hod was sitting up and looking as good as new. He glanced at the giant head lying not far from him.

"So Tagg finished him off."

"No. I did. When he turned on you, I shot him in the back." Hela's voice was a mixture of pride and shame. "I'm feeling a little sick to my stomach about it, though."

Hod grabbed her hand and forced her to meet his eyes. "Oh, no! I'm sorry! You should not have that burden on your heart. No girl should have to kill. It's terrible. I know!"

But Hela just shook her hair, thrust her jaw out, and gave her shoulders a quick shrug. As if wanting to change the subject, she ran her hand over the ragged place where the giant's sword had cut Hod's tunic.

"I am amazed at how your skin grew back so quickly. And I am so thankful. I thought you were dead."

"I almost was. I felt myself drift away into the dark."

"It was dark? I always wondered what it was like to be dead."

Hod threw his head back and gave out a short laugh. "Oh, I wasn't dead. I was just moving about in a misty place—trying to figure out where I was—when I saw a Watcher observing me."

"So you were dreaming?"

"I don't think so. It wasn't Remiel. It was another one. I said, 'Did you come for me,' and he said, 'no, you cannot stay.' Then I felt the water on my stomach and was back."

'"Do you think it was real?"

"Yes. But I'm going to ask Enoch about it. He knows so much about the Watchers."

When Tagg returned with word that no other nephilim were near, he hugged Hod and gave Hela a hand to help her up. They continued what was now an easy climb and were in Enoch's garden by dark.

◁12▷

Through the Passages

The nephil Radek and the two Lamechites he was leading entered Pazel's cave two days after Chay and Niute departed by way of the back passage. The group of three had left Kron's fortress from the northern side and traveled around the western end of the range, staying on level terrain until they could look up and see Pazel's door.

Afek, the lead tracker, motioned for the other two to stand back while he sniffed his way to the open doorway. Radek and the other Lamechite Rahm said nothing as they watched him. However, the nephil used the time to study the piles of boulders that made up this side of the mountain, so different from the harsh, upthrusted, monolithic northern side where the nephilim lived.

Rahm, the second Lamechite, made ever-widening circles as he checked for human trails at the base of the mountain. He had a rat-like face with a nose that soon ferreted out the place where Shani had hidden, but his sniffing only revealed that she had eventually gone up to the cave.

While Rahm was looking up at and studying the doorway above them, Afek came out of the cave and motioned for them to come up.

"No one's near, but several people have been here," he called down as they clambered up the mountainside.

When they all three stood in the light that filtered into the cave through the doorway, Radek glanced around and then ordered the Lamechites to explore all the passages and report back in an hour.

The first one to return, Rahm, went straight to the waiting giant. "The salt merchant has been here with a female companion, but not for several days. Also, I found my brother Niute's smell. He and a Sethian left together by way of a back passage."

"The salt merchant is a Cainite. So it wasn't him? Was it the fire-hair?"

Rahm shook his head. "No. It was another Sethian who came here with the fire-hair, a close relative from the smell."

"I too found the fire-hair's scent, but only near the door." Afek, who had joined them, pointed out his find.

Radek wheeled about. "Where? Where did he go?"

"He did not come far into this cave before leaving—and he had a woman with him. Give me a few more minutes, and I'll find out which direction he went."

"I scented a woman at the bottom of the mountain, but she left with the salt merchant," Rahm nodded. "I lost their trail in one of the passages. They never came back here."

While Afek sniffed his way slowly up the mountain to an overhanging rock, Radek and Rahm walked outside the cave and watched him work.

"The scent ends here. The fire-hair and one woman flew off on haraanis," Afek called out. "They never came back either."

"So there were two females," Radek said when Afek had come back down. "Maybe the salt merchant and his woman flew off too."

Afek gave the other Lamechite a questioning look. "What do you think, Rahm?"

"No, they did not fly. I lost their scent back in the passages. They have eluded us, but I smelled my brother Niute all over the place. He spent some days here, and I think he left with a Sethian—but not the fire-hair."

Radek clasped his hands behind his back and began to pace back and forth outside the cave.

"So three groups were here. The fire-hair and a woman, the salt merchant and a woman, and Niute with a Sethian. Were they all here at the same time?"

"I don't think so," Afek said. "I believe the salt merchant came here and was pursued by Niute, who lost him in the caverns. The salt merchant left and came back with the female. They were tracked by Niute but somehow escaped and left the cave."

"Yes, go on," Radek growled when Afek paused.

"Later the fire-hair arrived with the other Sethians, a male and a female. The fire-hair and the woman flew off on haraanis, leaving the other male in the cave, probably to wait for the salt merchant. This one was captured by Niute and taken out of the cave by a back way."

"Can we follow Niute?" The giant scowled and kept pacing.

"Easily. He made no effort to conceal his tracks."

"Good! You stay here, Afek. Rahm, you track Niute. I am going back to Kron. When he hears the fire-hair is riding haraanis, he will want to know who taught them how."

♓

A day after they had left Enoch's garden, Pazel and Shani had covered the distance between the garden and a small gap between boulders high in the mountains that provided the easiest access to his huge labyrinth of narrow passageways and caves stretching for half a league in all directions.

This route was very different from the Dark Passage, so Pazel hoped to meet no problems. He did not know this was the very passage Chay and Niute had left from just the day before or that Afek was now coming directly toward them on the same passage.

But since he did know the possibility that pursuers sent from Kron could be waiting in his cave, Pazel took no torch and moved carefully through this usually safe route. He was glad it contained none of the dangers found in the Dark Passage. He hated to think of taking Shani across the pit Hod had almost fallen into or through the lair of the giant bats, whose bites could be deadly.

It had been necessary then because Lamechites and Hartagga had been chasing Hod and he needed to get him as far up as possible before emerging on the mountainside. Still, this journey too could be perilous. The men sent by Kron could be waiting for him by now. But even if they were, they did not know their way in all the passages.

"How long will it take us to get to your main cave— the one you live in?" Shani asked.

"Ssh, don't talk," he warned. "I need to listen for footsteps. I fear the enemy is here."

"Sorry."

Shani held on more tightly to his hand and even gave it a little squeeze to show he had not offended her. They had proceeded for a few more minutes as soundlessly as they could when Pazel's hand stiffened and pulled Shani to an absolute halt.

"Stay here. Don't move." Pazel broke the silence to whisper, really more of a soft hiss, but it had the desired effect.

In the darkness Shani pressed her back against the stone wall and moved not a muscle while her husband explored the passage ahead. Her ears almost quivered as they strained to pick up any sound that could tell her what was happening.

Pazel removed his footwear and moved on panther-like feet in the total blackness until his acute ears heard the scrape of sandals on the stone floor some distance ahead.

The air outside was still this day, so he hoped no current was taking his scent toward the approaching enemy. When he saw the glow of a torch nearing a corner ahead, Pazel jumped back into a slight alcove his hand had found, held his sickle sword ready, and waited until the steps were almost upon him.

"Lamechite!" he screamed and was rewarded by hearing the man growl just as the sickening odor peculiar to these dirty men hit him in the face.

The torch was dropped and immediately went out on the cold stone floor.

Pazel had considered attacking him by surprise but the concern it might not be an enemy had stopped him. Now that he knew this must be one of the Lamechites in the group sent by Kron, Pazel jumped out and struck at what seemed to be head level.

The sword sliced through something soft and then bit into something hard. Pazel felt a warm liquid spurt onto his hand and instinctively jerked the sword back just as a sharp cry was followed by the sound of a body hitting the floor. When he heard nothing else after this, Pazel bent to the floor and felt for his opponent.

He touched what he knew was a bloody wound and then forced himself to touch the man's face to be sure he was no longer breathing. Next he picked up the man's fallen torch and used his flint to make a flame. Now that he had a light, he could easily scout all the way to the main cave to find out who else was there, but, fearing to leave his wife for so long, he turned and went back for her. When Pazel got back to the body of his attacker, he saw that he had slit the man's throat and that it was not Niute.

It must be one of those Kodi spoke of. That means there is another of these filthy dogs and a nephil near. I fear for Shani, but we must get the guano.

When he was close enough, Pazel called out in a loud whisper. "Shani! Are you there?"

"Yes. I see your torch. I'm just ahead. What happened? I've been so worried, but I dared not move."

Pazel said nothing until he reached his wife. Then he took her hand and began leading her back down the passage toward his home cave.

"Here is the man I heard coming," he whispered when they reached the body. "I struck at him in the dark and happened to hit him in the neck. Don't look at him. We have to keep moving."

"Do you think he was alone?"

"No. Kodi told us Kron was sending out three groups of one nephil and two Lamechites to find the healing water —and Hod and me. I'm sure the other two are here somewhere."

Shani's grip tightened, and her steps grew heavy as if she wanted to slow him down. Neither of them spoke. Pazel was listening in the close confines of the passage for any more approaching footsteps while Shani was worrying about what would happen if they did meet a nephil.

"Here." Pazel finally pulled her into a narrow side passage. "This opening leads to a cave where bats roost. I think we can collect the guano and get out of here before we are found by the other two."

He put out the torch at the entrance to the cave and then threw it far back down the passage. "Any tracker will follow this scent."

"I hope so."

They had been whispering, but now that they were in the bat cave, Pazel's voice was almost inaudible. He signaled for Shani to get down. "I don't want to disturb the bats. If they take flight, it might alert those looking for me. I'm going to crawl in and quietly fill the sacks. You stay here, but let me know if you hear anything."

While he was gone into the seeming oblivion of the cave's blackness, Shani sat at the entrance and listened. In her right ear, she heard the slight scraping of Pazel collecting guano and a squeaking sound she guessed was the bats. From the other ear she thought she heard an echo of voices at a distance but getting nearer.

It's my imagination, It is so quiet and so dark that I don't trust my own ears. I dare not move or call out to Pazel.

Still she kept her whole attention concentrated on that sound. Eventually she knew it was real. Far off, but not so far, a deep voice had clearly said, "Afek, can you hear me?"

"Pazel, Pazel," she dared to whisper. "There is someone out there—coming toward us."

Soon he was at her side—taking her hand. He listened a minute or two at the entrance before speaking. "Move this way a little."

When they had come back fifteen cubits from the entrance, he whispered again.

"Stay right here. I am going to spread some bat guano at the entrance to cover our scent. There is a back way out of this cave that leads to the Dark Passage. I never wanted to go this way, but I keep a torch there just in case. Even though it goes down at first, it will eventually take us high up on the mountain not far from Enoch's home."

By the time footsteps were near, Pazel and Shani had entered the small crevice that led out of the cave and into a narrow way that led downward.

"Shani, the Dark Passage is dangerous, so when we get to it, you must stay close to me. At least we'll be able to rest in a cavern before we enter the bad part."

"What dangers are there in the Dark Passage?"

"We will be past the nests of the giant, biting bats. I would not want to take you through there, but you will have to cross the pit. I'm terrified to even think about it."

Shani shuddered but made her voice as brave as she could. "I'll do it if I can."

"Here is the smaller sack. Can you can carry it?"

"Of course, I'm used to hard work, you know."

Pazel smiled, dropped the sack he was holding, and hugged her.

"I know, but I'm sorry that I can't carry both of them. I need to carry this torch."

He picked up the smaller bag and handed it to her before tossing the larger over his back. "Follow me."

The path they took was very tight. As small as they both were, Pazel and Shani were often forced to turn sideways to slip through. They eventually ended up in a cavern with sunlight filtering down through a hole overhead.

"Is this the cavern with the fifth river?" Shani asked.

"No. To get to the river from here, you have to go through that passage—past the bats." Pazel pointed to the right. "This is a smaller cave. We're going to the left. You wait here while I gather some things we will need. Try to rest."

Shani settled down on the floor and even dozed a bit until disturbed by her husband's return. She yawned and stretched before getting up from the ground.

"What is all this you've brought?"

"I went to my storeroom and got some rope and extra torches. When Hod and I crossed the pit, our torches were almost burnt out. We had to go on in the dark. I won't let that happen again."

"What is the rope for?"

Pazel came over and took her in his arms. For the first time during this busy and dangerous day, he gave her a kiss.

"Well, I have to get the bags across safely. I don't want to have to go into the giant bat lair for more guano. That's not my only reason, though. I almost lost my friend in the pit. I refuse to lose my wife. You will have a rope around your waist. If you fall, I'll be able pull you up."

When they reached the pit, Pazel threw two unlighted torches across to the other side. He stuck the flaming one in a crack before tying one end of the rope securely around the larger bag of guano and the other end around his waist.

"Now I will cross by climbing along the wall on the left. When I get to the other side, I'll light the two torches."

Then he carefully, with his face to the left wall, worked his way from one handhold and foothold to the next until he had reached the far side. Shani watched her husband find grips in the wall while his feet inched along the narrow lip of the pit.

When he was safely over and had lighted the torches, he untied the rope from his waist and pulled it until the bag of guano fell into the pit. He held on tightly as the weight of the bag jerked at his arms but would not let go of the load. Then he drew the bag up and set it safely against the wall of the passage leading away from the pit.

"How will you get the other sack over?"

"I'm coming back there."

Pazel coiled the rope and looped it over his head and arm before hurrying back to his bride. He then tied the rope to the second sack and repeated the method he had used to get the first one over. Eventually he had both bags of precious though smelly cargo safely stowed while Shani still waited to cross to his side.

"I'm trying to hurry," he called to his wife.

When back at her side, he tied the rope around her waist. "Now it's your turn. Wait until I'm across, so I can get a good hold on the rope in case you slip. Try to find the same handholds I use and don't be scared. I'm here to keep you safe."

She was almost across before she reached a place where she could not find a handhold. Pazel held the rope taut so that if she fell, he would be prepared to hold on to her.

"Stretch a little farther."

"I can't. I can't reach that rock."

"Try!"

"I'll find some place to grab. Give me a moment."

Just as Shani was finding a good enough rock knob to grasp, the sound of footsteps coming from the passage behind them set both their hearts racing.

"Hurry! Hurry!" Pazel gripped the rope tighter. "That must be the other Lamechite. No nephil could fit through the passage we took."

Shani froze in place, unable to move hand or foot. She glanced back to her left and was horrified to see a ferocious face just starting across the pit. He was coming after her and moving much more quickly than she had.

"Pazel!" she screamed and instinctively jumped away from the man who was reaching for her arm.

"Be careful!" But his warning was too late.

Shani's foot slipped, and she seemed to be grabbing at air as she slowly toppled backward down into the blackness of the pit.

"I've got you, Shani!" he yelled and instantly braced the rope across his back.

With one foot forward and the other back, he prepared to take the jerk of her body reaching the end of the rope's length. At the same time, he kept his eyes on the Lamechite, who had not slowed his pace and was nearly across the pit. Shani had screamed as she was falling, but when her body slammed hard into the pit wall at the far end of the rope, she grunted once and was silent.

"Shani! Are you all right?"

Pazel never took his eyes off the approaching enemy, yet he had to make a decision. The Lamechite was only steps from him, but if he held onto the rope, he would not be able to fight the enemy.

Shani might be unconscious or badly injured. From a previous time when he had dropped stones into the pit, Pazel knew it was no more than a body's length deeper than the end of his rope. With the hope that Shani was only knocked unconscious, he slowly let the rope slip through his fingers until he came to the end. Then he let it go. A second later he heard Shani's body hit the bottom.

Suddenly infuriated at the dirty man who had caused his wife's fall, Pazel pulled out his sword and launched a frenzied attack at his nemesis. The Lamechite, who had just stepped away from the pit, barely had time to draw his sword.

Never in all his life had Pazel felt such hatred. It was a fire burning a in his heart, driving him forward like an angry razor-tooth. Terrified for Shani, he did not let up until he had driven his opponent to the edge of the pit. But then he stopped. He could not allow this creature to fall on Shani. He was going to kill him—but not that way.

"Come on, you foul son of Lamech, you dirty assassin! Don't you know how to fight?"

"I'll show you who can fight!" Rage now drove the other man, who slashed his sword wildly back and forth.

Pazel allowed the man to drive him back many paces until they were almost beyond the torchlight. His own anger, however, was much stronger. At the right time, he lunged forward, not swinging wildly as his opponent did. Pazel made each move count and soon left a bleeding dead man on the stones.

Grabbing one of his lighted torches and rushing back to the edge of the pit, he held the light as far down as he could. But it was no use. It would take a stronger light than this to penetrate that darkness.

"Shani! Shani! Can you hear me?"

No sound came back to him from the depths—not a moan, not a cry, not a breath. Pazel slumped onto the stone floor, rolled onto his back, and sobbed until the tears flowed down the sides of his face and soaked his hair. Even then he was trying to think of a way to reach her. He tried to summon hope. Maybe she was not dead but only hurt. There had to be something he could do.

He must get to her. He would need help. He needed Hod. Again he held his ear over the pit. He thought he heard a low moan but could not be sure.

"Shani, if you hear me, I am dropping the healing water down by you. Drink it if you can. I will be back with help very soon. Remember I love you."

There was no sound from her, so he dropped the waterskin of healing water a few feet from where the rope had been. If she was alive, maybe she would find it.

With a last glance at the dead Lamechite and a long last look into the pit, Pazel turned and ran down the passage.

◁ 13 ▷

The Green Trail

After half a day spent crossing the higher reaches of the mountains with two bags of guano over his shoulders and his usual pack on his back, an exhausted Pazel looked down on the rock corral where he and Hod had met Kodi, Chay, and Mathu months before.

Terrified that Shani might be badly injured and waiting for him to save her, he had run whenever possible. All the while his mind had been planning how to get her out of the pit.

Why did I let Enoch make me take Shani? He said Elohim had a plan for her. But what is it? I don't understand. I have to get back right away. I hope Enoch has some rope I can use, or I could make a ladder from a tree. If the others have come back from their trip, I'll get someone to go with me.

He walked the rim of the corral and was looking down into the woods beyond when a high-pitched, drawn-out howl froze him for a moment.

What was that? Sounded like a wolf. I had better hurry.

Pazel's keen eyes spotted a silvery-gray wolf loping down toward him from the higher part of the mountainside. Pazel began to run through the woods and toward the stream. A look over his shoulder showed the wolf closer than he thought, so without pausing he waded on through the water.

By the time Pazel reached the other side—a length a tall man could have jumped—the wolf had caught up with him, but it stopped at the bank and snarled with its mouth drawn back to expose sharp fangs.

Pazel backed towards the wall, never taking his eyes off the wolf, which he now saw was different from any such animal he had ever seen. As large as a horse and with eyes that almost glowed red, it looked as if it were starving. Then the animal bunched its muscles to lunge across the rivulet; however, when it sprang, it seemed to run against an obstacle that knocked it down into the stream.

The wolf snarled and tried to crawl out of the water onto the bank but was unable to emerge from the shallow rivulet. Its paws slipped and slid on the rocky bank as if it had no control of its muscles. Before he stepped into the gap in the wall, Pazel stood still a moment and watched. The wolf was slinking out of the water on the other side of the rivulet when it suddenly cringed, looked up in the air above its head, and whined as if it had been kicked.

Once in the safety of the enclosure, Pazel dropped the bags of guano behind a bush and ran on until he reached Enoch's hut. To his great relief, Kodi and Chay were sitting down for a meal with their host.

"Pazel, you're just in time to share some bread and fruit," Enoch said as the Cainite ran up to them. "Where is Shani?"

"She . . . she . . . ." Pazel bent over double and held his side, his breath heaving in huge gulps. "I need . . . help . . ."

Kodi jumped to his feet. "Is she hurt?"

"She fell . . . down in the pit. I don't know if she's . . ." Tears started down Pazel's cheeks as he struggled to tell his tale. His words were swallowed up in his grief.

Enoch got up and put his arms around the young man. It was strange how his very touch breathed peace and hope into Pazel's heart. "She is alive. What do you need to get to her?"

"Thank you. I need a ladder. I thought I could make one from a tree—cut off the branches. And I need someone to help bring her up."

Again Kodi stepped forward. "I'll go with you. Chay can stay here to help Enoch until Hod and Hela get back. Is that all right?"

These last words were aimed directly at the old man, who nodded and put a hand on Kodi's arm while keeping his arm about Pazel's shoulder.

"This young fellow has been running a long time. He needs to eat and drink, and then you two must fly back to the cave on haraanis. Pazel is too tired to run and keep up with you."

Pazel let Enoch lead him back to the table. His breath was beginning to slow, and he knew he needed to slake his thirst even if he could not make himself eat. Although he wanted to start back immediately, he trusted this old man who also wanted Shani to live.

"Did you bring your ingredient?" Enoch asked him softly.

"Yes. I dropped two bags of it right inside your wall." He spoke so only the old man would hear and then raised his voice for all. "There is a huge wolf just across the rivulet."

"That's Varqr, Kron's new pet." Kodi's grim tone told them more than his words. "The king sent him after Hod. He must have tracked him here."

"We saw him back in the woods near Havilah," Chay added. "He was after us, but I thought we lost him when we flew away."

Pazel by now was guzzling water from one of Enoch's clay cups. He forced himself to eat an apple in large bites while Kodi sat down and finished his food at a slightly slower pace.

The nephil looked up at Pazel. "I was thinking about your idea for a ladder. We could make one by cutting the branches off a tall tree, but we can't get it back to the cave on the haraanis."

"I have a long rope ladder you can take," Enoch had walked back toward them in time to hear their words. "Is there some place above the pit to tie it?"

Pazel glanced up from his food and slowly shook his head. "I don't think so." His brown eyes were beginning to look desperate.

"Let's get going!" Kodi suddenly snapped. "I'll hold the rope if I have to! The important thing is to get to your wife."

At these words, Pazel jumped up and threw down his food. "I'm ready!"

"You sure you don't need me?" Chay asked hesitantly.

Pazel looked at this brother of his good friend and wondered if he really wanted to go. Then Enoch spoke for the Pazel and Kodi, who were now moving quickly toward the cliff edge where the haraanis waited.

"Your help is not needed, Chay. Finish eating. You can help me while we wait for Hod and Hela to bring the last ingredient. Now I need to get them the ladder."

Kodi and Pazel took off from the edge of the cliffs overlooking the Garden of Eden, swept down and up and circled about until they landed at the boulders where the Dark Passage began.

"A Lamechite was after me just after Shani fell," Pazel said as he lighted the torch he had left just inside the entrance. "I killed him, and I don't think there were any more."

"There could be. Remember I said Kron was sending out one nephil and two Lamechites in each group. Radek was the leader of the group coming after you. He should have one more warrior with him."

"I killed the other one in the upper passages when we first got back. I'm glad I did. I'm glad I killed them both!"

For the first time since he had known the little salt merchant, Kodi heard bitterness and cruelty in his voice. He reached out and put one hand on Pazel's shoulder as they walked side by side in the torchlight.

"Do you think Radek could be at the pit?"

"No. The passages leading there are too small for a ne-phil."

"Then I suggest we hurry before he finds another way to it."

Pazel grunted and picked up his pace, going forward as rapidly as possible considering the danger of unseen low -hanging rocks. He slowed as they neared the pit.

"Down there. She's down there. Shani! Can you hear me?"

While he was leaning down and calling into the dark depths, Kodi was looking for some place to attach the rope ladder.

"Where can we tie it?" Pazel asked when he noticed what Kodi was doing.

"These walls are too smooth. I'm going to have to hold it while you climb down."

"Hold it? Are you that strong?"

"Yes, I am. Now get on down there! I'll light another torch and, if you will bring me up your old rope, I'll use it to send the torch down."

Without further protest, Pazel backed carefully down the ladder, being sure not to make it harder than it had to be for Kodi. He felt around at the bottom, but Shani was not there. He did notice a glowing green trail, which he thought was made by cave slugs, leading away.

When he found the rope that he had tied around her, he scrambled back up the ladder.

"She's not there!" he panted out. "But the rope is on the ground—and it *was* tied around her waist! So she must be alive! I'm going back down. Give me the torch."

Pazel's first view of the bottom of the pit showed no sign of his wife except for a puddle of dried blood. The skin of healing water was gone. But where was Shani? Pazel put his face close to the floor and held the torch so he could study the green trail. He touched it with his fingertips, smelled it, and knew immediately it was the track of one of the huge slugs that found refuge from the sun in the lower caves.

These creatures—as long as a Cainite was tall—had yellow-green glowing skin and eyes that protruded on long appendages. Pazel had encountered them before and knew that their eyes worked better in the dark than in the light.

The gooey track was almost dry and stretched to a seemingly solid wall where it disappeared into a small, low opening. When he squeezed under the opening, he saw it led to a bigger area, big enough to move through.

He came back to where the ladder still dangled over the edge of the pit and called up to his cousin. "Kodi, Shani's not here, but I found an opening she must have gone through. Will you give me some time to search for her?"

"Of course, go ahead. Call me when you are ready to come up."

Pazel slipped through the opening and on through narrow, low-ceilinged passages and small caverns, always going downward, deep as his salt mine, always following the trail of slime. The green path often made sharp turns and circled cone-shaped formations, but it never came to an end.

Sometimes he could crouch, sometimes stand, and sometimes he had to crawl on his belly, always with his torch held out before him. He had been traveling a quarter of an hour when he came across the waterskin laying on top of the slime.

Shani must be following the slime since the skin is on top of it. I'm going on after her no matter where it takes me, but I don't want Kodi to wait. It could be a long journey.

Pazel quickly crawled back until he reached the pit. "Kodi! I've found where she dropped the waterskin. But I haven't found her. Can you find someplace to tie the ladder on the other side?"

"I think I can. I've been studying it. I'll find a place to tie the ladder and then come down and help find her."

"No. There are spots I can barely squeeze through. Leave the ladder and go back to help Enoch. Don't worry about us. She is alive, and all I have to do is lead her back here."

"If you two don't make it back to the garden before we leave—which will be soon—meet us at the river cave."

"All right." Pazel looked up from the bottom of the pit. "I won't give up until I find her. And, Kodi?"

"Yes."

"Thank you . . . for everything."

When Pazel had returned to where he had left the waterskin, he slipped it over his shoulder and continued on—more rapidly than before—eventually coming to what seemed to be the end of the trail. It was a larger cavern than any he had yet gone through, but still there was no sign of Shani.

Convinced she had to be close by, Pazel called out. "Shani! Shani! Can you hear me?"

The name echoed a little in the big cavern, as he expected; however, as he listened to the echo, Pazel thought he heard something out of place.

"Ahhhh . . . zel." That was not his echo.

"Shani! Is that you?"

No voice answered him, but he now saw a narrow gap in the cave wall. Although it was no wider than the span of three hands, Pazel knew she could have gotten through it. A scrap of her robe hanging from a spiky rock confirmed it. Pazel studied the floor around and beyond this gap and noticed the slimy trail continued on. He crawled through, calling out to his wife as he did. This time a voice—not an echo—returned to him. He went forward, even though his torch was beginning to sputter. He had to find her before the light was gone. He had to hurry!

The voice was louder—closer—maybe at the end of this passage. And then the torch went out.

Pazel stopped and reached for his flint. He struck it against the stone wall over and over, but not a spark flared in the pitch darkness of the tunnel. His pupils widened as he tried to orient himself.

Shani's voice floating to him pulled his head in the right direction. Now the glow of the slug's trail was the only thing visible. No wonder she had followed it.

"Pazel! Pazel! This way. Come this way!"

As quickly as he safely could, Pazel crawled beside the slime trail until it turned an invisible corner and opened up into the strangest cavern he had ever seen. It was decorated with swirling green lines that crossed each other hundreds of times. The lines went up the walls and across the roof crisscrossing until the entire cave was illuminated with a pale green glow.

Sitting in the middle of the room, on the top of a tall rock pedestal, was Shani. On the floor about her were hundreds of the giant slugs.

"Be careful," she called. "I'm afraid of these beasts."

"Shani! Thank the Creator you are all right! I've been so scared! Were you injured? You drank the water I left, right?"

"Yes. When I woke up all alone, it was dark except for the green marks. The waterskin was next to me, so I knew you left it for me. I called to you, but you were gone. I was so thirsty that I drank almost all of it. I waited for days."

All the time her sad voice spoke, Pazel had been carefully moving toward her. He had let her talk without responding in hopes that the slugs would not notice him moving through them, but her last words were too much.

"I had to go for help. I had no way to get to you! I was only gone a day. You were confused by the darkness — it does that."

His voice startled the slug he was stepping over, making it rear up and turn toward him. In the glowing light, the smooth, featureless face seemed harmless. Then it opened its wide maw and grabbed his leg with a smooth, sticky suction that felt as if it could tear the skin from his bone. Until now he had given no thought to whether this slug was a plant eater or a meat eater — now he knew.

"Watch out, Pazel. They want to make supper out of us!"

Pazel jerked his leg out of the creature's mouth before it could hurt him and ran the last few paces to Shani's rock.

He stepped on the up-rearing head of the last slug, and, disgusted to find it as soft as an over-ripe tomato, quickly vaulted onto the stone pedestal.

"Did one of the slugs bite you?" he asked Shani.

"Yes. The one I followed attacked me when I caught up with it, but when I hit it with the waterskin, it slithered off. I think they are cowardly. I poured some of the water on the bite. Then I fell asleep. When I woke up, I forgot to take the waterskin with me. I'm glad you found it."

He stopped her torrent of words with a laugh and a kiss. When he had kissed her enough to make up for all the fear and grief he had gone through since she fell, he stared at the slugs and the huge room.

"Do you hear something?" he asked.

"You mean besides their groaning?"

"Yes. I think I hear water!"

Pazel pointed toward a place on the far wall where the glowing light was more of a yellow. "I think the sound is coming from there. It's another opening, but on the other side could be our salvation."

"What do you mean?"

"That yellow means sunlight. The slugs have to absorb it before they can reflect it. And that sound is the river. We must be close to the big cavern where the river runs."

"How can we get past the slugs?"

Pazel grinned, and when Shani seemed confused, he began to laugh loudly. Then he reached into the pack that had never left his back. He pulled out a bag the size of his fist.

"You forget—I'm a salt merchant. I never go out without some salt."

"How will that help?"

"Watch." Pazel stood up and began to sprinkle salt right below them.

When the slugs began to scatter, moving faster than he ever thought they could, he jumped down onto the goo and reached up a hand to help Shani down. Then he turned and moved toward the yellow light, tossing salt ahead of them. When the salt landed on the creatures, they began to writhe and move quickly away. By the time they reached the small opening leading out of the green room, the rushing sound had grown much louder.

"You look in first. I'll keep an eye on the slugs."

"This is something special!" Shani cried when she put her head through the crack.

"Is it the river cavern?"

"No. You have to see this for yourself."

Pazel pulled her back, stepped through the opening, and was amazed to see a waterfall coming down the wall closest to them. It fell ten cubits from a hole near the top to the cave floor where it flowed on as a narrow stream. The light he had seen from the other room came from a hole directly above him. Pazel could tell this was not direct sunlight but only light coming from a room above.

"Shani, I think we are under the river," he said as he helped her through. "This water finds its way down here through a hole. I'm going to taste the water to be sure."

After checking that there were no slugs in this room, Pazel took Shani's hand and led her to the waterfall.

"I know how the healing water tastes and feels. This is from the fifth river," he said after tasting it. "Now we can clean up in the waterfall and find a place for you to rest. I'm going to climb up the wall and through that hole to make sure of where we are."

"I don't want to be left alone!" Shani protested while watching him fill his waterskin.

He hugged her again. "Let me just climb up through this hole above us. If it is the river cavern, you can wait there for the rest of the group while I look around down here. There are no slugs at that level. You'll be safe."

"Don't the others need you to guide them to us?"

"Hod knows the way through the Dark Passage. He will lead them to the fifth river. After I get you settled, I'm going to explore some of the passages leading out of this lower cavern. I might find another way to the outside that could come in handy when we blow up the upper cavern."

In a half hour, when he had Shani resting by the river above, Pazel took his torch and climbed back down to continue his explorations. He had no fear of getting lost as this was something he had done on his own since he first found himself in the cavern with the river when he was a small boy on his own. When he returned, it was with food for their dinner and his old wide grin on his face.

"Where did you find figs?" Shani exclaimed.

"Oh, I've been to my old home, retrieved some rope and these figs, and checked on my cave. It seems as if all our enemies have left."

"So we are finally safe—for now?"

"Yes, and I will make sure you are never again in danger."

Shani took his hand and held it to her cheek. "You cannot make such a promise. The mission must succeed, and I will make the necessary sacrifices just as Hela and the others do."

"I pray that you will never have to. Yet I am proud of you, my brave girl."

◁14▷

Back to the Dark Passage

The sun was beginning to set as Kodi flew back to Enoch's home. He saw the two Lamechites he had eluded two days ago circling their haraanis above the area outside the wall and waved to them to draw near as he circled near.

"Dolf! What happened to you two? I lost you somehow."

"We were told you never went back to the fortress. No one had seen you."

Even though he could read disbelief on Dolf's face, Kodi kept on with his story.

"The Sethian who was with me told me I could find the fire-hair—his brother—in northern Atlantia, so I ended up going there before I ever landed at the fortress."

"Did you find him?"

"No. I think the brother was lying."

"Why isn't he with you?"

"I was so disgusted with him that I threw him in the yellow fissure."

Again Kodi thought he read doubt in Dolf's expression, but, as they were flying and circling past each other it was hard to be sure. Maybe he had gone too far in claiming he had killed Chay. If they saw him alive, they would be certain Kodi was lying and report it to Kron.

"Where are you going now?" Dolf asked.

"Back to the old man to see if he is hiding the fire-hair. You two go back to the king and tell him what is going on. I am trying to get Enoch's trust. I'll have to stay here a while."

Only after he saw that the Lamechites were well on their way back to the fortress did Kodi turn back to the garden. Then he noticed that Varqr was still lurking back in the woods.

Hod and Hela had returned from their journey bringing Tagg and three iron pots by the time Keoaw landed in Enoch's home and had learned of Shani's fall.

"Where is Pazel?" Hod walked up to Kodi as soon as he dismounted. "Chay said you went with him to rescue Shani."

Kodi clapped a hand on the Sethian's shoulder and looked down at him with serious eyes.

"When he went down in the pit, she was gone, but he was sure she had drunk the healing water. She followed slug trails through a small opening. He did not know how far he would have to go to find her but said I would not fit through some of the gaps. He wanted me to leave the rope and come back here to help Enoch."

"Does he plan to come back here?"

"No, he said he and Shani would be waiting in the river cave."

"I pray he will be. Now come see what Enoch has done."

Kodi followed Hod back to the old man's table where three iron pots, each of which would be an armful for one human, were lined up in a row.

Hod introduced Kodi to Tagg and filled him in on the results of their mission before asking him to tell them all about Pazel. When he was finished, Kodi looked at Enoch.

"The wolf is still outside the wall. Do we leave soon for the rest of the mission?"

"Gather and I will explain it all."

At Enoch's urging Hod, Hela, Chay, Kodi, and Tagg crowded around the table. By now it was dark, so they studied the three pots by the light of Enoch's oil lamp. The round pots had swinging handles and openings at the top. These openings had been filled with circular oak plugs sealed with some type of resin. Greasy looking strips of linen hung from holes bored in the plugs.

"I am calling these eruptors," Enoch explained. "You will place one beside each of the main pillars holding up the roof of the cave. You will light the cloth with your torch. The fire will go inside the pot and ignite the powder. It will burn and expand and cause the pot to blow apart with such power that the pillar will crumble."

"Will that be enough to bring that rock roof down?" Hod asked. "It looked very firm."

"Appearances can fool you. The Watchers told me that the roof is thin limestone. If not for the pillars, the weight of a behemoth would cave it in."

"What if we are unable to blow up all three pillars—if one of the eruptors fails? Will the roof still collapse?" Chay asked.

Kodi thought Chay seemed worried. He tried to smile his encouragement but did not think his old friend noticed in the darkness.

"It is possible," Enoch replied. "But it will be better if they all work. I think they will."

Hod slammed a fist down on the table. The pots did not move. "We will make it work! No more negative thinking! This is our mission. There are five of us even without Pazel, for Hela will go with us."

"I think she should stay here." Chay frowned at Hod and put a protective arm around his sister.

Before Hela could protest Hod spoke again. "She will go. She is mighty with her bow and arrow and may be vital to our task. We will leave at dawn if Uncle Enoch agrees."

Enoch stroked his beard and seemed to be amused by the disagreement between his nephews. "That is good. All is at the ready, and Remiel has told me that Kron's army is marching on Pazel's cave at this very moment."

"Then we will leave at the first hint of light," Hod said. "Kodi, I will trust you to take care of the wolf."

"Of course. I will deal with Varqr."

"Good. Now everyone try to sleep."

Enoch held up one hand. "Before you go to bed, I have one warning. After you light the cloth on the eruptors, you must get out of the way. I want everyone to go to Pazel's cave or somewhere else safe. Only one man must stay behind to light the cloth, and then he must run away as fast as he can."

⋈

Hod woke before the rest. In fact, it was still dark, but once he was awake, he could no longer lie there on the ground. As quietly as possible, he got up and began getting his pack together. He went over to the table and checked on the eruptors. They looked as harmless as water jugs, yet inside them was this secret powder that would blow up stones and bring down caves.

What would this power do to a weak human body? He must do all he could to save the lives of his friends. Right then Hod decided he would be the one to light the cloths.

By the time the rest of his crew—he liked to think of them as the new Iron Fist—was up and ready to go, Kodi had slipped out ahead of them.

"Give me a few minutes to find and take care of Varqr. He will come to me, so it should be no problem to get him out of the way. I'll whistle when it's safe."

While Hod waited at the gap in the rock wall for the signal, he studied his sister and brother and Tagg. Hela's face had an expression of serious concentration in keeping with the trust he had shown by including her in this venture, Tagg's face showed his boyish eagerness for adventure. Chay, however, looked nervous, almost double-minded, as if he were not sure they should be trying to bring down the cave roof.

"Chay? Are you all right?"

His brother jumped at Hod's words, and his eyes went quickly from Hela to Tagg. "Of course`! Why do you ask?"

"Nothing really. You looked nervous."

Chay cleared his throat. "I'm just ready to get started. And I thought it might be a good idea if some of us carried some rope. At least I want to."

"While we're waiting, go back and get some rope from Enoch," Hod said, using his head to indicate the place they had just left.

When Chay returned a few minutes later, he had a long coil of rope over one shoulder. "I thought you'd be outside by now. I wonder what's keeping Kodi."

"I'll check on him." Hod motioned the others to wait before quietly stepping through the gap.

He scanned the landscape beyond the rivulet, feeling his pupils stretch wide in the murky morning light. Seeing nothing, he concentrated on listening. The birds were beginning to greet the day, but there was something else.

Scuffling sounds, as of two large bodies struggling to-gether, and then a high pitched whine. Moments later Kodi came striding out of the woods.

"Did you kill him?"

"Yes. He won't be following us anymore."

♓

Moving slowly, with Kodi easily carrying one pot and the rest taking turns with the other two, it took the entire day to reach the entry into the Dark Passage. While they walked, Hod filled them in on the twin perils of the pit and the colony of giant bats.

Kodi picked out a strong, slim tree on the way, cut it down, trimmed the branches, and carried it over one shoulder while holding the pot with the other hand.

"I think this will help us get the pots across," he explained. "You'll see what I mean."

When they arrived at the crevice between two boulders, Hod lit two torches from a pile of pine knots at the entrance and led his friends straight to the pit where they saw the rope ladder still tied on the far side.

Hod looked down into the black hole. "There's no sign Pazel and Shani climbed up. I think he would have untied the rope if he had and taken it with him."

"Maybe not," Kodi said. "Let's leave the rope in case he still needs it."

"We should go find them." Hela's insistent voice echoed Hod's own thoughts, but he shook his head and sighed at the burden of command.

"The mission is too important. We have to go on." He turned to Kodi. "Now show us what you're going to do with the tree."

Without a word Kodi took the heavy end of the tree, picked it up as easily as if it were his sword, hooked the smaller end under the handle of the pot he had been carrying and reached out across the pit where he easily set it down on the other side.

"Amazing! I never realized exactly how strong you are." Chay looked the young giant up and down as if it was the first time he had seen him.

"You never needed me to show you before." Kodi smiled and continued moving the pots to the other side. While he was working, he looked at Hod. "Let me cross over first and help everyone else."

"Are you sure? I've done this before."

"So have I," Chay added. "I know the hand and foot-holds."

Kodi laughed and headed for the right side of the pit where a small lip gave room for walking and a variety of knobby rocks provided something to grab. At different times both Hod and Chay had been guided across by Pazel and each was confident he could make the trip again. Hela, however, gave them some concern.

In two steps Kodi had reached the other side of the pit and was moving the pots farther from the edge. Chay and Hod looked at each other, wondering who would take the lead. Finally Hod spoke.

"Chay, you go first. I'm going to tie this rope around Hela's waist. You take the other end and let Kodi hold it. If she loses her hold, he will be able to keep her from falling."

"But—." When Hela started to protest, Hod turned and snapped his fingers.

"That's enough. Stop trying to prove yourself and do what you're told. I am the leader of this mission! If you fall, you'll delay us. Do you want that to happen?" His green eyes snapped and his red hair waved wildly as he threw his arms out wide. Hela gave him a long look before taking the end of the rope and tying it around her waist.

"I'm sorry. You're right." She handed the other end of the rope to Chay. "But I'm not going to fall."

Chay carefully made his way across the pit, the end of the rope clenched between his teeth. As soon as he reached the other side, he handed the rope to Kodi. With the story of Shani's fall fresh in his mind, Hod hovered near his sister as she began copying Chay's path. Tagg also stood nervously watching.

When she reached the other side, Hela hopped nimbly onto the stone floor and immediately untied the rope from her waist. Hod ignored the triumphant glance she gave him. Instead, he let Tagg cross and then followed him.

"Let's get moving," he said as he picked up one of the pots.

When they reached the small cavern with one overhead hole opening to the sky, it was dark and only three stars shone through.

"We'll sleep here." Hod put down the pot, took off his sword and pack. We'll need all our energy to get through the bats."

When they awoke the next morning, some weak early sunlight was coming in through the hole. After they had eaten something, Hod began discussing the coming trial.

"The bats, which are the size of hawks, are blood-thirsty. They will hold on once they sink their fangs into your skin. Pazel fought them off with his torch, but mine went out and I had half a dozen bites before we got out of the passage.

"So fire runs them off?" Tagg asked.

"Yes. They are used to the dark, I guess. The fire seems to startle them."

Kodi stood and looked about him. The cavern was growing lighter as the sun rose higher. "Do you know if Pazel has any torches stored near here? I want to take one in each hand and go in first. I'll beat them back and make them go out ahead of us."

"Yes, I saw where he keeps his torches. I'll get some. But the bats won't want to go into the other chamber," Hod explained. "It is brighter than this one."

"I'll force them to fly that way. When we get near the end, you can each run past me."

Hod nodded. "Good idea. If anyone gets bitten, we'll have the river for healing."

As they entered the tunnel-like passage, he heard the loud flapping sound he remembered from last time and knew it meant the bats were stirring. Then they began to emit a high pitched shrieking that curdled his blood. Kodi, however, showed no fear as he stalked with determination down the narrow path.

The plan worked. Kodi, with his two torches, led the way. After him came Chay, Hela, and Tagg—each holding a pot—while Hod carried another torch and guarded the rear. As he walked backward, Hod occasionally had to ward off a bat that had been left behind. When they were near enough to the exit from the passage to hear the river's sound, the bats suddenly rushed back at Kodi. He swung both torches around his head and turned to his companions.

"Run quickly into the cave! I'll try to hold them off."

Hela dropped her eruptor and grabbed Tagg's hand. Without protesting, they ran on ahead of the others. Chay paused a moment, glanced back at his brother, and then he too hurried past Kodi.

"I'm at your back," Hod said to the nephil when they were alone. "Keep moving. I'll stay with you—but move fast!"

Hod felt a bat attach itself to his foot and kicked out to shake it off. Those flying about his head he fought off with the swirling flame in his hand. As Kodi moved forward, Hod kept his back against him so they moved as one on out of the passage.

When they joined the others waiting for them outside in the great cavern, Hod saw that Hela was holding her arm and Chay's leg was bleeding.

"Were you bitten?" he asked them.

When they both nodded, Hod pointed them to the river, his own leg throbbing from the bite he had sustained.

"Bathe your wounds. If you want to get in the water entirely, be careful to hold onto the edge. The current is swift."

Kodi extinguished one of his torches and leaned the other against the wall. The sunlight coming through the three overhead holes lighted the cavern sufficiently. Hod put out his own torch before sitting at the river's side and soaking his leg. While the others bathed or drank the healing water, he refilled the waterskin he always carried. He noticed that Chay did the same.

"Hod, I dropped my eruptor in the passage," Hela said. "I'm sorry. I wasn't thinking."

"Let me go back and get it right now," Kodi said and immediately grabbed the still-lighted torch and headed for the opening they had just left. After bringing out the pot and setting it down outside the passage, he hurried back to the river—which the others had just climbed out of —and jumped in.

Before Hod could remind Kodi to be careful of the current, the river had pulled his feet out from under him and swept him down to the southern end.

"Kodi! Quick! Grab something," Hod yelled.

The four on the bank ran down the riverside, trying to keep up with Kodi, who was headed for a solid wall at the end. All were calling to him and horrified as his head seemed destined to slam into the rocks.

At the last minute, Kodi threw his arms up and caught onto the walkway that Pazel and Shani had used to cross the river. Using his tremendous strength, he pulled his torso up and on the bridge, and then drew his legs up after.

"Are you all right?" Chay, who had run ahead of the rest, grabbed Kodi's foot and pulled it up farther on the rocks.

Kodi sputtered and spit out water before answering. "I'm fine now. I had several bites, so I jumped into the middle of the water. Hod was right when he said to stay near the edge. I would have thought I was big enough, but that current is strong!"

Just then a merry face, grinning widely, stepped up on the bridge from the other side.

"I'm glad you're strong, cousin. If you had gone under the wall, I don't know if you would have ever surfaced."

Chay turned in surprise and put out his hand. "Pazel! We were wondering where you were."

"Shani and I have been here a while waiting." Pazel turned and called back to his wife before turning back to his friends. "It's about time you all showed up. I was starting to worry about you."

"Well, we're here now. Come on over. I was about to make plans for setting the eruptors," Hod said.

When the whole group was gathered in a circle, each sitting cross-legged on the cave floor, Hod leaned in and began to explain what they would do. "We'll set the three pots close to the base of each pillar, and then—when you have all run back through the Dark Passage, I'll light them one at a time and run after you."

Pazel held up a hand. "Wait! I've found another way out while we were waiting. The Dark Passage is too dangerous."

"We know!" Chay barked.

"Tell us what you found." Hod nodded at his Cainite friend. "And how you got here from the pit."

"I found that Shani had followed a slug trail out of the pit. It gave out a green glow, so I followed it too. I was far into the caves when I found her."

"He rescued me from killer slugs!" Shani broke in.

Pazel laughed and squeezed his wife's hand. "I suppose if we had fallen down they would have tried to make us their supper. Anyway, we got away from the slugs and went into a cave with a waterfall. It was healing water, so I knew we were near this cavern. I found an opening, climbed up, and discovered we were directly under the river."

Hod looked around. "You found a way up here? So we can escape that way? Back through the slugs?"

"No. I brought Shani up here to rest, but I continued on south in the lower passage and came out near the bottom of the mountains, not far from that well where I met you last year."

"Why is that better? No obstacles—no pits, bats, or slugs?" Hod asked.

"No! And the passage is wide enough for Kodi to go through. Once out, we could climb a hill and see if the cave roof collapses. While we hide in the rocks, we would also be able to see if the nephilim warriors have arrived."

When Pazel was done with his news, Hod considered his idea a moment. He looked about the cavern from one pillar to the next and finally back at his friend. "Do you think the lower cave will collapse when this roof falls?"

"I don't know. It might."

Hod thought some more. "All right, this is what we'll do. We'll set the eruptors. Then everyone will follow Pazel out this new passage. I'll give you time to get clear and then light the cloths on the pots starting at the south end. When I get to the last pillar, I'll take a torch and run into the Dark Passage and out the other end."

While Hod was speaking, Kodi was shaking his head. Finally, he slammed his fist into the palm of the other hand. "I won't let you do it! You are the leader. The group needs you. Besides, I am the best able to run through the bats!"

Chay, who had been watching closely, suddenly spoke up. "Kodi's right, but I insist on going with him. I'll take a torch and protect his back. I have a skin of healing water in case we get bitten. We can come back over the mountain and help you if you have to fight."

"That's right!" Kodi smiled at Chay. "We've been partners since he was a prisoner in the fortress. We can do it while you take the rest to safety. Don't worry about your brother. I'll take care of him."

While the nephil and his brother were speaking, Hod had looked from one to the other. The doubts that had been deviling him since he had left home now made him waver. There was something in his expression that made Hod uneasy. Finally, he gave a quick, decisive nod.

"I do not know how good a leader I am. Everyone seems to give me an argument." Hod's slight smile softened his words. "But, you're right. Kodi is faster and can handle the bats. Chay, you stick close to him. Now let's set the eruptors."

"If you want me to, I'll take Hela to the passage we'll escape through. We'll wait there for you," Shani said.

"All right." Hod glanced at Tagg. "Would you go with them just in case they have trouble?"

When Tagg signaled his agreement, Shani led them to the hole leading down to the lower cave. Meanwhile, the four remaining men began carrying and placing the iron pots in what they guessed would be the most effective positions.

"How will you do this?" Hod asked the nephil. "What is your plan?"

"I want Chay to wait at the opening to the passage with his torch burning. I'll start at the south and light one pot after another, running as fast as I can. Then we'll run by the bats and out, using our healing water if we are bitten."

"Good! We will leave now, so you can get started. And, Chay, you be careful." Hod and Pazel left Kodi and Chay to carry out the plan and hurried to catch up with the others.

◁15▷

The Serpent Loosed

After Pazel had led the others into the lower passage, Chay let out his breath in relief that he had been able to convince Hod to leave him behind. While his brother had been explaining his plan earlier, Chay was only halfway listening. Instead, he had been working out his own scheme.

His goal was to save one of the eruptors and bring it to Dracon to open his den enough for the serpent to escape. For days Chay had been looking for a way to get one of the pots and run away with it. But during the entire trip from Enoch's, there was never a time when someone was not holding on to or sitting beside the iron pots. Now he had to prevent one of them from being blown up. Since the pots would soon be set on fire, he had to stop the cloth strip from igniting the ingredients within. Once lighted, there would be little time to save the eruptor.

The plan he and Kodi had made was for the nephil to run with one torch in hand, pause to light each pot, and then run to the next pot. They hoped to be in the cover of the passage and safe from the collapse of the rock roof before the first eruptor went off.

Chay would have three lighted torches on hand ready to hand one to Kodi when he finished his run and came back with his first torch. Then Chay would take the other two and follow Kodi, who would drive the bats ahead of him.

"I'm not happy with the way this last eruptor is set. Don't start until I check it." Chay called across the huge cavern to where the nephil was waiting to begin.

As he knew Kodi wanted to make sure Hod's group had time to get to a safe place in the lower caves, Chay was sure he had the time to save one eruptor. Even though he was concerned for his brother and sister's safety, at the moment he was more worried about his own plan.

Pushing the coiled rope he had carried the whole trip higher up on his shoulder, Chay knelt over the last pot and pulled on the cloth until it slipped out of the small hole Enoch had pushed it through. He carefully tucked a little bit back in, making sure it looked as if it were still attached.

Then he waved to Kodi—signaling all was well—and went back to the cave opening. After waiting a few minutes more, Kodi began his run. He touched his torch to the first, ran as fast as he could as soon as he knew it was burning well, lighted the second pot, and was on his way to the third. After Kodi lit the rag on the last pot, Chay motioned urgently to him.

"Hurry! We need to get down the passage as quickly as we can."

Without taking more time than was needed to duck his head, Kodi grabbed the lighted torch from Chay and entered the tunnel.

"Run! Don't look back. I'm right behind you." Chay gave Kodi a little push.

Kodi immediately began running, waving his pine knot torches to push the bats ahead of them. Chay at first took a few steps after him, but stopped when he saw that Kodi was not looking back. After watching the nephil's receding light for a moment, Chay turned and went back into the cave. Just as he did, the first pot on the other side of the room exploded with an ear-shattering boom.

He threw his torches away as he was knocked to the ground and then glanced up in time to see the pillar beside it breaking into large pieces that crumbled to the floor. A creaking groan warned him the roof was about to follow.

Without another look, he ran and grabbed the last pot just as the second eruptor blew up. Although the noise made his eardrums ache, Chay ran with the pot toward the hole in the far northwestern corner where Pazel had taken the others. When shards of rock began to spatter his back, Chay dropped the pot and flattened himself on the ground, covering his head with both hands.

Knowing that Kodi could return at any time, Chay still waited until he was sure that nothing more would fall on him. Once the falling rock settled, he turned and saw that two-thirds or more of the rocky roof and fallen and filled in the southern and middle part of the river. The rest of the roof–about one-fourth of the cavern—was supported by the last pillar.

The cave was transformed into outdoors with the morning sun and blue sky shining behind a screen of rock dust. It was suddenly very quiet, and in the stillness he could hear Kodi calling his name far down the Dark Passage.

Chay stood up straight and looked around him. Not far away a large, smoking fragment of one of the other pots was spinning on the stones. Aware that Kodi could come back at any time and guess what had happened, Chay tore off one of his sandals and left it by the piece of eruptor.

Hoping that he could convince everyone he had been killed, Chay ran to the hole to the lower passage, quickly tied his rope to his pot's handle and lowered it down to the bottom. He then picked up the still-burning torch he had dropped, tossed it below, and followed it down to the lower passages.

Down below, Chay saw that the bottom of the river had been broken through and the water above was joining the water already flowing from a small waterfall down here. The lower cavern was rapidly filling up with water.

Chay quickly picked up his burning torch before it was engulfed by the flood. He saw that the water flowed on into more passages—probably the way Pazel had taken the others. He tossed his other sandal in the water, took his torch in one hand and the pot in the other, and looked around for the way out. Since he knew which direction he should be heading, it was not hard to find the gap leading out of this chamber.

Chay forced the pot through first, using his shoulder to move it. Once he had set the pot on the other side, he followed it with his body and waved the torch high to illuminate this new space. Pazel had said they had followed the glowing slug track and now Chay knew what he meant. The room was covered with green tracks—floor and ceiling. He immediately jerked back when he felt something soft against his leg. It was a giant slug.

"Ugh! Get away, ugly!" Chay swung the torch down and pushed it into the slug's head, which sizzled as the slug pulled away.

Behind him the water was beginning to ooze into the slug cave. Since it would soon be difficult getting through this place, Chay began to run, using his torch when needed to knock slugs out of his way.

On through the passages he dashed as fast as his bare feet could take him. By the time he arrived at the bottom of the pit with the rope ladder dangling down, he was standing in water over his ankles.

Chay tied the end of his rope to the handle of the pot and climbed the rope ladder, which was tied on the wrong side of the pit. Knowing he needed his light, Chay managed to climb using only his left hand and his right elbow while holding the torch in his right hand.

Seeing he would not be able to cross the pit with his torch, Chay put it in a crack in the wall beside the pit and studied the situation. Kodi could be approaching at any moment, so he had to hurry. If he left the torch burning on this side and continued in the dark, Kodi might guess he had been there.

Finally, Chay threw the lighted torch across the pit where it lay sputtering but still burning dimly on the rocks. Then he held the rope between his teeth and carefully worked his way across the pit. Once on the other side, he drew in the rope and pulled up the eruptor.

Carrying the coiled rope over his shoulder, the pot with his left hand, and the torch in his right, Chay started down the passage and was outside in a half hour. He was surprised to discover it was only early afternoon. While in the caverns, he had lost all track of time.

After making a careful scan of the area around him to be sure no one else was around, Chay took off as directly as he could for Dracon's cave and arrived shortly before sunset. As the last rays coming over the western peaks shown directly on the cave. Chay hurried into the cleft and on to the window opening into the serpent's den.

When he set the pot down, he was out of breath and panting from carrying the weight of the eruptor. He struck his flint against the wall and lighted the pine knot he had brought with him. The torch flaired with a sizzle and gave off a piney odor that filled the space around him and floated up to the window to Dracon's den.

"Is it you? Is that my Sethian friend?"

The deep, soft voice coming from the inner chamber shivered down Chay's spine even as it drew him to the window. When he had pulled himself up on the ledge until he could see Dracon's uplifted head, he paused. "Yes, it's me."

"Did you bring the powder?"

"I did."

"Why don't you come inside where I can see you better? Take your old seat and tell me what has been happening."

Chay slid a little farther back on the ledge. "No, I'll stay out here. I need to do some work on the eruptor before it is ready to use."

"All right, but tell me what happened with the old man. How were you able to take the powder?"

"I met Enoch and my friends at his garden. He sent us off for the ingredients, and then we made three eruptors and took them to the river cavern. I worked it so that I would be the last one inside and stole the third pot before it went off—actually, I fixed it so it would not go off. I left by another route and brought it to you."

"Very clever. I am proud of you. But the other ones did work ? They did bring down the roof."

Chay's mind went back to the cave roof, gaping open to the sky and the pile of rubble filling up and burying the river—the last sight he had of the destroyed cavern.

"They worked very well. Whatever is in those pots has great power for destruction."

"Do you know the ingredients?" Dracon's scales scraped against each other as he slithered back and forth with excitement. "That powder could be very useful to us."

"I know one of the three things used for sure, but I have a good idea of a second one—and a guess at the last."

While helping Enoch fill the pots, Chay had guessed charcoal was the ingredient Hela had almost revealed. The third was something sharp smelling but unrecognizable.

"Well, well. I suppose that will have to do for now. Now why don't you come in here where I can see you?"

"In a minute." By now Chay had slipped down to the cave floor where he was trying to decide how to replace the cloth he had pulled out of the pot to keep it from going off in the cave. He suddenly remembered Niute.

"Are you hungry?" Chay raised his voice to be heard.

"Oh, no. I am still digesting my last meal—the one you sent me."

Chay swallowed hard and put one hand across his mouth. At home in Garth, he had often seen that a mouse swallowed whole by a snake made a bulge in the predator's body for hours. "Niute?"

"Yesss. He was tasty although a little dirty. The next time I would prefer a Sethian."

"Don't expect me to provide you human food every time you are hungry," Chay called out.

Dracon gave a hiss that ended in his dry chuckle. "Do not worry. I will do fine with an occasional deer. Are you ready to break down that wall?"

Chay scurried up on the ledge and then stuck his head in the window. By now it was dusk outside, and all he could see were yellow eyes fixed on him.

"I have the eruptor ready. I think if I put it in this window ledge, it will blow a hole big enough for you to get through. I don't know what will happen to this outer cave, though. I think the rock above is thick enough to withstand it, but I don't know for sure.

Dracon's breathing, raspy and fast, seemed to indicate fear. He was silent a few minutes before finally speaking.

"Do it. Go ahead and light it."

"Maybe we should wait until morning when we have enough light to see where we are going."

The great serpent's chuckle came across the den to Chay's straining ears.

"I am used to the dark. It is my natural element now. Daylight will be my enemy."

"The whole den could fall in on top of you."

"I am going to the bottom of my den where my water oozes forth. If I am buried, I will drink deeply from my water. That should protect me from injury."

"I'll wait until you are ready. Call out to me. Once the eruptor is burning, I'll run as far as I can. My torch went out. I'll have to find something else to ignite."

Chay went searching in the near dark for some dry grass. When he had a handful, he returned to the cave and put the pot, with the cloth he had replaced hanging out, on the wide ledge. He pulled out his flint and struck it repeatedly against the rock wall until one of his sparks had lighted the dry grass.

Before he could change his mind, Chay held the burning grass to the cloth, grabbed his pack and waterskin, and fled the cleft. Uncertainty about how long it would take the fire to get to the eruptor sent him behind the first tall boulder he saw, a fairly near one. He was barely in time, for a moment later a loud boom shattered the peace of the night. When he saw a flash of light shooting upward, Chay immediately poked his head up over the boulder, but the light was gone and the darkness was lighted only by a storm of stars and a sliver of a moon.

A whistling noise made Chay look up in time to see hundreds of rocks raining down on him. They pelted his shoulders, his chest, his back, and—even though he instinctively threw his arms up—some began to strike his head.

Chay had just decided he was past the worst of the rocks when one very large stone struck his head and everything went black.

$$\text{⋈}$$

For half an hour all was silent. The young Sethian lay buried under a pile of rocks. Nothing was left to suggest where his body lay.

The night returned to darkness and silence. And then, if anyone had been watching and could have seen in the gloom, he would have seen something very large slither out of a great hole in the ground and move almost noiselessly over the pile of stone.

In the moonlight Dracon was searching for his accomplice.

"Perhaps I scared him. I was sure I had convinced him I could be trusted. I suppose he was wiser than I thought. Now I will never be able to get into the Garden unless I find another foolish enough to help me. At least I am finally free."

Aware that the sun would soon rise and knowing he needed to find someplace where he could hide from it until dark, Dracon moved off down the mountain toward his old familiar haunts from centuries ago.

◁ 16 ▷

After the Cave-in

While Chay was hurrying with his eruptor through the slug-filled passage, Pazel was leading Shani, Hela, Tagg, and Hod through a string of small caves and tunnels leading to the outside.

Their pathway went down under the river with occasional drips of moisture on the rock walls attesting to the body of water merely a sheet of rock away. Only Pazel held a torch, so the rest of them stayed as close to him as possible.

They heard the distant sound of the eruptors going off as faint muffled booms, but the walls around them did not even shake. They had gone first to the north end of the cavern, down the hole, and then east and south under the river, so no one could be sure exactly what they were hearing overhead.

Kodi had said he would wait until they were safe before lighting the cloths—and Hod was sure he had done exactly that.

"I only heard two explosions," Hod, who was the last in line, called to those around him. "Did anyone else hear the third one?"

"I didn't." Pazel halted the group and looked back at Hod.

No one could say they had heard a third one for sure, so Hod motioned for Pazel to lead them on. "We can't go back, anyway. We need to get out where we can see what has happened from the outside."

Soon the moisture on the walls disappeared, and the pathway began to climb steeply enough that they had to clamber up using their hands and feet. Hod was glad the path was going sharply upward as he feared that when the roof of the cave fell on the river, it might collapse and flood the lower passage.

Fresh air began to greet their noses, giving hope that they were near the surface, but Pazel's flaming pine knot was still the only light when Hod, from his spot at the back of the group, felt a place where a narrow passage opened up to the left.

"Pazel, did you see this opening?" When Hod called out to the Cainite, the torchlight halted and then illuminated Pazel's face as he turned back to look at Hod.

"I haven't had time to investigate that crevice. I only know it is narrow and seems to go upward."

Before following the group, Hod stuck his head and shoulders into the passage and was struck by an unusual scent wafting downward as if pushed by a breeze. The smell of cedar and roses reminded him of Enoch's garden. Hod felt a strong urge to explore this path; however, he did not have a torch and he had a mission to finish, so he turned back and hurried after the rest.

A little later Pazel led them through a tight opening halfway up a low hill on the southern edge of where the mountains met the desert. They followed him to the top of the hill, which was two hundred cubits above the desert floor and had a clear view of the distant ridge to the far south.

Hod immediately climbed onto a large rock slab overhanging to the west and found he had a clear view far to the west and down at the flat land between Pazel's dry well and the beginning of the mountain range.

"Look! The ground has caved in over there. That must be where the river cavern was."

When Hod pointed, they all gathered to see the amazing sight. From close to the dry well and almost to the first boulders that started the mountain range, the ground had collapsed like a titanic footprint. The great space was filled with rocks, dirt, and sand and slanted downward at the northern end. No hint of the river was visible from where they stood above it all.

Tagg was standing with the others when he noticed something much farther west. When his back stiffened and he sucked in his breath, the others turned to look at him, and then saw what he saw. Coming toward them, no more than half a league away, was a group of warriors made up of about two dozen nephilim and maybe half as many Lamechites.

"Get down behind the boulder, everyone, before they see us!" Hod motioned to them as he ducked down until he could just see over the rock.

He watched a while as the warriors drew closer to the area where the land had collapsed. The young people were as quiet as if they thought the distant enemy could hear them. Finally, Pazel, who had come up beside Hod, broke the silence.

"Hod, I have been studying the ground over the cave. I don't think the third pillar collapsed. Look at that rock ledge at the north end."

Hod turned his eyes on the crumbled land below and saw a ledge large enough for a score of Sethians to stand on protruding over the cave-in. A stone pillar held it up on the near end.

"Then I was right." Hod sighed. "The third eruptor didn't go off."

"That must be true," Pazel said. "We have a little time before they get here. Let me go down and see if the river is hidden. If it is not, we'll have to do something."

Hod gazed intently into Pazel's eyes. As the leader of the group, he thought this sounded like a good idea, but as a friend of this little Cainite, he feared making this decision.

"All right," he finally said. "But hurry and be careful."

"Don't worry! I know my way around that cave, even as it is now. I can hide if have to."

Pazel kissed his wife and handed her the waterskin. Wanting to keep everyone's strength up as there had been no time to rest, he and Hod had been sharing the water they had gotten from the river with the entire group, but both had at least half left.

Pazel quickly slipped around the boulder and out of their sight. While they all watched the area below, he worked his way around to the north and eventually appeared right above the crumbled pile of stone. They saw him crawl over the rocks until he slipped down between two boulders and disappeared into the ground.

Now there was nothing to do but hope he would get out of the collapsed cave before the approaching enemy arrived.

Hela, now noticing that Shani was shaking, put an arm around her shoulders and tried to comfort her while Hod, wishing there was something he could do, went around to the back of the promontory and climbed up higher where he could see without being seen.

As he scanned the sky, he spotted a haraani approaching from the north and quickly knelt down between two stones. But it was too late. The haraani and its rider changed directions slightly and flew straight toward him.

"Haraani coming! Everyone duck!"

When Hod called out his warning, Tagg put a hand on Hela's shoulder and pulled her down behind the boulder. Hela reached over and drew Shani near to them. From where he was, Hod tried to get a closer look at who was riding the haraani. He pulled his sword and prepared for a fight.

Although his attention was on the approaching bird, he heard his sister talking to the others behind him.

"Tagg, we could help Hod with our arrows. Let me go! He might need us."

Hod's sword was in hand as the bird landed, but then he recognized Keoaw.

"It's all right," he called back to the others. "It's Kodi."

When he motioned the nephil to get down behind a rock before he was seen by the nephilim approaching from the west, Kodi hurried over to Hod.

"Is Chay with you? He did not come through the passage behind me. I hoped he had gone out the other way."

"What happened to him?" Hela, who had finally slipped away from Tagg and joined her brother, clutched Kodi's arm.

"I'm not sure now. He ran back into the cavern as the eruptors were going off. When I went back, he was gone, but one of his sandals was there. I don't know what happened to him. So he didn't come here?"

"We haven't seen him." Hod began to chew his lower lip.

"Where is Pazel?" Kodi asked.

Hod pointed off down the hill, trying to keep his mind on the situation at hand, even though he was beginning to fear for his brother.

"It looks as if the third eruptor did not go off. He went down to see if the water had been covered by the rocks."

Kodi stood up straight, showing no fear for his own safety. He looked off at the crumbled ground with an assessing eye.

"I think it went off but did not destroy the pillar. I saw a piece of the pot beside it when I went back. I better go down to Pazel before those nephilim and Lamechites find him."

Before Kodi could leave, Hod laid a detaining hand on his arm. "I counted over twenty nephilim in that group. Is that all Kron has? I mean, how many nephilim are there?"

"There were close to eighty of us at one time. Some were executed by Kron for failing him and some have died of disease and old age. We don't live as long as you humans. That's why Kron wants the water. Anyway, the answer is maybe fifty left."

"So if we kill these, we will be cutting the number almost in half. All right, you go on to help Pazel. I'm worried about him.

ℋ

Once he had ducked under the tumbled slabs of rock that had made up the huge domed roof of the cavern where the fifth river emerged from underground, Pazel worked his way to the northern end to see if any of the river was exposed.

At the place where the river came from the rocks, he found the third pillar still standing and beside it a shattered piece of one of the iron pots. Near it he spotted a sandal that looked as if it had been torn from someone's foot.

"I hope Chay wasn't hurt in the eruption!"

Just as Pazel spoke, he heard voices with Lamechite accents coming from the area above the cave and knew the enemy was near. He looked quickly from the pillar to the river and saw that most of it was filled in and buried under slabs of rocks. Only a bit of the river—maybe ten paces long—was left.

When he hurried over to the place where the water came from under the northern wall, he saw that a few cubits from the source, the river poured through a very large hole that had been knocked in the bottom of the rock channel through which the water had run.

It looks like the river is now going further underground. I wonder where it will go from there. Will it fill up all those deep caves?

Pazel had noticed more caves and tunnels going deeper underground and looking as if they were heading southwest. He assumed these would become new channels for the river. But there was still pure water gushing out of this northern wall, and it could be easily accessed by the nephilim above.

We have failed. Kron will have the water very soon. How can the four of us stop them?

Pazel went over to the last pillar and leaned against it with one shoulder before looking up at the remnants of the domed ceiling. He was sure that if they could bring down this column, the rest of the ceiling would collapse and cover the last part of the river.

The voices above were growing closer, so Pazel ducked back out of sight close to the entrance to the Dark Passage. From there he saw a Lamechite come down the slope, approach the gushing water, taste it, and then scratch a small cut on his arm with his curved sword. Next, he stuck the wound under the flowing water and pulled it back to watch what would happen.

As Pazel knew it would, the cut healed and the Lamechite went scurrying back to report his finding. Pazel hesitated. If he hurried, he might be able to follow this man out and be back with his friends. If he did not act quickly, the cave could soon be swarming with Lamechites and nephilim.

Before he made up his mind, the first man returned with several more Lamechites. Three nephilim stood at the top of the rubble calling down instructions for them to fill their waterskins with water. From his hiding place, Pazel watched them as they washed their hands and faces and took large drinks from the refreshing liquid

"This is delicious water," one of the men said.

"I'm glad it's healing water," another one laughed. "I've had an upset stomach all day!"

While the Lamechites took turns filling their water-skins, they laughed and joked. Obviously they didn't think anyone was around, at least no one they should worry about. Pazel scrunched back further just in case they caught a glimpse of him.

I need to get back to the others to let them know what is going on here. There is no way out but the way I came in, and I cannot do that without being seen.

Pazel finally decided that when the Lamechites started up, he would go behind them. He hoped none of the nephilim or Lamechites would notice before he had a chance to run to his friends. When the last one was halfway up, Pazel took one step out of his hiding place, but before he could start a large group of the giants began to come down. Pazel quickly hunched back into his hiding place.

As he watched this new development, he was thrilled and concerned to see that Kodi was the last nephil coming down. The other nephilim, who evidently did not notice Kodi lagging far behind them, went immediately to the water and started drinking it.

While they were occupied, Pazel hissed at Kodi, who immediately looked over. When Kodi saw who it was, he darted over to hide with Pazel.

Pazel grabbed his cousin's arm and pulled him close. "You were taking a big chance coming down here! Someone is sure to notice that you were not with them earlier!"

"Yes, I know, I expect them to. I have a story to explain how I got here."

"Why did you come down in the cave?"

"To help you! What do you think?"

Although they were whispering, Pazel pulled Kodi farther back into the debris. "I've been trying to find a way out, to tell everyone the water was still exposed. When did you get here?"

"Just a few minutes ago. After I came out of the Dark Passage, I whistled for Keoaw—I knew he would stay near until I needed him—and we flew down to where Hod and the rest are."

Pazel's face became pensive. "Where is Chay? I saw a sandal by the remains of the eruptor. Was it his?""

"I saw that too. I know he followed me into the passage, But then he ran back into the cavern. I'm afraid he was killed by the last eruptor."

"Hod did not hear the third eruptor go off." Pazel said. "He thinks that's why the roof is not completely caved in."

Kodi's brow crimped into a sad frown as his shoulders sagged. "My conclusion was that Chay thought it had not exploded and picked it up. When I saw his sandal, I was sure it had blown up in his hands and obliterated him."

"That would be horrible—if it happened. I know he was a good friend of yours. Kodi, do you see our mission has failed? The nephilim are getting the water! Look, they are taking out bags full."

"We can't let that happen. I've been thinking I might be able to push the pillar down, but we need more weight on top of it. You need to go back to Hod and tell him to lure the nephilim on to the last part of the roof."

"But you—you could be—." Pazel did not like to think what would happen to Kodi when the roof caved in.

"I'll be fine. Don't worry." As Kodi spoke, Pazel looked around the area. The group of nephilim were eventually joined by the rest of the giants, who were laughing as they drank and played in the water. He saw that they had sent their Lamechites back to the top, where they were no longer in view.

"The Lamechites seem to be gone for the time, and all the nephilim are down here, I think. Maybe I can make it out while they are playing in the water."

"I'll go down and talk to them. While I am distracting them with some story about what I am doing here, you slip on up to the top. They are standing under the remaining roof. Since all the nephilim are down here, you'll have to lure the entire group of Lamechites onto the roof. When I see them moving there, I will put my weight against the pillar."

"But—!"

"I know what you are thinking. Don't worry about me. I have an idea to save myself. We have to hide the water from Kron—that's our mission. Now get going!"

"All right, but you'll need my help. How will you know when we have enough Lamechites on the roof? Listen for my signal. I'll give a shrill whistle when it's time to push."

"What if I don't recognize it?"

"You will. My whistle cuts through anything."

Pazel waited until Kodi had approached the group of nephilim, who seemed very surprised to see him back but unsuspecting of his motives. While the nephilim were listening to Kodi's story, Pazel slipped around the rock pile, keeping low, and worked his way to his friends.

"Pazel, I was so worried!" Shani threw her arms around her husband and would not let him go when he tried to turn to the others.

"I'm fine, darling, but I need to talk to Hod."

Hod pulled his old friend close and out of view of any enemy scout. "Did you see Kodi? Is the water still visible?"

"Yes to both your questions. Kodi is down there right now. The nephilim are drinking the water. They and the Lamechites are filling containers with healing water. We can't let them carry any of it off."

"I agree. Did Kodi have any ideas for stopping them?"

Pazel paused and cleared his throat while he looked around at the area below where his cousin was ready to give his life for the mission. He knew he had to pass on Kodi's desire for Hod to help bring the roof down on him, yet he hated to be a part of his possible death.

"Kodi thinks he can push on the last pillar and bring it down—if you can get the Lamechites to gather on the last bit of roof and add weight to help it collapse. He said not to worry about him. He has a plan to save himself."

"Hmm, let me think a minute," Hod said. "The Lamechites have gone back a way to the west and look like they are setting up a camp. It will be hard to get them on the roof without alerting the nephilim down below."

"It might work, but I don't think all the Lamechites weigh enough to bring the roof down." Hod looked across the desert southward to the ridge he had crossed when he was running from Niute and the other Lamechites.

"On the other side of the ridge are some behemoths. One of them would be heavy enough to collapse the roof. If I had a haraani, I could try to lure one across the desert and get him to stand on the roof."

"Keoaw is still roosting on the rocks over there," Pazel said. "Do you think he would let you fly him?"

"I don't know, but I'll try."

Hela and Tagg had been listening to the conversation between Hod and Pazel without interrupting. However, before her brother could look for the haraani, Hela stepped toward them.

"We'll be ready with our arrows. We can distract and kill some of the Lamechites if they try to interfere. We have made many arrows, so we will keep the nephilim down in the cave where they will be caught when the roof comes down."

Hod nodded briefly. "All right. But wait until I come back with a behemoth. I'm leaving you my waterskin in case anyone gets hurt."

"I still have some," Pazel said. "We've been drinking mine, but it's not all gone. Don't worry about us. I'll take care of things here. Just hurry!"

◁ 17 ▷

Keoaw the Brave

As he moved toward Keoaw, who was perched nearby, Hod expected the bird to take off, to avoid this
human who was not Kodi; however, to his surprise
the creature merely cocked its feathered head and gave him
a quizzical stare from a wide-open eye.

"You know me, don't you, my friend? You've seen me with Kodi." Hod spoke in a soft, soothing voice as he moved with one hand out toward Keoaw.

When the haraani allowed him to touch its head, Hod let his hand slide down its feathered neck until he reached the leather rein. Carefully, very carefully, he took the reins in his hand and held it as if he had no intention of mastering this magnificent creature—which he did not.

I will be honored if this noble bird will accept me as a partner. I pray that Elohim will guide him.

Still talking softly, he gently slipped his right leg over the squatting bird's back, being sure to put his weight on his toes.

Although Keoaw did not move, Hod detected a trembling deep within the bird, almost like a silent purr. Slowly he let his full weight come down on the leather saddle and took a firm hold of the reins.

"Come on, you king of the skies." Hod made his voice quiet and cajoling as he urged the haraani to step off the boulder. "Let's go. Let's do this for Kodi."

Almost as if he recognized the name or sensed the importance of this flight, the bird moved toward the precipice. Due perhaps to the slight weight of this rider compared to Kodi, Keoaw did not fall far before veering up into the sky.

"Yes!" Hod spurred his mount on, thrilled it had accepted him. "Good boy! Now, let's hurry!"

By swinging to the east in a wide arc before going south, Hod got away from the mountains without alerting the Lamechites, who were setting up camp a quarter of a league away from the cave-in.

All the nephilim were now down in the cave playing in the water, obviously with no fear of attack. Since none appeared to see what was going on above, Hod believed his plan should work. He only hoped Kodi would wait until he got back before he tried to push down the pillar.

Hod's stomach knotted tightly as he flew through the beauty of the afternoon sky. The waning sun warming his right cheek reminded him that he had to hurry if this mission was to be completed before dark.

So much depended on him now. Chay may have died trying to destroy the river, and Kodi was down there ready to give his life for the same cause. Hod's thoughts raced along with his body.

I should be the one to die. I allowed Chay and Kodi to talk me into letting them stay behind to fire the eruptors. I should not have given in.

Below him was the strip of desert separating the Eden Mountains from the first ridge. He quickly crossed to the savannah that stretched as far as the Pishon River. Days before, when flying over this area, he had unsuccessfully tried to feed Varqr to the razor-tooth behemoth. Now he hoped he could as easily find that same beast.

Flying low over this land of grass and trees, Hod and Keoaw searched to the east and then south to the Pishon. It was while making this last turn that he a saw the behemoth drinking at a water hole.

"There he is!" Hod guided Keoaw to the west.

In moments they were circling the head of the razor-tooth, allowing him to get a good look at who was on the bird. The behemoth threw his head up and back showing rows of jagged teeth. The beast's gray, leathery skin was caked with mud, probably from rolling in one of the ponds that dotted this land, and the eyes in his square head were bloodshot with anger. But he did not seem interested in following Hod.

Seeing it was going to take something drastic to lure creature after him, Hod flew Keoaw high above the razor-tooth's head, pulled his sword, and then darted down at the animal's peacefully-drinking snout. He was amazed at the fearlessness of the bird and somehow proud he had been allowed to ride him.

Buzzing downward like some type of gigantic mosquito, Hod used his weapon to sting the behemoth directly above its nostrils. The behemoth jerked its head up and stared stupidly at its attacker but still made no move to follow him.

"Watch out, you brute! I'll sting you again!"

To punctuate his declaration, Hod swung around the behemoth's neck and gave him jab as he passed. Then he dashed away on Keoaw, circling only once to make sure his enraged prey would give chase.

As the animal roared and almost jumped at him, one curved claw reached high in the air. It turned from the waterhole and began to go after its tormentor.

"Whooee! That was close! All right, Keoaw, let's head back to find Kodi." By now the razor-tooth was lumbering after them faster than Hod thought possible for such a large animal. As the beast ran on immense and powerful hind legs, he continually reached for Keoaw with his much smaller forelegs.

Hod could have led his mount higher in the air where they would be well out of reach of the razor-tooth, but he wanted the monster to think it could catch them. For this reason, he circled back whenever he thought his pursuer was losing interest. It took some dodging in and buzzing around the hungry teeth to encourage the creature to follow him up the ridge.

When at the top, the behemoth balanced its over-sized form on the narrow cusp of the ridge while it reached for the haraani flying about its head. Hod thought it was going to give up and go back, perhaps discouraged by the sight of miles of bare rock and sand, so he dived down, dodged the claws, and stabbed the beast in the back before zooming upward again.

The behemoth took a step forward, rolled head over heels down the loose soil of the ridge, and then seemed to gain a second wind. Roaring out its anger, it ran faster than ever across the stretch of rock and sand leading to the mountains. Hod no longer had to stay within range of the grasping claws to keep his quarry interested.

Instead, he made a beeline straight toward the dry well, all the while leaning low across Keoaw, whose wings were surging through the air. While the wind blew his red locks back from his face, Hod looked over his left shoulder one last time to make sure the beast was still there.

It was only a hundred paces behind him and intent on following this pesky human to the end. Hod could now see his goal clearly enough to assess the situation. The Lame-chites were running back toward the cave-in and would be there in minutes, Hela and Tagg were standing on the promontory shooting arrows down toward the nephilim, and Pazel was standing a little lower waving at Hod and pointing out the activity below. Kodi was nowhere in sight.

I have to do this right. This is not just a test of my leadership. This is for the success or failure of the mission. I cannot fail.

♓

As soon as Hod left on Keoaw, Hela and Tagg began preparing their bowed staffs and arrows. They bent the staffs, attached the strings, and then began counting out arrows. Tagg had tied some sharp, pointed rocks to his arrows at Enoch's home and while waiting on the mountain.

"Tagg, I was thinking that if we can keep the nephilim down in the cave, they might be killed when the roof collapses," Hela said.

"All right." Tagg did not take a minute to think about her idea. "Let's tell Pazel and Shani what we are doing."

When Hela turned back and explained their plan to the other two, Pazel nodded and pointed to the south.

"I've been watching the ridge Hod crossed. He is on his way back—with a razor-tooth following. Be ready to start shooting."

"The Lamechites are coming back," Tagg added. "You take them, and I'll shoot at any nephilim who come out."

As she was already concentrating on the pile of rocks below, Hela nodded. "I wish we had more arrows. Make every one count."

"I have my sword if we need it," Pazel said with a grim set of his jaw as he pulled his weapon.

"Let's hope it does not come to that." Tagg turned and looked at his fellow Cainite. "But if it does, I have my sword too."

Just as two nephilim began to climb out of the cave-in, the Lamechites arrived and began to go down. Wanting to keep as many of the giants in the pit and under the roof as possible, Hela began to fire her arrows. The first one embedded squarely in the neck of the first nephil to leave. He screamed and fell backward.

"That was easy," Hela said as she drew another arrow from her pack and fitted it to the string.

Tagg, who had already shot two of his arrows toward the Lamechites, looked over at her a moment. "It's harder than you think—or maybe I'm just not as good as you."

"Well, you haven't had much practice." Hela kept her eye on the enemy below as she talked, and when another nephil came out to check on the first, she let fly an arrow, which got him in his thigh.

"I think I just made that one angry. But at least he went back down under the roof."

Hela looked over at Tagg, who had finally hit one of the Lamechites running around in circles, looking up and pointing at their attackers and dumbfounded by this new weapon taking them out one or two at a time.

She looked back at Pazel. "Is Hod still coming this way?"

"Yes! He is halfway across the desert, and the razor-tooth is still with him."

Hela looked once more at the Lamechites, who were swarming over the top of the tumbled rocks of the cave-in, and then at the nephilim who were staying down under the roof.

"I have an idea! Let's shoot all the arrows we have down on the Lamechites. They will think there are many of us. We need to drive them down under the roof so they will be crushed with the nephilim."

"Good idea!"

Tagg and Hela immediately began raining arrows on the enemy below, pushing them down and under the roof. Meanwhile, Hod had arrived with the behemoth. The sight of the huge body and sharp teeth coming their way seemed to encourage the Lamechites to move even faster down into the last bit of cavern.

Hela watched breathlessly as Hod swung Keoaw in a circle toward the remaining roof on the north side. The beast stayed with him, roaring with rage all the while.

"Be careful! Oh, Hod, be careful!" She screamed at her brother even though she knew he could not hear her.

H

Kodi came out from his hiding place at a moment when all the nephilim were busy drinking and washing in the healing water. Seeing that they feared no enemy and were excited to have discovered the water their king wanted, he was sure they would not have any concerns about his sudden appearance. He walked up to them as nonchalantly as if he had been with them for days, scooped a handful of water from the fountain spurting from the rock wall, and rubbed it over his dusty face. It took a moment before the others noticed him.

"Kodi! When did you get here?" Radek, the nephil who was leading this group, was the first to turn in surprise at the sight of the newcomer.

Careful to appear as his old self before these giants who knew him, Kodi did not answer until he had taken a long drink. The immediate thrill of invigoration assured him that the healing power was still effective.

"I've been searching for the salt merchant on this side of the mountain. It looks like he has moved away—doesn't live here anymore. Then I saw all of you and this sunken spot. What do you think happened?"

"It looks like a cavern with an underground river caved in. See that big slab of roof over us. That is what is left of the cavern. That rock column over there kept this part from collapsing. We found the healing water, though."

Kodi studied the scene around him as if he were seeing it for the first time. The rubble was a combination of large, jagged rocks and huge stone slabs, and chunks of the pillars. Even getting to the bottom of the cave-in involved climbing down a sloping pile leading to the last pillar still holding up the remaining roof.

"Kron will be happy. I wonder what happened?" he asked Radek.

"I don't know, but I suspect the fire-hair had a hand in it. He was probably trying to hide the water."

"Do you really think this is the water Kron is looking for?" Kodi knew the answer but wanted to be sure what Radek thought. He ignored the mention of Hod.

"Yes, this water coming out of the wall is healing water. I already tested it."

Kodi grunted before glancing around at the pillar supporting the cave roof. He was sure that the amount of rock left above, if it came down on them, would kill all the nephilim standing below. If he brought it down, he would rid the world of some of the most vicious of his comrades, none his friends. None of them had ever treated anyone with kindness.

The column stood only a long step from what was left of the river. Kodi made that step and stood looking down at the place where a sharp edge of a slab had broken out the bottom of the riverbed, allowing the water to rush into a big hole leading down to the lower chamber.

Hoping to stall the nephilim long enough for Hod to find a way to get the Lamechite warriors gathered on the roof, Kodi continued to engage them in conversation. "Has Kron heard back from either of the other groups he sent out searching for the fire-hair?"

"Yes, Gradrach came back from Garth. He tracked the family westward, but their trail suddenly disappeared. The Lamechites could not pick it up."

"How about you, Radek? Your group was coming this way to look for the salt merchant."

Radek's answer sounded like a growl. He gnashed his sharp teeth and pulled at his shaggy beard. "I never saw him in his cave, but he or someone else must have killed my two Lamechites. They disappeared in that labyrinth of passages."

"I doubt if it was him. I looked all around, and I'm pretty sure he had moved on." Kodi hoped his lie would deflect attention from Pazel.

"Maybe so. Anyway, I started back to the fortress and found this group sent by the king. When I led them back, we discovered this cave-in. Right now we are trying to get all the water we can to take back to him."

"What do you have to carry it in?"

"They brought five barrels in case they found water. The Lamechites were filling waterskins down here and taking them up to fill the barrels, but right now I have them setting up camp. Borien, go tell them to hurry back."

Kodi, who had noticed that a few of the Lamechites were standing at the top of the slope, watched as the nephil Borien obediently began climbing out of the cave-in. He had not gone halfway up before he screamed and fell back on the rocks.

Radek instinctively started up to help the other giant but then cried out as a sharp stick slammed into his leg. By now a storm of arrows was coming down on them. While the Lamechites above hurried down the rocks, the nephilim below tried to get as far back under the roof as possible.

Kodi knew this was the work of Hela and Tagg, yet he also knew that with most of the Lamechites below, he might not get the weight he needed on the roof.

Above the screaming of Lamechites, his ears strained for Pazel's whistle meaning that they had gotten weight on top.

"Hurry! Everyone get back. There is a razor-tooth coming right at us." The last of the Lamechites to make it to the nephilim yelled out a warning.

Wondering what this meant, Kodi stationed himself beside the pillar where he could see around the ragged edge of the roof and up at the southern sky. As he peered up, he saw Keoaw and Hod flying over the western edge of the cave-in. Below and right behind came the behemoth, just as the Lamechites had said. Kodi instantly knew this was Hod's solution to the problem of finding weight to help him bring down the roof.

And a very good solution it is! Now I'm ready.

Suddenly Pazel's promised signal, a shrill whistle, cut through the noise around him. While everyone else in the last of the cavern was screaming and huddling together, Kodi began to push with all his strength on the pillar. He felt it give a little, and then he heard a snapping crack. Finally, a piece of the column shot away from his hand and flew off toward the rest of the crumbled rocks.

"Kodi! What are you doing?"

He heard a nephil's horrified scream but did not even bother to look at him or the rest of those huddled against the wall. For a half minute, he thought the roof was going to withstand not only the loss of the supporting column but also the weight of the razor-tooth now stomping on it.

It is not going to work!

And then the roof groaned like a woman in labor. He heard the cracking of the rocks breaking up and scraping against each other just as he dived toward the river.

As Kodi was executing his plan to get into the hole where the river ran into the lower cavern, the whole weight of the roof above came down upon him. He heard the Lamechites and nephilim screaming, and he heard the razor-tooth shrieking in terror. He felt his bones being crushed by the weight. And then he heard and felt no more.

Ж

While the four up on the promontory cheered him on, Hod lured the behemoth toward the cave roof and circled above to keep it there. The monster turned around and around while it snatched and bit up at him.

I hope the roof gives soon. It looks as if all the nephilim and most of the Lamechites are under it. If it does not go now, our plan will fail.

Suddenly a sound unlike anything he had ever heard rang out above the yelling of the enemy below. He looked down in time to see the flat sheet of rock breaking into many pieces that seemed to hang suspended in a waving motion before crumbling crazily into the cavern.

The behemoth on top flailed at the air, and then, just before it followed the slabs of stone to the bottom, one of its claws struck out to snag Keoaw's wing and fling bird and rider toward the ground. They were hurled in a wide arc that propelled them over the cave-in and onto the piled up boulders at the base of the mountain.

Hod cried out and, although he rolled off the haraani at the last moment, felt his ribs crack and his face crushed as he smashed into the rocks. Bleeding and unable to move anything except his right arm, he reached out and felt for Keoaw, who lay still beside him.

While Hod could not open his eyes, his ears were alert to the roaring crash of rock, screaming of dying nephilim and Lamechites, as well as the protesting roars of the razor-tooth. Gradually these sounds lessened, yet Hod could do nothing more to discover whether or not the mission was successfully completed.

Was the water buried under the great weight of stone? Was it enough to prevent the nephilim from digging it up again? Had the enemy been destroyed or would the survivors come after him and the rest of the Iron Fist?

I can do nothing more. Elohim gave me a mission, and I have done what I could. I did my best. Now I am ready for whatever lies ahead, be it life or death. May Elohim bless Kodi. He is without a doubt a man.

◁ 18 ▷

Mission Complete

ook! Hod is luring the behemoth to the cavern roof!"
Pazel pointed out the scene below to the others on
the mountainside.

"But he's getting too close!" Hela grabbed Pazel's arm.
"The razor-tooth is going to get him!"

Tagg moved to stand close to Hela, his bow held un-
needed now in one hand. "It's working, though. See how
he keeps the behemoth on the roof by circling close. It's
starting to break up—and all the nephilim are under it!"

"Oh, no!" Pazel cried. "Hod! Keoaw! The razor-tooth knocked them down."

Hela screamed and jumped away from Pazel's grip. "He's hurt. He's not getting up!"

As soon as he saw the haraani and its rider fall to the ground and felt Hela pull away, Pazel snatched up his less than half-filled waterskin and started down the mountain. When he realized the other three were following, however, he stopped and looked back.

"Hela, let me check on him. It is getting close to sunset and the footing will be dangerous. Tagg, you retrieve some of your arrows that landed on the rocks. We will have to fight." He pointed to where the rest of the Lamechites were rushing back from their camp.

"I'm going with you," Hela protested. "He is my brother."

"You at least will stay up here." Pazel said to Shani before signaling Hela to follow him.

His wife nodded and stepped back just as Hela moved forward and held up her bow. "I have three arrows left. I'm bringing this just in case we need it."

At the new cave-in below, plumes of rock dust mingling with the screams of the injured behemoth made a horrifying scene. Pazel saw and heard it all even though his mind was intent on getting to Hod as quickly as he could. Lamechites already were scrambling down into the debris to see if any of their people had survived. More than one saw them, but they were on the western side and would have to skirt the cave-in before they could reach him.

"We have to hurry. They will be coming after us even though it's getting dark. We have only a short time to get him out of here," Pazel called back to Hela just moments before they got to Hod.

"Is he alive?" As she knelt beside her brother, Hela's voice sounded like a sob.

Pazel's felt a stinging in his eyes but would not allow himself to give in to the emotions simmering in his heart. His friend needed him desperately and needed him to be as cool-headed as possible.

He gently ran his hands over Hod's back. "I can't tell if he is breathing, but I think he moved his right hand."

The Cainite gently turned his friend onto his back and winced when he saw the unrecognizable face. Then he saw Hod's swollen lips move. "Hod, if you can hear me, don't try to talk. You are badly hurt and there are Lamechites coming after us. We need to act quickly."

Although his eyes were swollen shut and covered with blood, Hod grabbed Pazel's tunic with a weak grip and tried to speak. His friend leaned closer.

"Water . . .?"

"Yes, I have some water—healing water. I'm going to use it now. But then we have to get out of here."

"Save . . . some . . . for . . . Keoaw . . . deserves it."

Pazel looked at the limp pile of feathers beside them and shook his head. "Well—I don't have that much."

"Please." Hod's voice fell to a whisper. "Save enough for him."

"I will, but then I'll have to move you quickly!"

While Hela knelt over her brother and held his head in her arms, Pazel wasted no time pouring more than half of the precious contents of his waterskin on Hod's face and body and then spilling the rest almost haphazardly on the haraani's seemingly dead carcass. Without watching to see what happened, he scooped Hod up, turned, and began carrying him like a baby in his arms back up the mountain.

Hod was so badly injured and there had been such a small amount of water that Pazel did not expect the usual amazing results. He knew Hod had at least half a skin of water at the top of the mountain, and he was desperate to get him back to it.

With Hela behind him, her bow and arrows ready in case they were attacked from behind, they managed to get quite a way up the mountain before the Lamechites reached Keoaw. Pazel, intent on navigating in the near dark, did not look back, but Hela stopped to see what the men would do. She could tell they were gathered around the crumpled bird, but then the night closed in and hid them from sight.

"I don't think those men will come after us until sunrise," Hela told Pazel when she caught up with him. "They will not be able to see well enough to get over these rocks."

"I have to get Hod to his waterskin. He has passed out."

Pazel was staggering a little as he struggled up the mountain, so Hela lifted Hod's legs to bear part his weight. Before long they could see Tagg coming toward them. He immediately took Hod's almost lifeless body from Pazel and carried it the rest of the way up.

"I'll take care of him," Pazel said when they were all at the overhanging rock. He laid Hod on a patch of sandy soil in a flat area between boulders, lit the torch he had brought with him, and then held it where he could study Hod.

Let me not be too late, Pazel prayed as he gently stretched out the twisted limbs and crushed face covered with drying blood.

Hela quickly joined him beside the still body. "Is he gone?"

The despair in her voice made the tears Pazel had been holding back start down his face, but he wiped them away with bloody hands.

"I am afraid he is. He was alive when we found him, but his body was crushed. I didn't have enough water for him and Keoaw. I shouldn't have poured any on that bird."

"It's what he wanted." Hela sobbed as she spoke. "Do not blame yourself. And don't give up on him."

"It is too late by now."

"I have Hod's healing water here. Please try it. Maybe it's not too late."

With little hope of reviving Hod, Pazel took the waterskin from her hand. Just then he heard a loud squawk followed by the flapping of great wings coming from above him. He looked up to see Keoaw—whole and healthy—settling on the rocks above them.

"It's Keoaw! The water worked! You just poured a little on him, and he is whole!" Hela cried out as, with glossy wings pulled close to its sides, the haraani stood erect and proud on taloned feet.

It stretched its gold-capped head as it surveyed the scene beneath. Hela was sure it looked from Pazel to Hod as if it were asking why he did not help him. The sight of the reborn bird seeming to fill him with new hope, Pazel poured a little water over the bloody face, making sure that some went into the mouth. Then he generously poured what was left up and down Hod's body.

When Hod did not move after several minutes, Pazel jumped to his feet. "It's no use. I should never have poured the water on Keoaw!"

His face contorted with pain and unable to bear standing here watching his dead friend, he went to where Tagg stood watch.

"Do you see or hear anything?" Pazel asked.

"No. I think they gave up—at least for tonight."

With shoulders drooping, Pazel slowly went back to Hod's body. As he thought about what he could say to comfort Hela, he paused and then took a deep breath before taking the last step. At the last minute, he lifted his head and was stopped in his tracks by what he saw. Instead of a scene of sorrow, his friend was sitting up slightly, his head against Hela's shoulder and his eyes wide open.

Pazel went down on one knee beside him. "You're alive! Praise Elohim! I thought you were gone."

"No, I was alive. I heard everything. I knew you were carrying me up the mountain. I just could not open my eyes or talk. Did you pour some of the water on Keoaw?"

Pazel chuckled and looked up and over Hod at where the haraani perched. "Against my own judgment! And it worked! That is what made me hope you had a chance. I was so sure you were dead that I almost did not use the healing water, but when Keoaw flew up and looked down at you, I knew he wanted me to try."

Slowly Hod stood to his feet, stretching out one limb at a time. He felt his face gingerly and brushed at the blood that had dried in streaks after Pazel had poured the water on it. Then he looked up at the magnificent bird who appeared to be watching over them.

"Keoaw is a wonderful haraani. He never flinched from flying right at the razor-tooth. I wish he were mine instead of . . . Kodi! Has anyone heard from Kodi?"

Pazel's face fell and his shoulders drooped. "He must have been crushed to death with the rest of the nephilim when the roof fell under the weight of the monster. Could we go down to see if we can find him?"

"Yes, we must go down and look for him," Hod said. "I had hoped we could complete this mission without losing a life. I should have been the one to light the eruptors,"

"You made the right decision. Only you knew about the razor-tooth, and you risked your life to bring him here. You have been a good leader, Hod. Now sleep for a while. We might have a battle on our hands in the morning."

ℋ

When the first rays of light hit the mountainside, Hod was immediately awake. He found his sister getting out some food. "Is there any water left? I'm so thirsty."

Hela handed her brother the waterskin, and then she called to Tagg, who stood where he could check out the enemy. "Can you see any Lamechites?"

"There are six of them coming up."

Tagg handed Hela half of the dozen or so arrows he had found below the day before. "I know a good spot where we can see them come around that big boulder. We can shoot them one at a time."

They both stationed themselves at a place where they could shoot downhill and aim their deadly weapons at the chests of the approaching men. They shot arrows at each Lamechite who came into sight around the last bend in the mountain until they ran out. Hearing them call out, Hod pulled his sword and motioned to Pazel.

"I'm going to help them. You stay with Shani."

"I'll be fine," Shani said. "Pazel, you go with him. He needs you."

When they got to the scene of the battle, Hod saw that Hela and Tagg were out of arrows and that Tagg was holding off the last three Lamechites with his sword while the unarmed Hela stayed behind him.

"Hela, you go back to Shani." Hod touched her on the shoulder and pushed her farther back.

Pazel instantly began attacking one of the men, who turned on him with fiercely slashing blows. Hod took on the next man and forced his opponent back down the mountainside. After he cut down the Lamechite with one vicious stroke and was sure the man was finished, Hod ran back up to help Tagg, who he knew was tiring.

Together they fought the enemy to the edge of a sheer drop-off. The man kept backing off until he lost his footing and toppled backwards to his certain death.

Hod leaned over the edge of the mountain to make sure his opponent had truly fallen to his death. When he sighted the crumpled body a hundred cubits below, he turned and looked for Pazel, whom he soon saw walking slowly back up the mountain.

"I lost mine. He ran off. I guess you finished off those last two Lamechites."

"Yes, Hod killed one and the other fell off the mountain." Tagg looked at Pazel, who by now was scanning the scene below.

"I see him running west. There are no other Lamechites or nephilim around. But that one got away."

Hod sighed and shook his head. "That's too bad. He will be able to tell Kron about finding the water."

"And they were going back and forth with full waterskins to their camp earlier." Pazel frowned as he strained to see all the way to the Lamechite base.

"Doubly bad. If that one takes a skin full of water to Kron, he will use it for evil. Let's go down and see if the water is fully hidden."

Hod picked up his empty waterskin and headed down the mountain with the others while Pazel held Shani's hand and protectively guided her over every obstacle that might have caused her to trip and fall. Hod saw this and considered helping his sister but knowing her determination to be self-sufficient, he hesitated.

Nevertheless, he looked back at her to see how she was faring. "Are you all right, Hela?"

Hod grinned when he saw that she was allowing Tagg to hold her hand and guide her down the mountain. Hela blushed but did not let go of Tagg.

"Yes. I'm fine."

By the time they reached the bottom, most of the dust had settled back into the cave-in. When they studied the scene, they saw no bodies, just the behemoth's legs. He was alive but pinned under a large slab of rock. The bellowing roars coming from underneath the debris convinced them the razor-tooth was not badly wounded.

"He might be able to get out from under those boulders," Tagg said.

Hod looked thoughtful. "I think he is trapped for the moment. We have time to look around, and then we need to get out of sight. He can't hurt us right now."

"Then I am going down to look for Kodi," Pazel said.

"I am too." Hod put his hand on Pazel's shoulder. "Tagg, you stay here with the girls."

The two friends began climbing down into the mess of broken rocks, careful to stay away from where the behemoth was buried. There was no sign of the water below. Not even the sound of rushing water came up through the rubble.

"The bottom of the river had broken out and the water was pouring into the lower passages and caverns when I saw it," Pazel said. "I think the last cave-in closed off the fountain where the water came from the mountain."

"Do you think Kodi could have survived this?"

"Only if he made it into that hole. The rocks would have come down on him even if he made it."

Hod took a few more minutes to look around the area. Finally, he came back over to Pazel.

"There's nothing to be done here. It is totally dry. I think all the water was forced down lower. I have two concerns, though. First, I want to go back to that passage we took under the river. If the healing water can be accessed there, we need to close that off. Also, if it's not flooded, I want to look for Kodi in the lower chamber."

They all followed Pazel back to the place where they all had emerged from the lower passage. Hod stopped and turned to the two girls.

"I want you to stay here where you can get out quickly if you need to. Tagg, I want you to stand watch outside just to be sure the enemy is gone. Pazel and I can do this ourselves."

So the two old friends worked their way slowly down the sloping path until they neared the lowest point that went under the old riverbed. But now they found standing water blocking the way and reaching to a cubit from the low ceiling.

"Kodi was right to think the river filled the lower passages," Pazel said. "It has probably flooded that cavern below the cave-in and back into the slug caves."

"Yes, but is this still healing water? It is now mixed with animal waste from bats and slugs."

"And the water here is not even moving."

Hod stroked his chin and pondered the situation. If it was still healing water, they would have to collapse this passage. If not, their mission was done. "How can we tell if it still heals?"

"I'll just do what I saw the Lamechite do up in the cave-in." Pazel chuckled, handed the torch to Hod, and pulled out his curved sword.

Hod watched as his friend used the sharp point of his sword to scratch a short cut onto the back of his forearm. Immediately a thin red line welled up on his skin. Then Pazel bent down and washed the blood off in the water at their feet. When he stood and showed his arm to Hod, they both saw the red line reappear.

Just to be sure, Pazel repeated the action, with the same results. Before he stood, though, he scooped up a mouthful of water. "It doesn't seem the same."

Holding the torch to one side, Hod went to the water's edge and bent down to try it.

"Doesn't even taste good." He made a face and shook the remaining water from his hand. He was amazed at how quickly the wonderful healing water had become worthless.

"I wish we could get past here and look for Kodi farther in, but it's impossible. If he was not crushed, he is surely drowned." Pazel looked at Hod with grief in his eyes.

"I know. I'm sorry you lost your cousin, but he gave himself for the mission." Hod put one hand on his friend's shoulder. "We should go now. At least we don't have to worry about destroying this entrance."

Hod turned and, holding the torch before him, led the way out of the cave. "Now let find those barrels of water the Lamechites were filling."

They left the passage and told the others they were going after the surviving Lamechites.

"We'll go, too," Hela said and Tagg nodded in agreement.

The group were at the south of the cave-in so walked west until they reached the beginnings of a camp containing a few tents made of animal hides stretched over poles, a small store of food supplies, and five barrels.

"Let's see if they have filled all these barrels." Hod went to one barrel and pointed out another to his companions.

While Hod was prying the lid off the first, Pazel and Tagg were pushing the others over on their sides.

"These are empty," Pazel said.

Hod put the lid back on his barrel. "Well, this one is full. They must not have had enough time to fill the rest."

Shani clapped her hands and threw her arms around Hela. "Isn't this wonderful! That last Lamechite was afraid, so he ran off without taking the water. We can pour this out, and the healing water is gone. We've completed the mission."

"We can go home!" As she looked over the other girl's shoulder, Hela saw a large form emerging from the cave-in. "Look! The razor-tooth got out!"

Everyone stopped and turned to see the beast staring back at them. The behemoth shook its head as if still a little dazed and then, before any of the young people could move, swung its head to the south and began running toward home. They all followed with their eyes until it was a small figure in the distance.

"I'm glad the razor-tooth survived," Hod finally said. "He served my purpose. Now he can go back to his life."

Tagg brought the attention back to what they had been doing before the behemoth appeared. "Shall we pour this water out now?"

"We could do that, but maybe we should fill our waterskins first."

Pazel looked at Hod for an answer. Their eyes met and locked. Each knew what the other was thinking. If the mission was to destroy the water, would they be within the will of Elohim to take two bags of water? They asked the question of each other silently while the rest watched.

"I wish we could ask Enoch," Hod said.

"I do too, but we can't. You are our leader. You have to decide."

"I need time. You all watch for the enemy. I will make a decision soon."

Hod left the group and walked back to the cave-in where he sat on a broken edge of stone jutting out over the depression. After thinking a moment, he turned his eyes heavenward.

"Elohim, I need your guidance. You have given me this task, but how can I make this decision? I do not know Your will. I fear my own choice could lead to disaster. Already my decisions have led to the loss of two of our number. Please send me a counselor."

Hod dropped his eyes to the crumbled rocks before him and sat waiting for an answer. It had to come. And then a voice spoke behind him. "Hod, do you need help?"

The young man started from his seat and turned in amazement to see Enoch walking toward him.

"How did you get here, Uncle?"

"Remiel brought me through the air. He said you needed me."

Without thinking, Hod threw his arms around Enoch and wept on his shoulder. "Uncle! I lost Chay—and Kodi!"

"This is sad news, indeed." Enoch looked up to heaven as if he were asking for understanding. "Was it your fault? Did you needlessly put them in danger or did they willingly risk their lives?"

Hod stood back from him and dashed the tears from his eyes with his fingertips. He cleared his throat before looking back into the cave-in where his brother and the nephil had been lost.

"Both of them chose to do what they did, but I should have taken their places. After all, I was their leader."

"Then they did what they were led to do. They are in the hands of Elohim."

"How can I tell my father that I let Chay die? And, Uncle, my brother and I were just beginning to understand each other. I already miss him so much."

Enoch put an arm around Hod and led him over to a more comfortable place to sit than the rock overhanging the depression. "Tell me how it all went from the time you left me. Tell me how Chay and Kodi died."

While Hod recounted the mission from their entrance into the Dark Passage, to when they placed the eruptors, to their escape through the lower passage, and finally ending with the fall of the behemoth on top of Kodi, the rest of the nephilim and Lamechites.

At the end of his tale, he told about their discovery of the barrel of water and his dilemma over what to do with the contents. For a few moments, Enoch sat stroking his beard and contemplating the destruction in front of him. Eventually he spoke.

"You did not see either of them die. Perhaps they have been spared. I have no word on this. It seems to me that their stories are incomplete. Both still have choices to make. However, all will be as He wills. We must wait and see."

When Hod gazed at his uncle, he was impressed once again with the aura of another world that surrounded him. He was reminded of when he first met him and had asked him how one walked with Elohim. Enoch had told him that his first thought every morning was of the Creator, that he talked to Him all day, and that he put Him ahead of everything.

I made an effort to follow his example, but I have failed. I love Elohim, but I want to have a wife and family, and they will take up much of my time. Even Enoch said he did not reach this state until his wife died.

Hod decided he needed to ask his question. "I didn't know if Elohim wanted us to have the water or if He wanted it all destroyed."

"Remiel told me of your concern, and I have spoken with Elohim about it. It is His will that you and Pazel each take one skin of water with you. The barrel remaining is to be hidden by Pazel somewhere very secret in his caves. He is not to use it until it is called for at a special time."

Enoch walked with Hod back to the Lamechites' camp where he repeated the words of Elohim to them all. Hod and Pazel immediately filled their waterskins and handed them to the women. Then they rolled the barrel across the ground until they were below Pazel's door where they lifted the barrel between them and carried it up to the cave.

Q

◁19▷

Meeting Mehri

"Will you go with me to the home of Seth," Enoch asked Hod when he and Pazel returned from hiding the water barrel. "I want to see him before I go to my own family."

"I will be happy to. Doing that very thing has been on my mind as I want Hela to meet Mehri. After that, we need to go home. I am sure my parents are worried about us. And I must tell them about losing Chay."

When Hela, who stood by him, put her head on his shoulder and started to cry, Hod drew her closer with one hand. Her tears made his own eyes redden.

"He might not be gone," he said. "We don't know. Isn't that right, Pazel?"

The little Cainite was silent as he looked from Hela to Hod and then to Enoch. It was almost as if he were unsure of what to say.

"He could be alive. I only saw his sandal next to a fragment of the eruptor. That's all Kodi or I knew when we were down there. Shani and I will keep a look out for him on our way to Havilah. If we find him, we'll tell him you will be going home soon."

Hod touched Pazel's shoulder and turned his friend to face him. "Aren't you going with us to Seth?"

"No, I'm taking Shani back to her family and staying there with them until I know it is safe for her to come back to live on the mountain. I have almost lost her once. I'm not taking any more risks. We will travel cautiously and get home as quickly as possible. In fact, we are leaving right now."

The two men grasped hands and looked each other squarely in the eye. Hod gave Pazel's hand a tight squeeze.

"I still plan to visit you in Havilah, but I have to take Hela home first. Expect me within a few months."

"We will. Good-bye for now, my friend."

Pazel turned now to Enoch. "Did we succeed in our mission? We know the water below is no longer pure. Will Kron be able to get to the healing water?"

"No. Remiel has told me that the channel the water ran through collapsed far up into the mountain as a result of the eruptors. It seeps down into the lower chamber, but it is no longer pure."

"I'm glad we succeeded, and I hope this is the end of our work."

The young people looked questioningly at Enoch, eager to hear his answer, but his words only added anxiety rather than peace.

"No. This is not the end. Most of the nephilim, including Kron, must be destroyed. A few will survive to be wiped out in the great judgment; however, Elohim has sent me to the Dark Watchers to tell them His patience with *them* is over. At the end of your final mission, those Dark Watchers who created children with human women will be bound by the good Watchers in the bottom of the yellow fissure until the end of time. No more nephilim will be born once the final mission is complete."

"When will that be?" Hod asked.

"I do not know. When the time is right, Elohim will bring you to me. Once more, you will be the leader. There will be five—but not all the same. No more questions now. Wait until the fullness of time for all to be revealed."

When Enoch had finished, he, Hod, Hela, and Tagg watched Pazel and Shani walk to the west. All seemed to agree that they did not want to turn their faces eastward until their friends were out of sight. Then Enoch moved first, shepherding the young people with his arms like a mother hen with her baby chicks.

"It is still early. If we make steady progress, we will make the banks of the Pishon by sunset. But we will get nowhere if we don't start."

Together they walked steadily, only taking a sip of healing water when they tired. After a quick meal out on the desert, they reached the banks of the Pishon when the sun was low behind them. The water rushed with heart-stopping speed, so Hod and Tagg used their ropes and knowledge of crossing rivers to get everyone across.

They were surprised at the strength in Enoch's arms as he pulled himself along the rope they had stretched to taut-ness over the churning stream. Hod had crossed first and Tagg crossed just behind Hela, ready to help if she were swept away.

Hod laughed to himself to think of what a change the last week had made in his sister. When she had first caught up with him and Chay, Hela had belligerently insisted she could hold her own as a warrior and did not need any help climbing hills.

Now she allowed Tagg to assist her as if she were helpless. Hod, from his position on the far bank, watched Hela look back at her escort and smile as if she were so grateful for his aid.

The silly girl is pretending. She could pull herself across the river as easily as Tagg can. I suppose she cares for him, and I know he cares for her. He never takes his eyes off her. If he were to want to marry her, what would I do? It is not my place to give permission, and Father is so far away.

Some of Seth's men who noticed them crossing came to lend a hand. All were awed and excited to see Enoch, who rarely came back to Seth's home. Enoch's own children lived half a day's walk to the south.

"Uncle Enoch," Hod said as they were walking toward Seth's house. "Do your children mind that you do not spend much time with them?"

"I do not think so. My eldest son, Methuselah, is almost three hundred years old and has many children and grandchildren of his own to occupy his time. And my father Jared lives with them. I am not much missed, I think."

"Oh, I am sure that's not true! You are the greatest man who has ever lived. Why, you walk with Elohim!"

Enoch threw one companionable arm over his nephew's shoulder.

"First, I do not claim such a standing for myself as "greatest man who ever lived." Also, imagine how difficult it would be to live with someone who bears such a reputation. I think they must be relieved when I go back to my mountaintop."

"I can't understand that! You know so much. You talk to Watchers!"

"And my father and son do not. They worry about feeding and clothing their families while I am off talking to heavenly beings. I am sure they are proud of me but glad they do not have to live in my shadow every day."

Hod shook his head as they walked. They were almost to the house, yet he wanted to understand what his uncle was saying, so he stopped and held Enoch's arm.

"How does that make you feel? Are you ashamed that they think this way? Do you try to make them be like you?"

"Most definitely not!" Enoch laughed, but Hod knew it was not at Hod's words. It was almost as if he laughed at the frailty of man.

"Hod, you do not understand. It is all the work of Elohim. He calls whom He will. They must find their own way to Him as He wills."

"That is hard to understand. How can they find their own way if He does not call?"

"Yes. It is a mystery I do not completely comprehend. Now let us go on to our ancestor."

By the time they got to the house, Hela and Tagg had already reached it. Mehri had come out and greeted her friend Tagg, whom she had met during the first mission, and Tagg had introduced the two young women. Hod found that they were on the way to becoming friends when he walked up.

Enoch hugged Mehri and then went immediately into the house, but Hod stayed with his sister, who took his hand while still holding Mehri's hand.

"Hod, Mehri is as sweet and beautiful as you said she was!"

Hod glanced quickly at Mehri and then away. He saw that she was blushing and her eyes could not meet his, so he forced himself to answer with more calmness then he felt. "Oh, yes. We all agree that she is the most beautiful girl in the world."

"Please, don't say that." Mehri's blush deepened as she now looked at Hod directly. "Beauty is meaningless. I would rather be righteous."

Hod reached for her hand and pulled her toward him. "As you are. I have something to tell you. Could we walk up on the hill that looks at the Garden gate?"

When they reached the top of the hill several minutes later, Hod and Mehri gazed a while at the vee-shaped cleft in the ringed cliffs a quarter of a league in front of them. Both knew that inside the cleft was the Garden of Eden, which Enoch could look down on from his home on the far side.

"What do you want to tell me?"

"This is hard to tell. I know you cared for Kodi. He saved you from Azazel and was a good friend—."

Mehri gasped and grabbed Hod's arm. "'Was' . . . 'cared' . . . do not tell me he is dead!"

"We think he is. He sacrificed himself to bring down the roof of the cavern where the healing water flowed. We hope he dove down into the river, but even if he did, he most certainly was drowned or crushed by rocks."

When Mehri immediately broke into tears, Hod was horrified. Not only was he uncomfortable with a crying woman, but he became convinced she must have been in love with Kodi. Hod now realized that he had come in hopes of asking Seth for her hand.

If she loved Kodi and was grieving for his loss, how could he even approach the subject of marriage? "I am so sorry to have to tell you this bad news. I did not know how much you cared for him."

"I cared for him . . . like a brother. He was so good to me."

"I thought maybe your feelings for him were more serious." Hod looked away from her, letting his gaze wander over the opening to the Garden.

Mehri also turned her eyes away from him. They stood side by side watching the river gush through the crevice and splash on the rocks below. The silence between them seemed full of importance, so much so that he could not bring himself to speak.

"Oh, well, perhaps it is possible I cared for him," Mehri said. "But he is a nephil. I do not suppose anything could have come of it."

"But you are grieving for him?"

Mehri finally turned to face him, smiling slightly as she put one tentative hand on his arm. "Yes, I am, but I am glad to have you here with me."

"I have a greater reason to mourn. My brother Chay also disappeared, and we have reason to believe he also was killed trying to bring down the roof of the cavern."

"How awful! Poor Chay! I am so sorry."

"Thank you." He covered her hand that rested on his arm. "I dread having to tell my parents."

"I will pray that you will have the strength to do what you must do."

With a nod and a smile, Hod took her hand in his and led her back to Seth's home. The eldest member of their family and the second surviving son of the original parents, Adam and Eve, Seth sat on a low cushion beside a fire just as he had last time. The oldest man alive had white, wispy hair, watery blue eyes blue rimmed with red eyelids, and skin like dried leaves wrapped around a boney skull.

"Come, my children. Sit close so that I can see you." Seth's voice was more of a dry whisper than Hod remembered.

The aged patriarch looked at Enoch. "My favorite child of my grandchild's grandchild has returned to visit me and has been telling me tales of his visits with Watchers."

"Yes, Elohim has lately sent me on journeys around the world and into the very dwelling of the Dark Watchers." Enoch gestured widely with his arms. "While we waited for the rest of you, I have been telling Seth of Elohim's plans for the future. Now I will make way for Hod to speak."

Seth nodded slowly and turned to the young man. "Tell me all about this new mission of yours. When you visit you bring more excitement into my life than I ever know these days."

With Hela and Tagg adding details when he forgot them, Hod explained to the patriarch all they had done since leaving the family's new home. Seth occasionally chuckled or asked a question, but most of the time he allowed the young ones to talk. When they came to the place where Chay disappeared, he reached out and patted Hela's knee.

"If he did not survive, he has gone to join my father and mother and my eldest brother Abel, whom I never knew. It is my belief that we will all meet again."

Hod felt like crying as his mind once again dwelt on his brother. He found it hard to imagine him gone, gathered to his fathers. In the Sethian line, men and women of honor lived for centuries. It was almost shameful to die young due to carelessness or sickness. Chay was but twenty and had only begun to live.

"Death is horrible!" Hod's words held bitterness and fear.

Enoch began to answer but Seth, putting out a hand to stop him, spoke instead. "I think about death all the time. I am more than eight hundred years old, and I feel my time growing short. My body aches, my eyes and ears fail me, others must wait on me. Sometimes I welcome death. I am ready to go. To me, death is not so horrible."

Now Enoch, who had been listening closely, added his thoughts. All of the young ones hung on every word.

"Remiel and I have spoken of death. The Watchers do not understand it because they cannot die. They say they wonder why we fear it since it is the only way for our souls to be freed from our bodies."

"But where do our souls go?" Tagg asked, and Enoch turned a kind eye on him.

"Remiel calls it the place of the dead. He says it is divided in two parts—paradise and hell. Those who have faith and worship Elohim go to the first, the rest to the second."

All Enoch's listeners, even Seth, pondered this revelation in silence.

Finally Hela spoke. "Faith in what?"

"Faith that He is, that He loves and provides, that He knows best."

Hela shrugged and giggled. "That should be easy."

While Hod cast a reproving gaze at his sister, Enoch nodded. Seth, however, shook his head and responded. "No, it is hard—very hard."

After the visit with Seth, Enoch left them to go to his family while Hod and Hela chose to remain a few days before going home. Hod paid little attention to the amount of time his sister spent walking and talking with Tagg since he was spending the same time with Mehri.

One day he and Mehri were seated on the banks of the Gihon looking over at the place where the Lamechites had attacked them when they were coming to Seth's home on the first mission.

"Look! Right over there. That was where the cherubim saved us." Hod pointed toward the northeast.

"Really! I wish I had seen it, but I was already being taken to Seth's house. It seems so long ago, doesn't it?"

"Yes. When I left here last time, I thought I would never see you again. I was sure you would be married by now."

Mehri dropped her eyes to her lap where her hands were twisted together. "Seth is waiting for the right man. He says Elohim will let him know somehow."

"Do you think I could possibly be the right man?"

"What? Oh!" Mehri's hands quickly untangled and flew to her lips. "Hod! Do you want to marry me?"

"Of course, I do! I always have, but I never imagined I would be chosen for you. I still doubt Seth would approve. Would you want me if he did?"

Hod was sure he was doing this all wrong. He had no idea how a man was supposed to tell a girl he cared for her, that he never wanted to be separated from her. He held his breath while she thought about his question.

"I think I would, but I'm not sure. I don't know whether my choice matters."

"Is it because of Kodi that you are not sure?" Hod looked closely into her beautiful blue eyes.

Mehri shook her head, but he saw tears on her cheeks.

"I told you that he would never be considered as my husband because he was a nephil. Anyway, he is probably dead."

"Would you mind if I asked Seth for your hand in marriage?"

This time she smiled and shyly took his hand. Where before she had entwined her own fingers, now she mixed hers with his and then lifted his hand to her lips. "I will marry you if Seth approves."

"Then let us talk to him right now."

Together they walked to the house where the patriarch lived and found him seated outside.

"Great father," Hod began when they found him. "I would like to know if you would consider me as a husband for Mehri. She is willing."

When Seth looked at her, Mehri gave him her shy smile and nodded. The old man studied her a while before turning his eyes back to the Garden.

"You are both very young. Hod, you must obtain the approval of your parents and hers, and you must wait one year. Much could change during that time. Ask me again at that time."

"I will, and I understand. I need to talk to my parents and hers. Mehri must stay here until all danger is over. And I have a final mission. I would not make a good husband until then. I leave with Hela tomorrow. But I will be back."

When he told Hela the plans, she agreed more readily than he expected.

"Are you sure you are ready to leave Tagg. You two have become very close."

"Oh, I meant to tell you. He is coming with us. One of the men here is going to tell his family that he is safe and going west with us."

"Well! What does this mean?"

Hela began to laugh as she watched the expressions on his face. "It means that if Father approves, you will have a new brother-in-law."

Q

◁Epilogue▷

As the heavy slabs of rock began to slam into Kodi's strong body, he instinctively tightened his muscles and forced himself to aim straight for the hole the rocks had broken through the river bottom.

The jagged edges tore his wide shoulders, and Kodi wanted to scream at the pain. He was consumed with the need to stay in the stream of icy water and avoid inhaling it on the way to the bottom of the lower cavern. When rushing water slammed him into a stone floor, he finally gasped in pain.

The large chunks of the roof and pillar that had followed him through the hole, began to hit and punch at him like blows from an angry behemoth. Kodi felt his bones snapping and heard his teeth crunching together as the agonizing pain shot through his body. The next sensation, which seemed to alleviate the pain, was of whirling sideways in a fast current that spun him forward and then downward.

I am drowning. My body is crushed and ruined and my life is ebbing away. Cannot hold my breath any longer. Might as well breathe in the water and end it.

All was dark, so dark Kodi could not tell whether or not his eyes were open. He knew it was a narrow passage this river took into the bowels of the earth because every so often both sides of his body would scrape on rocks. Since his giant lungs held a great deal of air, many minutes passed before he knew they would burst if he did not expel his breath.

When he finally exhaled in the water, his body was propelled upward as if he were riding a fountain from the deep. The speed with which he arose prevented him from taking the breath he so desperately wanted.

And then he was bobbing on the surface of a pool of water with bright sunlight shining down on him. Kodi immediately sucked in a deep breath while his mind spun faster than his body had done earlier. He was very confused.

I don't understand. How could I be alive? I know the rocks broke my bones. But I'm not in pain. I must be dead. This must be the afterlife.

Looking around, Kodi saw that the water from the pool ran as a river through a gigantic cavern. He grabbed for the edge of the pool and hoisted himself up on the edge. He ran his hands over his body, and then he studied his reflection in the still water at the side of the pool.

"I'm not injured! I *am* in the afterlife!"

Kodi looked straight up and saw that the sunlight coming down in a wide shaft through a perfectly round hole overhead. His eyes were caught by brilliant flashes of red, blue, and green, and, as his eyes focused, he noticed the walls of the cave were thickly encrusted with jewels more beautiful than any he had ever seen in Kron's throne room.

And then, coming at him from the far end of the cavern, Kodi saw a whirling cloud of light. The luminous figure shimmering before him seemed like confirmation of his conjectures. He watched as the creature materialized in spinning rings of what looked like shiny clouds. The face was the last thing to clarify.

"Greetings, my son." The figure, which was twice as tall as Kodi, moved closer, close enough for him to see its face. "I have been looking for you. Tell me how you ended up here."

"Azazel! Then I *am* dead? I am in the afterlife where Dark Watchers live."

"No, this is not the afterlife—if there is such a thing for you mortal beings. Why did you think that?"

Kodi shook his head slightly as if he were trying to order his thoughts. Azazel's appearance here did not make sense. He had seen his father, one of the leaders of the Dark

Watchers, many times, but he had never called him 'my son.' What was he doing here just when they had completed their mission?

Or did we complete it? I know the roof came down on me, but I don't know if the river was safely hidden. What does Azazel know about my actions lately?

By now Azazel was close enough to Kodi to look directly down on him. He slowly shrank small enough to put his arm around the young nephil.

"I have come looking for you, my son. Your brother Kron is wondering what had happened to you. He has reason to suspect you are no longer loyal to him—and so do I."

"Why do you think that?" Kodi, who had always feared this being, could not immediately tell him the truth, but the Dark Watcher would not let him dissemble.

"Tell me!"

Kodi trembled throughout his entire body. He had thought the time would come when he would have to declare himself on the side of Elohim, but he had never thought he would make this confession to his terrible father.

Somehow he knew that this moment was extremely important to his soul. He must either declare for or against Elohim and then take the consequences from either side. He clenched his fists, his nails cutting into his hands, and forced himself to speak.

"If you demand to know, I will tell you. I am a follower of Elohim. Since I have come to know Him, I have aided the Sethians in their missions against the nephilim."

As soon as Kodi spoke, Azazel changed from translucent whiteness to the darkness of a storm. His body swelled rapidly to its former size and his voice boomed throughout the cavern.

"Traitor! Denier of your own people! You have made a foolish choice. You will never help them again!"

Kodi jumped back as rapidly as he could; however, he could not escape the black claws which came for his throat. He could not outrun this supernatural being. The claws tightened around his neck and threw him with such power against the cavern wall that Kodi's breath was forced from his lungs. He struggled to draw in enough air to speak.

"You are my father. Why do you want to kill me?"

Azazel's face, contorted with hideous evil, was close, and Kodi's words elicited only a scornful sneer.

"I have many sons who are glad to obey me. You are my one failure. You are too human—and I hate humans!"

Sharp teeth suddenly grew in the Azazel's gums, and these teeth were aimed directly at Kodi's neck.

"Elohim, save me!" Kodi closed his eyes and called out just as the fangs touched his neck.

And then he was free. One moment he was on the edge of death, the next his attacker was jerked away from him. Kodi immediately opened his eyes and saw Azazel locked in a wrestling match with another Watcher.

One struggling figure was white, the other was gray. Kodi retreated to a far corner and watched until the white form had his father pinned beneath him. Just then two more huge white forms came and grabbed Azazel by his arms.

While Azazel screeched out blasphemies, the two newly arrived beings carried him up and out through the hole in the roof. When the Dark Watcher disappeared from his view, Kodi jerked his head back to the white form before him. At the sight of this Watcher regarding him with eyes that shone with love, Kodi fell on his face.

"Stand up, friend. I am only a creation as you are. You should not worship me. I am happy to see you are unhurt."

Kodi stood and felt his neck and the places on his arms and chest where the rocks had hit him. "Azazel did not have the chance to hurt me, but I know I was injured by the falling roof. How is it that I am whole?"

"You fell into the healing water while it was still pure. As you were swept along, you were being healed."

"Oh," Kodi laughed at himself. "I forgot about the water. Who are you and how is it that you came here?"

"I am Remiel. When you made your choice aloud to Azazel and called on Elohim, He sent me to save you, for your work is not yet complete."

"What must I do?"

Remiel pointed upward. "You will go back to your world, back to Kron. Azazel will never have an opportunity to tell him about you. When the time comes for the last mission, you will be called."

"Is that all you can tell me about what is to come?"

"For your encouragement when you are faint of heart in the fortress of evil, I will tell you one thing." Remiel took hold of Kodi's arm as he spoke. Then they began to ascend together upward toward the source of the sunlight.

"When the great judgment comes, many centuries from now, eight humans will be saved. One of these will be the child of your grandson."

With a heart full of wonder, gratitude, and hope, Kodi emerged from the cave on the banks of the Pishon, far south of the Eden Mountains. Without another word, Remiel disappeared from sight, leaving Kodi to make his own way back to Atlantia.

Jeanne Desautel Foster

About the Author

Quest for Eden: The Fifth River, Jeanne Desautel Foster's sixth book, is the second in a three-part series set in pre-flood days. The third part, *The Tree of Life*, will be published in the fall of 2011.

Foster, a retired teacher and journalist with degrees in English and education, writes many types of novels including Christian historical and romances.

For more information about Foster's books, see her website, www.jeannedesautelfoster.com.

Jeanne Desautel Foster

Coming in the fall of 2011, *The Tree of Life* will complete the adventures of Hod and his friends. Ask your bookstore to order it or find information at jeanne desautelfoster.com.

Jeanne Desautel Foster